MARGARET FORSTER

Born in Carlisle, Margaret Forster was the author of many successful and acclaimed novels, including *Have the Men Had Enough?*, *Lady's Maid*, *Diary of an Ordinary Woman*, *Is There Anything You Want?*, *Keeping the World Away*, *Over* and *The Unknown Bridesmaid*. She also wrote bestselling memoirs – *Hidden Lives*, *Precious Lives* and, most recently, *My Life in Houses* – and biographies. She was married to writer and journalist Hunter Davies and lived in London and the Lake District. She died in 2016, just before *How to Measure a Cow* was published.

ALSO BY MARGARET FORSTER

Fiction

Dame's Delight
Georgy Girl
The Bogeyman
The Travels of Maudie Tipstaff
The Park
Miss Owen-Owen is At Home
Fenella Phizackery
Mr Bone's Retreat
The Seduction of Mrs Pendlebury
Mother Can You Hear Me?
The Bride of Lowther Fell
Marital Rites
Private Papers
Have the Men Had Enough?
Lady's Maid
The Battle for Christabel
Mothers' Boys
Shadow Baby
The Memory Box
Diary of an Ordinary Woman
Is There Anything You Want?
Keeping the World Away
Over
Isa & May
The Unknown Bridesmaid

Non-fiction

The Rash Adventurer
William Makepeace Thackeray
Significant Sisters
Elizabeth Barrett Browning
Daphne du Maurier
Hidden Lives
Rich Desserts & Captain's Thin
Precious Lives
Good Wives?
My Life in Houses

Poetry

Selected Poems of Elizabeth Barrett Browning (editor)

MARGARET FORSTER

How to Measure a Cow

VINTAGE

1 3 5 7 9 10 8 6 4 2

Vintage
20 Vauxhall Bridge Road,
London SW1V 2SA

Vintage is part of the Penguin Random House
group of companies whose addresses can be found at
global.penguinrandomhouse.com

First published in Vintage in 2017
First published in hardback by Chatto & Windus in 2016

penguin.co.uk/vintage

A CIP catalogue record for this book is available from the British Library

ISBN 9781784702304

Printed and bound by Clays Ltd, St Ives plc

I

THE FIRST day, free. She walked in a public park, her legs heavy, and yet she felt untethered, floating, waiting for a wind to blow her along. All the green of the trees ahead made her eyes feel muzzy. She blinked constantly, to clear the shimmering. There were groups of people about, sitting on the grass having picnics, or sauntering along the pathways in the full sun. She came to a pond. She took in a woman throwing sticks for a dog, and another, watched by a child in a buggy, feeding ducks. She swayed slightly, and wondered which path she should take. Then she registered a man, all in black, standing on a hillock above the pond. He had a phone held to his ear, and was talking, though he was too far away for her to hear any words. She turned, and began to go up a hill opposite the pond, up a path with no one on it. Suddenly, halfway up, she realised someone was walking in step with her, saying something.

His voice was quiet. He was now so absolutely in step with her that she couldn't see him properly.

'Are you her?' he said.

Calm, she told herself, calm. She didn't reply. This was mid-afternoon in a public park, plenty of people about.

'Are you her?' he asked again.

He still had the phone pressed to his ear though this ear was covered by the flap of a hat, the sort pilots used to wear. She decided to turn and walk back the way she had come. He turned with her.

'Who are you then?' he said, voice still soft. 'If you aren't that bitch, who are you?'

She quickened her pace. He quickened his. He might follow her out of the park. Panic made her stumble. He took hold of her arm.

'What's wrong with you?' he said. 'Eh? What's wrong? You dozy bitch.'

All this time, his voice remained low. No one passing would be able to hear it. Common sense told her he was either merely eccentric or else harmlessly mad, but her body was reacting differently. She was trembling. He was talking again, but she couldn't take in what he was saying. It was ten years ago. He couldn't possibly have recognised her. She took a deep breath. Probably this was some sort of game he regularly played. 'Are you her?' meant nothing.

It was merely an opening gambit. She was nearly out of the park and into the road. She turned left, towards the bus stop, and he turned and went back into the park.

She sat down at the bus stop, flushed and sweating, and closed her eyes. She would have to leave London. They had told her it would be advisable, but she hadn't listened. London was full of weird people. Once, that had been part of the thrill of living here, but not now.

Where should she go?

She bought a map of the British Isles and opened it out flat on the floor of the room they'd given her. Somewhere north would be best, but she didn't know anything about the North, or even the Midlands. She took out a clip from her hair and, closing her eyes, she jabbed it on the map. It had landed on a blue shaded area of sea, somewhere between Wales and Ireland. She turned the map round and shut her eyes again. This time the point of the clip hit land, just south of a town she saw was called Workington, near the sea. She liked the idea of being on the coast and she liked the name of the town. Workington – a working town, honest, straightforward. It appealed to her. Did Workington, too, have deranged people wandering in parks? Surely not in the way London did. Nowhere was safe, but for her, this Workington might be safer than London.

She would have to ask if she could move there. That was one of the conditions. There would probably be objections, all of them justified, all made with her welfare in mind, as she would repeatedly be told. It made her tired, just thinking of the meetings there would have to be, all the reasoning she would have to listen to, how 'good' she would have to be. She wouldn't dare tell them that she wanted to go to this northern town because she'd hit on it with the point of a hairclip pressed on to a map. With her eyes shut. She would have to invent some reason, some connection, however vague. Well, invention was her forte. It shouldn't be too difficult. A great-grandmother, perhaps, now dead? But they were suspicious enough to go to the bother of checking that. Oh, never mind, she'd think of something.

She made the necessary phone call.

At first, Nancy couldn't be absolutely sure that someone had moved into Amy's old house. No removal van had arrived. Nobody had been seen unloading a van or car or getting out of a minicab laden with suitcases. But the upstairs curtain wasn't right. Nancy was quite shocked to realise it had taken her twenty-four hours to notice this. 'I must be slipping,' she said to herself, aloud. (Talking to yourself was fine so long as you knew you were doing it.)

The little terraced house had been empty a whole year, ever since Amy went into hospital and then a nursing home and then died and was buried in that awful cemetery full of miners, the last place she would have wanted to end up. There were cemeteries and cemeteries and this wasn't one of them. No tidy graves, everything overgrown and ugly. No white marble angels or crosses, only ugly black lumps of some granite-like substance with the lettering on them barely discernible. No flowers. Nobody came to this cemetery to put flowers on the neglected graves. It was a scandal that Amy had been bunged in there. The nephew said it was a family grave. That's what he told Nancy.

'Family?' Nancy said, knowing she was laying on the sarcasm heavily. 'Family? Don't make me laugh.' And she shut the door in his face.

A mistake, really. She always acknowledged her own mistakes afterwards, when it was much too late. She could have said nothing. It would have been quite enough to raise her eyebrows, and stare. But she'd spoken her mind, though by no means all of it, and she'd shut the door on the nephew. The obvious consequence was that she wasn't told what was going to happen to Amy's house. It wasn't rented. Amy owned it, definitely. Most of the houses in their street, either side, were rented, but Amy and Nancy both owned theirs. It was a link between them. They were householders, and they were widows, and they were both childless. Nancy had made her will as soon as her husband died. She wanted no disputes over who was to get her house. But had Amy made hers? Was the nephew to inherit it?

He'd been in and out of the house several times but that wasn't necessarily significant. First thing he did was close the curtains in Amy's old bedroom, the room directly facing Nancy's. It annoyed her. There was no need to do this. There was already a net curtain decorously draping the window, and nobody except Nancy could see into that room anyway. But the nephew had closed the other, thicker red velour curtains over it, and they stayed closed. Every night, closing her own curtains, it upset Nancy to look out on that dark square opposite. She tried not to mind, but she did mind, and she minded most of all not knowing why she minded. It was silly, she was silly. There were all kinds of trivial things like this that made her feel silly, a feeling to which she objected but failed to do anything to correct.

One of the red curtains had been pulled aside. Only one. Did this mean there was someone now in residence? Or had the nephew been in, looking round, and had he opened the curtains to get a better view of the room and then forgotten to close both afterwards? Nancy contemplated going to knock on the door. Where would the harm be in that? Suppose burglars had got in. It would look bad if she'd noticed the curtains, but had done nothing. Was that being a responsible citizen? No, it was not. And if someone had moved in, then it would be proper to welcome them to the street, to introduce herself. What was the worst that could happen? Only that she could have the door shut in her face. Well, if so, she would know where she stood. Definitely.

The rent was cheap. She hadn't yet adjusted to the prices of things but even she could tell it was cheap, so cheap she thought she'd misheard. But once she was inside the house, she understood why. There was no central heating. In the living room, there was an electric fire, and that was it. The kitchen, described as 'basic', was primitive, but that didn't upset her. She hardly needed a kitchen. She didn't mind the small size of the rooms either, or the lack of light. The house came furnished and the furniture was shabby, ugly and uncomfortable. Except for the bed in the front bedroom. It didn't fit in with everything else. It seemed new, one of those divans with a deep mattress. How odd, to find such a bed here. She lay down on it, relishing the comfort. So important, a good bed, something she hadn't enjoyed for a long time. There were no sheets on it, no duvet or blankets. It had been stripped. Everything else left untouched, but the bed stripped.

One of the red velour curtains was pulled back. She got up, and stood looking out of the window, though not directly in front of it. She didn't think she'd ever seen a street of houses quite like this one. The bricks were all blackened, a long, tight-fitting terrace of squashed houses, only the doors distinguishing one from another. The bright blue of two of them spoke of valiant attempts to brighten the street up, but they failed, only emphasising its general dreariness. The door of the house she was in hadn't been painted for many years. It was a brown colour almost as dark as the blackened bricks either side.

She had a job all fixed up for her. It was a humble one, but she knew she was lucky to have it, this being an area, and a time, when there was fierce competition for any job. In fact, especially for mundane jobs that anyone could do. She was to have an induction day, and then she would be issued with an overall, which it would be up to her to wash at the end of every week. Getting to work would involve taking a bus from the end of her street, and then a ten-minute walk. That would suit her fine. She thought she might walk the whole way. It would take maybe as long as an hour, she hadn't tried it yet, it was just an estimate. But she was an early riser now, after all the years of being forced to rise early, and she could leave for work at seven in the morning. Coming back, if she were tired, as she expected to be after spending most of the day on her feet, might be different. She might get the bus then.

There was someone opposite peering out of the window. It was only a shape, but it was there.

Well, she had anticipated having to face up to neighbours. She'd been advised what to do, how to handle inevitable interest. She must not be evasive or hostile, but neither must she attempt to be too friendly. Polite, distant, but wanting to keep herself to herself. That should be easy.

The town helped, the house helped, the dreadful furniture helped, but the job didn't. She would have to stick it out, though. For the time being.

For the time being, for the time being . . . being what? The bus windows were steamed up. She rubbed a circle on the glass but she still couldn't see out clearly. The bus was packed, people standing in the aisle. The coughing was like barking, deep rattling coughs.

'Germs,' the woman next to her muttered.

Was there any need to reply to that one word? To be safe, she made an 'mm' sound. The woman was large, her thighs bulging over her share of the double seat. She had a large plastic shopping bag on her knee and another between her feet. She was a smoker, the smell clinging to her clothes, her fingers discernibly yellow. This bus would be an ordeal for her. What smokers had to endure these days, now the comfort of a fag was denied to them. Rightly, of course. Rightly. The law was right. It always was. She'd heard a great deal about how the law, or laws, was, or were, *right*.

'You all right?' the woman asked. The word seemed to echo, right, right . . .

'Yes,' she said.

'Only you're shaking. Cold, eh? Nowt like it will be though.'

She tried to smile. This only encouraged the woman. She was saying something about the cost of heating her flat, how she dreaded winter and wouldn't be able to pay her bills, but if there was one thing she couldn't face it was being cold in her own home and . . . On and on she droned, not seeming to care that she was getting no response. People like her just want to speak aloud, get rid of all the ranting in their head. The bus stopped. Two people got off, four got on. So many stops, and they were only halfway to hers. Long before it was reached she'd have to disturb this woman next to her and start edging her way to the exit doors or else she'd never get there in time. At every stop, there were shouts of 'Here! I want off!' and sometimes the driver ignored them. Once, he shouted back, 'You had yer chance.' She thought there would be a riot, but no, this subdued people, though at the next stop there was a rush, and a lot of swearing in the driver's direction.

'Excuse me,' she said.

The woman groaned. 'You'll have to hold this, pet,' she said, and passed over the bag on her knee. It was very heavy. Once the woman was on her feet, she slipped it on to the vacant seat. The woman was now in the aisle, the standing passengers protesting as she picked up her other bag from the floor and swung it carelessly round. Eventually, the manoeuvre was complete. Someone sat down beside the woman and a conversation was immediately begun. The voices thickened, the accents strengthened, and she could hardly make out a word. Did she herself talk posh? It was a constant worry. To sound 'southern', or even 'cockney', or 'Essex' was OK, but not posh, not here. The way round this was to talk very little at all.

The relief to be off the bus! She stood for a minute, in the rain, staring at a puddle she'd stepped into, an oily swirl on its surface. Somewhere in her bag she had a small collapsible umbrella, but she didn't think she'd get it out and put it up. She'd just get wet. There was a certain curious pleasure in feeling the rain quickly beginning to drip down the neck of her coat, running in a steady trickle down her spine. She had no hat or scarf. Her hair was soon plastered to her head, and her ungloved hands and poorly shod feet were soon cold. But hadn't she, not so long ago, longed to be out like this in the rain? They were never allowed out in the rain, not in a downpour like this.

She walked past her own front door twice. The number, 18, was not visible anywhere, and with the exception of one or two brightly painted doors, they all looked the same. There were probably other distinguishing features but she hadn't learned them yet, and had to work out which was number 18 by counting from a clearly marked 22, white numbers on a slate at the side. Inside, she went straight to the kettle and put it on. Her cold, wet hands shook as she fumbled for a teabag and dropped it into a mug. She was shivering, knowing she should get out of her sodden clothes but incapable of moving until the tea was ready and she had something hot to cling on to. After the first sip, she held the mug up to her cheek, pressing it against her skin.

Twice today she'd forgotten her name. It still meant nothing to her.

'Like a drowned rat,' Nancy said to herself (but, as ever, aloud). 'Not a hat to her name, not a decent pair of shoes, not an umbrella in sight. In the name of God, didn't even know her own house.' Oh, the entertainment was there in plenty. 'Some folk have no sense,' she went on. 'What did the weather forecast say? Rain, heavy rain, this afternoon and all night. Some folk . . .' The sooner she went over there the better, but she delayed, not wanting to seem pushy. There was being welcoming and friendly, and there was being nosy, and she wanted no confusion. There'd been talk at the pensioners' club that afternoon but she'd kept schtum. Rumours flew around like wasps, each with its sting. This new neighbour was a widow/divorcee/from London/Manchester, renting/buying/job at Tesco's/at Morrisons.

'She's in number eighteen, Nancy,' someone said, 'opposite you. Have you seen her, eh?'

'Of course I've seen her,' Nancy said scornfully.

'Did that lad of Amy's tell you she was coming?'

'I'm not saying,' Nancy said which was correctly interpreted as a 'no'. After that, interest in the newcomer waned. For the moment.

It annoyed Nancy that the nephew was referred to as 'Amy's lad'. He was not her lad. He was not even a proper nephew, not a blood relative. The nephew was the stepson of Amy's brother, who lived in Carlisle. The brother and his wife, and her son by her first marriage, hardly ever visited but when they did Amy made a big fuss. It had taken many years for Nancy to find out that this 'nephew', this golden boy (in Amy's opinion), was not in fact properly related. Amy adored him. Photographs of him were all over her house, the ones taken annually at school and sent to her in their grey cardboard frames. She'd told Nancy she intended to leave him everything she had. Nancy expected she'd told the nephew that too. It kept him visiting, if infrequently, once he was grown up. He was at the funeral, of course, with his stepfather (his mother didn't bother). Very appropriately dressed in dark suit, white shirt, black tie, well-polished black shoes. He had at least shown respect. The service was disgracefully brief. No hymns, not one. A prayer so hastily mumbled by the vicar that there might as well not have been one. The mourners who weren't family were not mourners. Nancy recognised them all, women who scanned the local paper and turned up for the show, hoping for a sight of some genuine grief. They would be disappointed this time, except for the treat of the dead woman being buried, a real hole dug and the coffin lowered in. Rare, these days, with folk mostly whipped off to be cremated after the church service. And the nephew did throw a white rose in which would have cost him, it being winter.

There was no funeral tea, or if there was Nancy was not invited, and if there was it wasn't held in Amy's house or at any of the venues well known locally for hosting such events. The nephew and his father shook hands with the vicar, got into their car, and drove off. Nancy walked home thinking how thoughtless some people were. No consideration. No speck of kindness. No thanks for all she'd done for Amy Taylor. She'd worked herself up into such a rage about the nephew and his father's lack of appreciation by the time she reached her own door that she knew she was red in the face. There was a plant pot on the doorstep, enclosed in cellophane. She opened her front door without disturbing it, then cautiously nudged it inside using the toe of her shoe. It toppled over. She picked it up by the cellophane wrapper, dislodging a card. The handwritten message said, 'With thanks to Mrs Armstrong for the help given to our beloved sister and aunt.' Beloved! Beloved!

Left on her doorstep. Not *given* to her, properly. Just left. And only a chrysanthemum, bright yellow and slightly wilted. She would rather have had a pot of bulbs. For a moment, she wondered if she could change it. She knew the shop. Even if she hadn't known it, the address was on the card. Could she go straight away into town and say she was allergic to chrysanths and would like to change this plant for something of similar value, preferably a pot of daffodil bulbs (not hyacinths – she couldn't abide the smell)? It made her agitated, this idea. Backwards and forwards she walked in her little house, her coat and hat still on, the chrysanthemum in her arms. She badly wanted to act on her idea of an exchange, especially as it would mean that she'd find out how much the nephew had spent. What had he reckoned she was worth?

She didn't go. She had a better idea. As soon as she calmed down and had a cup of tea, she'd give it to the woman who'd moved into Amy's house – a welcome present. Then, if the nephew came again, as he was surely bound to if, as reliable rumour had it, the house was rented, not sold, then he would see the plant and get the message. Nancy wasn't sure quite what this message said, but it amounted to a slap in the face.

'A slap in the face!' she said (out loud).

*

The rain had stopped. There was a sudden lightening of the sky, a pale whiteness edging out from under the black clouds. Standing at the bedroom window, she saw the chimney pots opposite outlined against this whiteness. Smoke came from a few of them, gently curling upwards, pale grey against the white. Pretty. She'd never thought to see anything pretty here. Her hands were on the red curtains, to draw them shut, when she saw the door of the house opposite open. An old woman stood there, contemplating a puddle in the road, watching it intently. She was clad in a curious assortment of clothes and was holding a plant pot. Over her head, which already wore a hat, she had a plastic scarf, tied under her chin. Her maroon overcoat had a belt round it, and she had a black bag with a long strap worn diagonally across her chest with the belt, going round her waist, on top of it. She looked to right and then left and waited, though there was no traffic, and then she skirted the deep puddle and walked across the road. The knock was loud.

There was no possibility of ignoring it. Too risky, too certain to provoke the very curiosity which should not be encouraged. Tara practised saying, 'My name is Sarah Scott.' She'd wanted it to be Smith, but Smith was rejected, being too obvious. She'd thought it might be clever to be obvious, a sort of double bluff, but no, Smith would not do. Sarah was fine. A common name, everyone knew a Sarah, and it transcended age and class. It was safe, readily agreed to.

'Hello,' she practised again, as she went down the stairs, 'my name is Sarah Scott.' But she wouldn't be asked for her name. Never volunteer more than is asked for. Hello would be sufficient. Would keeping this neighbour on the doorstep be sufficient? Was it a test? Would she be expecting to be asked in? Hello. Then wait. Let her visitor dictate what should happen next. Listen to what she says and take your cue from it. Maybe just 'hello', and then, if the plant was a gift, 'thank you', and a smile. And close the door.

The woman was somehow inside and the front door closed before Tara realised what was happening.

'Wet, out,' the woman said, wiping her feet energetically on the threadbare mat. The narrow, dark passageway – it wasn't a hall – was full of her. 'Brought you this,' she said, thrusting the plant pot at her.

'Oh,' said Tara, 'thank you.'

'I live across the way, number nineteen,' the woman said. 'Been there near fifty years.'

Tara found herself nodding, as though she'd always known this. They were standing so close together, confined in the small space, that she could see every line on her neighbour's face. It was embarrassing. She hadn't yet said, 'My name is Sarah Scott,' but the visitor hadn't given her name either. They couldn't go on standing there. 'Come in,' Tara said, her voice weak, the invitation unconvincing. She started to lead the way into the living room, but was not followed.

'I'm not stopping,' the woman said, and opened the front door. 'I'll be seeing you, I expect.'

And she was gone. The wretched plant pot slipped out of Tara's hands, the yellow petals fluttering to the floor at her feet. Picking it up, her hands slipping on the wet cellophane wrapping, she felt dizzy, and let herself slide down. She'd done everything wrong. Hadn't she? Had she? She went over what her neighbour had said and what she herself had said and she couldn't decide. She'd given nothing away. That was surely good. She'd said 'thank you'. That was good, polite. It was the visitor who had dictated the short interchange. She was the one in control.

She put the plant pot on the table in front of the living-room window so that it could be seen.

The first meeting was in Morrisons café. There were no introductions. They both knew the drill, identified in each other's appearances what they had expected to identify. Tara had tea, the Man had a cappuccino. It looked rather too full of froth, but since he hardly touched it, just played with the froth, it probably didn't matter.

'Well, *Sarah*,' he said, emphasising the name, 'how's things?'

'Fine,' she said, maybe a little too quickly.

'Settled in?'

'Yes.'

'No problems?'

'No.'

'Good.'

He was looking at her carefully. She knew he would note that she'd made an effort but not so that she stood out. Her clothes were the ones provided, which he would almost certainly know about, but she had added a scarf she'd bought the day before. Cheap but colourful, the blue background calling attention to the blue of her eyes. They were not the sort of clothes she had been used to wearing, but then those would have been hopelessly dated. Her shoes were her own, though. Extraordinary to think they had been kept. She had almost wept when she slipped them on and they fitted so beautifully, so comfortably, just as they always had. Even now, when they were becoming so worn, literally down-at-heel, she loved them.

'Friends?' he asked.

She shook her head.

'Neighbours?'

She hesitated. 'One woman, she lives across from me, an elderly woman. She brought me a plant.'

'That was kind. Did she ask your name, where you were from, where you worked – anything like that?'

'No. She just gave me the plant. A chrysanthemum.'

'Not a nosy neighbour, then.'

'No.'

She thought that if he messed up the froth on his coffee one more time she'd scream. She should be meeting his eyes, but she wasn't. Her eyes were either lowered, or else she was looking over his shoulder at the queue for food. Evasive, she was being evasive. Evasive was bad. And there were silences, long silences, while he studied her and played with his coffee. Should she be trying to fill them? Should she initiate conversation? Wasn't that his job? Resentment built up in her mind, the feeling that whatever she said, however she acted, tiny things that were completely insignificant would be pounced on and interpreted to her disadvantage.

'There is a letter,' he said, 'but you don't have to receive it.'

This made her look at him properly, trying to read his expression. His voice gave nothing away. Flat, imparting the information but nothing more. He waited, raised his eyebrows slightly. She should ask who this letter was from, did he know, and to which address it had been sent. But she didn't. She was being offered a letter and it could only, she thought, be from one of three people, so she wanted it. She hadn't had a letter for years, except for official communications which, though they came in envelopes, hardly seemed letters, or what she judged to be letters. Personal, handwritten, private.

'It can be sent to your new address,' he was saying. 'Just say the word.'

He smiled slightly and she hated his smile. It was the kind of patronising smile she'd seen too often on the faces of people like him. There was even, within it, a trace of enjoying his power over her. He'd probably read this letter, or someone had. It would look unopened when it came to her but it would not have been. Already, it was spoiled, but she told him that of course she would like it. She did not add 'please'.

He nodded, said he or a colleague would see her in three months' time, but that he hoped she knew she could contact him at any time. She need never feel she had to manage on her own; she had support. It was her turn to nod. She wasn't going to say 'thank you', or how grateful she was, or how she appreciated this 'support'. She stayed at the table while he walked away through the crowded café, wondering how far he'd come. She could have asked him that, but she'd asked nothing. Had that been clever of her? Or had it made her seem hostile? She was so tired of constantly wondering how she looked and sounded, aware that in trying so hard to be anonymous she was presenting herself as odd, a strange, nervous, bland woman who was Sarah Scott.

It went on and on in her head, a desperate litany repeated so that it could become second nature, but it never did. She didn't recognise this woman's life except for the few bits that matched her own.

I am Sarah Scott.

I am forty-three years old.

I am divorced, with no living children.

I am from Canterbury originally.

I have no siblings alive.

I trained as a nurse but retired through ill health.

My mother is dead.

My father is dead.

I like to read, mainly non-fiction.

I am nine stone four pounds.

I am five foot six inches.

There was more, lots more. She was bound to have forgotten half of it. Did it matter? It might, they'd said.

The new neighbour was a creature of regular habits. A creature of rigorously regular habits herself, Nancy gave her credit for that. Left her house at 7.00 in the morning on the dot, returned between 5.45 and 6.10, which suggested the time depended on getting either the 5.20 bus or, if she missed it, or it was too crowded to board, the next one. She never put the light on in the hall. Nancy herself automatically snapped the light on as she entered. Everyone did. The hallways were dark even on the sunniest days, what with the front doors being solid wood with no glass panels and no fanlights above. This woman entered her house in the dark and put no light on for a full ten minutes or more. How did she manage to see her way round? Nancy couldn't understand it. When a light did go on, it was always in the bedroom. The curtains, the thick red curtains, remained open even though the light was on. Nancy, standing well back from her own bedroom window, and with only the staircase light on, could see straight in. It was not her fault.

The woman, who she had learned was called Sarah Scott, lay on the bed, on Amy's practically new, expensive bed which she had hardly had time to enjoy. Nancy knew it was Amy's bed because she had enquired after its fate when the nephew came round. This news pleased her. It would have been shocking if the brand new, costly bed had been carted off to a sale room, or even taken off by one of those house-clearance people. But the bed stayed, and this Scott woman obviously appreciated its comforts. She lay on it, every evening, for at least half an hour. Nancy couldn't see if her eyes were closed, but she certainly gave the appearance of being asleep, lying, as she did, so very still. Odd, though, to have the light on if she was sleeping. She must come in extremely tired, to have to go and lie down like that. Her job must be exhausting, but what could it be? Nancy had not yet found out, though it would emerge through the usual channels. She'd hear soon enough. Meanwhile, she was content to know her neighbour's name before anyone else. The postman told her. He was young and careless, and if she had had any letters sent to her, beyond bills, Nancy would not have trusted him to deliver them. He put letters through her own letter box which were quite clearly addressed to number 29 and not 19, and she had reprimanded him for it, making him take them back the next day and redeliver them to number 29. He laughed and said, 'Righto, missus.'

He had a red cart he pulled along. So lazy. Nancy saw no need for it. He was big and strong as well as young and could quite easily have carried a sack as postmen had done all her life. So lazy. And the way he left the cart at one end of their long street while he carried a bundle of letters for the first twenty houses was irresponsible. Anyone could pilfer from it in the time it took him to return. But he had told her the name of the woman who now lived opposite her. She hadn't asked, she would *never* have asked. He'd delivered just one letter to her but nevertheless had noted her name. That, in Nancy's opinion, was fishy, but she could hardly complain considering he had passed the information on to her which he most certainly had no right to do. She'd badly wanted to ask was it Miss or Mrs Sarah Scott, but of course she hadn't. Of course she hadn't. It was the novelty value, she supposed. New people hardly ever moved into their street. It was not that sort of street. He liked having a new name, he said. Made delivering more interesting. What nonsense. He made it sound like something special when it was a job any fool could do, just sticking stuff through letter boxes.

Sarah Scott: Nancy quite liked the name. Sort of posh, she thought, though she knew plenty of very ordinary, decidedly unposh Sarahs. Scott was not a local name. It wasn't, she reckoned, any kind of local name, even if it must have originated, she supposed, in Scotland, surely. Sarah Scott wasn't Scottish, though. The two words she'd spoken when the plant was given to her proved that. She was from away. Away? Nancy realised 'away' was a very vague term. She decided that what she meant was that Sarah Scott was not Cumbrian, or even northern. So what had brought her here? And on her own. No visitors in six weeks. Was she to be temporary? Someone drafted here for a limited amount of time to do some particular job? Nancy didn't think so. Sarah Scott didn't look important enough. She didn't look as if she did any sort of work that might rate her being sent for specially.

One day, sooner or later, she would need help of some sort. This knowledge was a great comfort to Nancy. It didn't matter how stand-offish or reclusive people were, the time always came when they couldn't manage on their own. It was a rule of life, one she'd learned over many years of acute observation. Sarah Scott's time would come.

Tara waited for the promised letter with a mixture of apprehension – though she didn't know what she was apprehensive about – and something that was near to excitement. She suspected it might be from Claire. Claire had written once. She hadn't replied to this letter, resenting, as she did, its tone. Neither Liz nor Molly had written at all. They'd never been letter-writers. They were phone people, regular calls, which in Molly's case were liable to go on a long time. If they had made calls, she never heard about them. Who would they have called, anyway? They didn't visit either. None of the three. She'd been surprised by that, but got used to it. There would be reasons, she expected, though this realisation hadn't stopped her being resentful. She knew how *she* would have responded.

She tired herself to the point of numbness, thinking about this letter. All day, standing at the conveyor belt, her hands automatically lifting, pressing down, she shook slightly with all this absurd agitation about its arrival. Repetitive jobs, she'd already learned, needed attentive minds. Such a simple action she was performing, so easy it could be done, surely, in her sleep. But it couldn't, that was the shock. To think she'd been educated for this. Nobody would believe it. She didn't believe it herself. Tara couldn't be doing this, not with her talents, her qualifications. It was Sarah Scott doing it, stupid Sarah Scott, silent Sarah Scott. She talked to no one, except for the obvious pleasantries, the polite good mornings, the comments on the weather. Her silence didn't seem to bother the women she worked with. One or two of them, in the brief breaks, made an attempt at communicating but nobody asked direct questions. They were all tired, as she was herself. They wanted their shifts over, and then home as quickly as possible.

There was no spark in this Sarah Scott. Tara was startled by how completely she'd given in to this woman, how that had been part of the plan, for her, Tara, to fade away and be resurrected as another, better person. A plan that was succeeding too well.

It was why the letter loomed ahead as so significant. A link to a life left behind, but still hers.

II

A REUNION: Claire wanted to have a reunion, a celebration, twenty-five years on, but of course Tara should be present or it would have no true meaning. It was Tara, after all, walking on the opposite bank, who had dived into the fast-flowing river and grabbed hold of the child's foot. Liz quickly followed, and together they hauled the little boy out and Molly began the life-saving procedure she'd only just learned at a first-aid class. Claire was the one who ran back along the river path to the pub, the Bull's Head, to get them to phone for an ambulance. Oh, how fast she had run, heart thudding, breath coming in such gasps because she wasn't used to running. Her finest hour . . . that was what Dan said, sarcastically, every time she reminisced, which she did once a year, remembering the date of this dramatic event all too clearly, a summer's day, perfect blue, cloudless sky. And the boy's life was saved.

They were local heroes for a while, even Claire who had merely run for help which, by the time it came, had not really been needed. Molly had done the necessary. But all four of them were photographed with the boy they'd saved and a piece was written about them in the newspapers. That was how they became friends with Tara Fraser. They were already all in the same sixth form but Claire and Molly and Liz had known each other since nursery school. Their mothers were friends, their fathers commuted to London on the same train. Tara Fraser didn't have these connections. She was thought of as a bit wild, known to 'give cheek' to teachers, known to be defiant in the face of authority. She dyed her auburn hair black, then purple, and had ways of getting round all sorts of rules about uniform that irritated teachers.

But after the famous rescue, Tara became part of their set. They began to move around as a quartet, Tara influencing the others in all kinds of subtle and not-so-subtle ways. Her language was awful. She used the F-word frequently, quite shocking the other three, but there was no stopping her. Led by Tara, they too began circumnavigating rules and regulations, enjoying the small thrill it gave them. Claire was called into the headmistress's office and told that she was now proving 'a disappointment'.

'You are a prefect, Claire,' the headmistress said. 'It is up to you to set an example.'

Claire hung her head and apologised, but the moment she left the room she rushed to the others and mimicked the headmistress, basking in Tara's approval. Such good times they had, and then school ended, and they all went off to different places but kept in touch, always.

Claire was the best at keeping in touch, at rounding them all up, two or three times a year, and organising a lunch or supper. She sent handwritten notes, thought quaint by the others. She liked writing them, she still did. It was a habit of hers to drop a short note, expressing concern, when she heard someone was ill, or that a husband/wife/partner had died. Often, the recipients of these notes were neighbours she didn't know at all well, but still, they deserved some compassion. It didn't matter if they were never acknowledged. Well, it did, but Claire knew it shouldn't, not to a truly caring person. She stifled a slight disappointment when, if she later met a person to whom she'd sent a sympathetic note, nothing was said, no mention made of her thoughtfulness. Some people were like that. She was not.

She had written to Tara, after deep thought, when she read in the newspapers what she was said to have done. She'd spent ages toiling over this missive, trying to convey sympathy without attaching blame, even though it looked as though

Tara was very much to blame. There had been no reply. She didn't write again, and she didn't go to the trial. Of that she was deeply ashamed, but when she had tentatively floated the idea of going her husband had been adamant that she should not. It would do no good, Dan had said. Far from being a gesture of solidarity, it would be acting like a voyeur. But at least, when one newspaper dug out the old story of the rescue of the boy, and tracked Claire and the others down, she had stood by Tara, emphasising all her good qualities. There had been some pretty close questioning, though, and she knew she hadn't come out of it well. Did she keep in touch with Tara Fraser? Oh yes, she certainly did. So when had she last seen her? Claire struggled . . . Six months ago, maybe a little longer. Last talk on the phone? She couldn't be sure. At this point, Dan had arrived home, furious to find she was letting herself be interviewed, and dragged her inside.

Then there were the prison years. She'd written straight away, when Tara was sentenced, and posted it without reading it through because she knew if she did read it she'd probably tear it up and this would go on and on. There was no reply. In a way, this was a relief. She'd done her bit. But she knew that was a lie. Guilt about how she, as a friend, should have behaved, troubled her for months, at the strangest moments, and then, over the years, she began to forgive herself and forget.

Now the guilt returned, the moment she decided to plan a reunion. Tara would have to be invited. It was time to make up for lost opportunities (Claire liked that phrase, 'lost opportunities', so soothingly vague, so meaningless). She had no address to write to but she'd read about Tara being transferred to an open prison a few years ago and she sent her letter to the governor there, with a covering note.

Molly and Liz thought Claire's letter a waste of time. They were hard on her about it because she was so self-righteous and pleased with herself.

'She'll never get it,' Liz said, 'and if she does, it will annoy her.'

'You don't know what I said,' objected Claire.

'I can guess,' said Liz, with a smirk.

Claire flushed, and tried not to react.

'I don't think she'll want to see us anyway,' Molly said. 'We were proved to be broken reeds.'

'Oh, for God's sake,' Liz laughed. 'Broken reeds? Really, Molly.'

'Well, you know what I mean. She'll think we let her down, and we did – she won't want anything to do with us. The very idea of a reunion would probably make her sick.'

'It will be like sticking a message into a bottle and throwing it into the sea,' said Liz.

'Well,' said Claire, 'I'm going to throw it.'

*

Slowly, slowly, Tara grew into the house, the street, the job. She began to make small changes which she thought had a significance she couldn't quite work out. Buying a cup and saucer in a charity shop and bringing it home to put on the shelf she'd emptied of hideous crockery seemed bold and defiant. This was *her* cup and saucer, Sarah Scott's. It had nothing to do with Tara Fraser, even if Tara too had preferred cups to mugs. She would never have chosen this one, though. Tara liked colour. She wouldn't have picked a plain cream cup and saucer, large enough for a very generous amount of coffee. Just looking at it pleased Tara. When she used it for the first time her hand trembled slightly with the unexpected pleasure. She bought a cushion (again, in a charity shop) and a cafetière (new). Then she took down both the net half-curtain and the red velour curtains in the bedroom and put up a blind. It thrilled her to be able to manage this herself. Tara would never have tried, but Sarah bought the necessary tools, a screwdriver and a small hammer, and followed the instructions carefully, and there it was, working perfectly, a plain blue blind which went smoothly up and down. She liked it best at half-mast during the day, but fully down at night. If there was a moon, the blue turned paler and gave the room a strange, unearthly atmosphere which she liked, though it made her shiver. Tara would have thought that she, Sarah, was a weird

saying 'Good morning' or 'Cold, isn't it?' but didn't. Nodding was enough. They were right.

She was by now on those sorts of terms at work, though, the 'Cold, isn't it?' sort of pleasantry. Back came a torrent of agreement, tales of individual experiences of cold, of having no heating, no hot water, and at least in the factory it was warm. Nobody, she noticed, ever asked her a direct question. Nobody wondered why she'd come to work here, or where she'd worked before. It was a relief, this lack of curiosity (if that was what it was) but it made her feel even more isolated than she already was. Maybe, she thought, these women were merely biding their time. Maybe this was how they did things here: softly, softly, catchee . . . But that, she knew, was her paranoia showing. She should just be thankful and treat others as they treated her.

It was easy enough. She found that Sarah Scott didn't have much interest in her fellow workers. She didn't want to know more about them than the scraps of information which they let drop told her. She didn't, apparently, want friends. She had enough of them. A blatant lie. She had none, and though Tara had had real friends, close friends, they had long since melted away. She was poisonous to them, she'd supposed. Untouchable. They'd shuddered, she expected, at having been associated with her in the past. But there was a letter coming, to Tara, not Sarah, so perhaps this was not quite true. Someone had risked writing to her. Why? After all these years. Why? When no effort had been made, so far as she knew, before, except for that irritating letter years ago from Claire. A week had gone by since she'd been told about a letter on the way. Not a long time, especially to her, a blink of an eye to one who had learned the true meaning of enforced patience, who had experienced the numbing monotony of endless empty days, days ruled by meals, by lights going on and off, by the noise of footsteps, the sound of bells, shouted orders. A week was nothing once, yet now it seemed interminable. Each day she returned from work barely able to breathe as she opened her front door, and then stood and stared at the empty mat. No post. Another twenty-four hours to get through before there was any chance of there being something on the mat. Anger followed the disappointment. What were they playing at? Why were they tormenting her like this? They'd asked if she wanted the letter and she'd said yes. What did they want her to do? Beg for it? She would not beg. Begging, of any kind, reduced her. She had very little left to lose but what she had, that thin sliver of self-respect which had somehow survived, she would not give up.

She closed the front door carefully.

The curtains had gone. Nancy could not believe it. A *blind*! Perfectly good curtains, just discarded, as though of no value. What had been done with them? If Amy's curtains were not good enough for this Scott woman then she would be happy to have them, very happy. The blind upset her, its blue blankness an offence. Most of the time it was three-quarters of the way down, leaving only a small gap through which nothing at all could be seen. When a light came on, the blue glowed brightly but no shadow appeared behind it. A thick blind, then, thick material. Like blackout stuff. Nancy remembered it well, black and thick, not a chink of light showing from within in case German bombers were guided by it.

But this Scott woman was much too young. She'd have no memory of blackout blinds, or of the war. Why had she taken down curtains and put up a blind? It meant something, but Nancy couldn't figure out what. She wondered if other changes were going on in Amy's house, concealed from view. Maybe the whole place was being revamped, modernised. Maybe next thing she'd see a plumber arriving with a new bath and sink. That kind of thing had just begun in their street, at the far end, things being done to these houses which were unbelievable. There was no knowing where it would end. Nobody was content any more with what they had. It was the television which had started it, all those adverts, giving people ideas, and then there were those card things, bits of plastic with numbers on, and if you had one you didn't need cash, it just went in a machine and the deal was done. Well, she had a television, course she did, but she would never, never stoop to having a plastic card.

A woman who took down good-quality curtains and put up a blind would have a plastic card. Nancy was certain about this. She looked at the blind, and was convinced. She badly wanted to discuss this with someone but feared she might be laughed at, thought hopelessly behind the times.

'An old fuddy-duddy,' she said aloud, not like the new woman across the road. Amy would've understood, even though she'd been proud of her nephew keeping her, she said, 'up with the times'. So far as Nancy had been able to make out this meant getting her a television – for heaven's sake, everyone had a TV, Amy had simply been thirty years behind everyone else. The way she'd boasted about getting it, about the nephew buying and installing it, had been ridiculous, misplaced gratitude. Why was it misplaced? Nancy fretted over why. The words had sprung into her head unbidden and lay lumpily there, waiting to be explained. She tired herself so with this kind of thing, wondering where words came from, what they meant, and the more she fretted the more inexplicable combinations of ordinary words seemed. She needed to say them to someone else to give them a chance to mean more than their ordinariness suggested.

'Misplaced gratitude,' she said loudly, and left it at that.

The house, his now, had been let for six months, the rent paid in advance. The cheque was not signed by the occupant but by a man. It was none of his business who this man was, or how he was connected to Sarah Scott, so he never enquired. He had stipulated in the tenancy agreement, though, that he would have the right to enter the premises to see all was as it should be, with notice of his intended visit given beforehand. He didn't know why he'd insisted on this. The house was in a shabby state, nothing much to damage there, and one single woman would hardly be likely to wreck it further, but you never knew. She might be a cat lover and the place could become infested with cats or she could take in lodgers, pack them in. Neither of these possibilities was likely, and he knew that he would be quickly informed by that old bitch across the road if either happened. She missed nothing, and would get a kick out of letting him know if his tenant did anything odd. She'd wait until she was sure damage was already done, and then delight in telling him, relishing what she saw as the Good Neighbour act.

He glimpsed her at her window as he walked down the street, watering an ugly dark green plant she had there. She was always using this watering as an excuse to stand at her window, checking out any activity. He deliberately waved, knowing she would ignore him, pretending she hadn't seen him. When he got to the house, *his* house now, he stopped and turned towards her window, and waved again. She straightened her lace curtain and disappeared.

The house was tidy. He'd said what time he would call, so he expected an effort would've been made, but the impression was that it was always tidy. No sign of hastily cleared-away clutter. No clutter at all. It was as if no one lived there. Quickly, he looked into the kitchen, after he'd scanned the living room from the doorway, smiling on registering the chrysanthemum plant, and then went upstairs. The curtains had been taken down and a blind put up. This surprised him. Why go to the bother? He looked around and saw the curtains, both sets, neatly folded on a chair. No harm done. When Sarah Scott had gone, the curtains could go back up if she took the blind with her. Coming down the stairs again, ready to leave the house, he detected a faint smell. It wasn't unpleasant, nothing like the smell from blocked drains or rotting food, but something slightly spicy. Cigarette smoke? Some foreign brand? Or perfume lingering? By the time he got to the bottom of the stairs, it had gone. As he went to open the front door and leave, a letter came through the letter box. He picked it up. For his tenant, of course. He put it back down on the mat, together with a note he'd written before he came, saying he'd called as arranged, and everything was satisfactory.

Out of a desire to be annoying, he went across the street and knocked on Mrs Armstrong's door. She didn't have a bell, just a large brass knocker, kept gleaming with Brasso applied every Monday morning at eleven. He fairly hammered with the knocker, knowing perfectly well it was unnecessary to do so. He knew he wouldn't be asked in, and that the door, when it opened, would only open a crack.

'Hello, Mrs Armstrong,' he bellowed when it did. 'Just thought I'd see how you are. Well, I hope?' There was no proper reply to his harmless enquiry, just a grunt. And now, being really mischievous, he said, 'Have you got to know your new neighbour yet? Nice lady, isn't she?'

The door opened a little bit further.

'I keep myself to myself,' she said, 'and so does she.'

'Well,' he said, enjoying himself, 'that is a most agreeable state of affairs. Well done. I'll be on my way, keep myself to myself, too. Good day, Mrs Armstrong,' and he tipped an imaginary hat.

Seething, Nancy slammed her door shut. He was so cheeky. Thought she didn't get the sarcasm, didn't know he was making fun. Smart alec, that was what he was.

'He just likes a joke,' Amy had said, failing to recognise the nastiness in him. Trust him to come and snoop around when Sarah Scott was out. She wouldn't put it beyond him to have gone through drawers trying to find things out about her. She ought to tell her neighbour that he'd been in the house fourteen minutes precisely, and he'd been in her bedroom too. She might not know, and she should be told. You couldn't be too careful.

It was a white envelope, oblong, the name Sarah Scott, her name now, and address typed upon it, dead centre. First-class stamp. The thickness, when she picked it up, told her the other letter, the real letter, was inside. Smaller. Different shape.

She should take her wet coat off, make a cup of coffee, settle herself beside the electric fire, both bars on, before she opened the outer envelope. Of course she should. But she didn't. She leaned against the wall, just inside the front door, and ripped open the white envelope, taking no care at all, letting it flutter to the floor and then lifting her foot and stamping on it. The sight of her real name, her old name, and the handwriting, both made her head swim. Sarah Scott, she told herself, get a grip. There is no need to upset yourself. Claire is harmless. She always was. The nicest, kindest, most straightforward of the four of them. Whatever she'd written, why ever she'd written (at last) there would be no cause for alarm. She had nothing to fear from Claire. Tara had nothing to fear, Sarah had nothing to fear.

Then she did take her coat off and hang it on the hook behind the door where it could drip on to the old doormat. She slipped her shoes off too, leaving them there, and padded through to the kitchen to put the kettle on. As usual, she didn't turn on a light. There was no need. The chrome of the kettle glowed, guiding her to its switch. She was in no hurry, was no longer disturbed. She was not excited or hopeful either. All this time, since the Man had told her about the letter coming, she realised what a state of nerves she'd been in, and now it had gone. It was odd, she thought, how, instead of being relieved that she was calm, she missed the tension of waiting for this letter. It had come. Now nothing else was likely to happen.

She opened this envelope more carefully, examining the sticker on the back. It had Claire's name and address on it and a little rose printed in the top left-hand corner. She imagined Claire having them done, several sheets of them, perforated for easy tearing off. She peeled this one away from the flap and held the tiny label between finger and thumb. She was not going to reply, whatever was in the letter, so she didn't need to keep this scrap, and in any case Claire being Claire would have written her address on the letter itself too. But all the same, she laid it on the wooden arm of the chair she was sitting on. The sheet of paper she then took out of the envelope, blue, pale blue, and sure enough there was Claire's address and phone number and email all printed at the top of the paper, the lettering a darker blue. All very proper, all very formal, all very Claire. Who else, today, would have printed stationery? It was old-fashioned enough, middle class enough, to be touching. Poor Claire, so correct, clinging to the rules by which she'd been brought up.

A reunion. The letter was to tell her (to tell Tara – not, of course, Sarah) that there was to be a reunion. A sort of silver wedding thing, twenty-five years, though no wedding had been involved. It was just a thought Claire had had, how lovely it would be to meet up after all this time, twenty-five years to the day, though not precisely to the day because that would be a Monday this year and so it was to be the day before, or rather two days before. The Saturday, and after all *the* day had been a Saturday, did Tara remember? Her memory, quite unnecessarily, was jogged. It wasn't the sort of day, or event, anyone involved in could ever forget. Four teenagers had acted in such a way that a child's life was saved. Tara remembered enjoying the drama of it, though she tried to hide it, tried to be modest and self-effacing, announcing that it was nothing. Anyone would have done the same. But they wouldn't have. She'd been wandering along the grassy track beside the riverbank bored out of her skull, nowhere to go, nothing to do, and on the opposite bank she'd seen that stuck-up trio approaching and she'd hated them. When the little boy fell in the river her instant reaction was that she would show those three what she was made of. So she dived in and grabbed the child, and all else followed from that. Oh, how she enjoyed the aftermath! The fuss! The acclaim! And new friendships. Especially that: the new friends. She seemed, up to that point, to have gone through life without friends, real friends. Other children mostly bored her, refusing, as they so often did, to play the games she wanted to play. So she made a point of declaring that she was quite happy on her own and didn't need friends. Teachers, noticing her solitary state in the playground as they were bound to do, questioned her tactfully about this, but got nowhere. Grammar school was better. She was good at all sports, and was soon in teams, and that meant she wasn't on her own so much, she wasn't so obviously without friends. But, suddenly, the desire to have a little gang around her grew, which was why she watched Claire and Molly and Liz so enviously. She couldn't break into that clique, she knew that – they wouldn't let her – but she could perhaps form her own gang.

It proved impossible. No sooner had she made overtures to a girl she thought promising than Tara got tired of her, and wanted free of the expectations she'd just raised, hurting the chosen girl in the process. After this had happened a few times, she earned the reputation of being bitchy and arrogant and best steered clear of. She concentrated on scoring goals galore in hockey matches, and outplaying everyone at tennis, and taking part in swimming galas where she won race after race. So she was busy, involved in plenty of action, but still essentially solitary. Then came the day of the child's rescue, and everything changed. She had friends, bound to them by her own bravery.

This reunion was to be a lunch at the riverside pub to which Claire had run, shouting for someone to call for an ambulance. It was, wrote Claire, a gastropub now. It had rooms available which were not expensive, and she could book one for Tara if she would be travelling any distance, if, from wherever she was, a day trip would not be possible. A day trip, indeed – enough to make Tara smile at the idea. The smile, weak and a little bitter though it was, helped her see how absurd the whole idea of this 'reunion' was. And yet . . . it was tempting. She could slip back to being Tara again, just for a weekend. How uncomfortable they would all surely be. They wouldn't know how to treat her. They would want to ask the Big Question, the one they wanted to ask, she was certain, at the time but hadn't done so: how had it happened? She'd pleaded guilty, but how had it happened, what exactly had brought her to that point? And she had her own question: why had none of them offered a shred of support (she didn't count

Claire's pathetic letter)? Why had friendship not overridden all else?

Tara told Sarah that this was nothing to do with her, and that she should tear the letter up. Sarah did not know this person who had sent the letter. Sarah has a different life, a new life. Sarah is safe here. What happened in the past cannot be allowed to intrude into her existence here. So, Sarah, Tara said, tear this letter up. Old friends do not matter. They are deluded if they think they do.

Sarah was slow to obey, but eventually, to Tara's relief, she did. She tore Claire's letter up. Good girl. But Tara wasn't fooled.

Nancy waited and watched. Saturdays and Sundays there was no activity. No coming and going. Sarah Scott stayed inside the whole weekend, unless she went in and out during Nancy's own brief hour when she went shopping on Saturday morning. This seemed to her unlikely. The blind in the bedroom was still fully down when she left at nine o'clock and when she returned, just before ten, it was still down. It didn't get half-lifted until about eleven. So, Sarah Scott had a lie-in on Saturday mornings. Perfectly reasonable. Nancy allowed that. But what about the rest of every weekend? Rain or shine, the woman shut herself up in that house. It wasn't healthy. There was no television there any more – the nephew, typically, had removed it, and there had definitely been no delivery of another – and if there was a radio surely listening to that couldn't fill the whole weekend.

There was no sign of her new neighbour making any church attendance on Sunday, but that wasn't unusual. Nancy didn't go any more herself, except to funerals sometimes. She thought about resuming her old habit, ingrained since childhood, of going to morning service but then she remembered how it had depressed her for years before she gave up. So few people there, lost in the echoing place, coughing and shuffling, hardly one of them able to sing a hymn. And the vicar was pathetic, his sermons mumbled with head down, barely audible and without meaning. If it had not been for the white surplice, always pristine (she gave him that) he could have been a tramp who'd wandered in. The first Sunday she didn't go, Nancy felt defiant. If the vicar came to enquire about her, she was ready with her criticisms and he would just have to accept them. But he never came. She could have been lying dead. It was no good saying to herself that maybe he hadn't noticed her absence. Not noticed? She sat in the front left-hand pew, right in front of his pulpit, the only one who ever did. Not noticed, when he never had more than eight people in his congregation? Not noticed, when she was always the last out, the last to shake his hand? The only one who looked him in the eye and was in no hurry to scurry off?

But a gap was created. Nancy had felt restless every Sunday morning since. There were lots of shops open on Sundays these days, but it would have seemed wrong to go shopping, even window shopping. Shopping was Saturdays. She tried going for a walk and sometimes still did. It meant getting ready, which was good, and being out, which was good, but she always felt self-conscious going for a walk that had no objective. If it rained, or was exceptionally cold, as it often was, an aimless walk was not an option. She stayed in and played patience. This seemed almost wicked, on a Sunday, but it filled an hour. Very occasionally, she had a visitor, and even less frequently she made a visit herself. Those were satisfactory Sundays. She got bored, though, with the women who visited her and whom she visited. They all knew each other too well, the connection between them of long standing but never running very deep. There was nothing new to discover, and these days all of them repeated themselves. Nancy didn't, but the others did. Even when she said yes, they'd told her whatever it was before, again and again, they still carried on. It was highly irritating. She missed Amy, with whom she had been totally at ease.

Sarah Scott would be new. Everything about her would be fresh. However ordinary she might turn out to be there was a whole unknown life there. Nancy craved knowing it. She wouldn't, given the opportunity, do anything as crass as ask direct questions. She didn't wish to interrogate Sarah Scott. She would be quite content to let her history unfold, bit by bit, year by year. And she would be perfectly happy to share her own story, if Sarah Scott showed any interest. She had nothing to hide. Maybe she hadn't had an exciting life, but she'd had her moments, as a child, during the war. Sarah Scott might be interested in those experiences. Possibly.

What Nancy needed, she realised only too well, was an excuse to invite her new neighbour for a cup of tea. An excuse, a convincing one, was essential, otherwise it would be embarrassing. She couldn't openly admit that she was intrigued by Sarah Scott and wanted to know about her. That would be terrible bad manners. Giving her the nephew's plant had been a mistake, a miscalculation. It had seemed, and indeed was, false, and Sarah Scott had sensed this, which was why she'd seemed so shaken. Something natural was needed, some casual, friendly overture which arose without effort, and could not be misinterpreted.

Nancy went on watching and waiting, afraid that she might miss some significant sign which would direct her to the solution of this puzzle, this desire to find a way to approach Sarah Scott. Her presence in Amy's old house was becoming unbearably tantalising, especially on a Sunday.

*

Claire worried about the fate of her letter, but then she worried, fretted, about so many things. She worried silently, her head so often filled with this internalised anxiety. Those upon whom all this worry was lavished knew nothing about it. Tara, for example, had never known of all the nights Claire stayed wide awake thinking about her. Why had she done what she'd done? It was impossible to understand. Molly thought Tara must have experienced some sort of mental breakdown. She'd done what she'd done in a frenzy. Claire didn't agree. True, Tara had a temper, and she was often unpredictable, often hyper, but the evidence was that the act she'd committed had been carried out with a cool efficiency. Liz said that they all had to remember that they hadn't really been close to Tara any more after she married Tom and moved to London.

They had all been to the wedding, though it was hardly what could be called a proper wedding. Claire's wedding, a couple of months after Tara's, had been the real thing, six bridesmaids, a hundred and twenty guests, church service, the lot. Tara refused to be a bridesmaid. Liz and Molly agreed, but Tara said nothing on earth would make her wear a long pink dress. In fact, the dresses were not pink. They were a pinky lavender, quite different. Tara had deliberately appeared in black. Short, very short, tight skirt (and this was by now the nineties when short skirts were rarely seen except on young teenagers) with tights and boots, and an appalling shiny black PVC thing, neither top nor coat, that crackled during the service. At her own register-office affair Tara had been in white. A demure *broderie anglaise* dress. Tom, apparently, had chosen it, suitable, he said (or so Tara told them) for his 'adorable child bride'. What Tara saw in this Tom, none of them could fathom. It wasn't his looks – that was for sure. Or his charm, since he had none. It must, the three of them decided, be the sense of danger he had about him. They struggled to define this, but couldn't. He more or less ignored them, but they could see how intensely he concentrated on Tara. He had, Liz thought, a magnetism about him, attracting Tara to him in a way none of them could understand. It was disturbing.

Weeks passed, and gradually Claire began to accept that she was not going to get a reply to her letter, whether or not it had reached Tara now she was free. This 'freedom' was much discussed by the friends. What did it amount to? She had paid the penalty for her crime.

'The past is behind her, over,' Claire said.

Liz said that sort of thinking was naive. The past would never be over for Tara. It would have to be lived with, accommodated. That was the most that could be done with it.

'She's had to do it before,' Molly reminded them. 'Block out the past.'

'Yes,' said Liz, 'but that was a past she couldn't remember. She was only three when she went to live with the Frasers. She said herself she couldn't remember anything however hard she tried. She just had to believe what the Frasers told her. It isn't the same.'

They were silent for a while after Liz said that. How shocking it had seemed to them that Tara lived with foster parents. They were curious, but too well brought up to ask direct questions, especially one: why? Nobody else they knew had foster parents. They half wanted Tara to reveal that she hated the Frasers, and longed for her real parents, but she didn't. She complained about her foster mother in the way they all complained about their mothers, but she didn't ever say, or hint, that she hated her, any more than they did (except in odd moments of fury). And she loved her foster father, John, always going on about his sporting prowess. He was the one who taught her to swim when she was still tiny, and coached her to become the school champion. They swam in the Thames together and entered races which Tara always won.

'I wonder,' Molly suddenly said, 'if she's thought about us at all. Maybe we just faded from her mind the last ten years.'

'Unlikely,' Liz said. 'She might be full of resentment about us not rallying round when she needed us – and even before that, once she'd moved to

London, we didn't make the effort to go to her, just expected her to come to us.'

'But that was natural, surely,' said Claire. 'We all live within twenty miles of each other.'

'Still,' said Liz.

It was a quiet lunch, that time. They were all a bit depressed. They'd gone over and over the good times they'd had with Tara and then they'd had to face what had happened all over again. They didn't, now, expect Tara to turn up. But Claire noticed that neither Molly nor Liz was as upset about this as she was.

Snow at the end of January, snow well into February, and then constant rain the whole of March. The house was freezing the entire time. Coming home each day, Tara kept her coat and scarf and boots on right up to the moment when she went to bed. Only then was she ever warm and that was due to the electric blanket she'd bought. Once in bed, only her nose was still cold, and as the night wore on, and the blanket was switched off, she pulled the duvet over her head.

But she slept, and without sleeping pills. She had no nightmares any more either, or even proper dreams, the sort of dreams she'd been used to having. Something was changing, then. Peace of mind would come eventually, they'd said. In time. A new rhythm would establish itself and sweep away the old order. This will be slow, they'd said, and you have to do your bit, give yourself to your new life. So she must be giving herself more successfully than she had estimated. How had she done it? By not struggling against Sarah Scott, she supposed. Sarah was so dull, so obedient, so entirely without any spark. She ate, she worked, she slept, and that was about it. She didn't seem to notice anything, react to anything. She tottered through each day keeping her head down, doing what she had to do, never making any complaint. But she didn't have nightmares, she was calm. There was no pain any more. That, she told herself, made being Sarah Scott worthwhile.

She'd always known there were people like that in the world, those fortunate few who drifted placidly through their lives, untroubled by rages or depressions or ambition, but she hadn't known how they did it, what the trick was. Now, as Sarah Scott, she should know, but she still didn't quite grasp the essential secret to such harmony. Sticking to a rigid, and easy, routine was, she could see, part of it. If you had a routine, there was no need to think, and it was thinking, especially wild random thinking of the sort that Tara had indulged in, which caused havoc. But following a routine couldn't, she felt, explain everything. There was an element in this woman Sarah Scott which was about self-abasement, which was not commendable. It made the price too high. She thought she couldn't go on being so terribly humble and feeble without starting to hate herself. Hate Sarah Scott. Surely, somewhere in this creature she could find a flash of individuality to make her existence worthwhile? It might be dangerous for her to attempt to deviate from what she had allowed to become the new norm but a little risk was what Sarah needed to take or she would drown in her own dreariness.

She couldn't explain any of this to the Woman when she met her (a woman this time, though it was supposed to be the same person every three months for the first year). They met in Morrisons café, as before when she met the Man, and followed the same procedure. The Woman was quite smiley, very pleasant, or at least determined to appear so. She had tea, nothing fancy, no Earl Grey or anything. She said Sarah was doing well. Tara kept her expression blank, wondering how this judgement was made. Did it rest on the fact that she'd kept her excruciatingly boring job? Was it because she'd caused no trouble of any kind, or none that had come to the notice of any of the authorities? Or was it because she hadn't had a nervous breakdown with the strain of becoming a new person? It didn't matter, really, but she would like to have known how the assessment that she was 'doing well' was made.

The Woman asked if there was anything she needed help with, any difficulties she was experiencing. Tara took the opportunity to say she would like to get her driving licence back and she would like to have a car which she thought she could afford. She wanted to get out at the weekends and see something of what she'd heard was beautiful countryside. Ah. This was a problem. She couldn't have her old licence back, because of the name. She'd have to apply, as Sarah Scott, for a licence and this would mean, of course, sitting the test. Did she think she was up to it? Not just the driving, but the mental strain of it all? Tara said she thought she was. Very well, the Woman said, though she looked doubtful. It's more complicated these days, she added, there's an online test first. Tara raised her eyebrows and smiled. I didn't mean, the Woman said, that you wouldn't be up to it, just thought I'd point it out in case, with being out of circulation, you hadn't realised. Thank you, Tara said. She was a nice person, this one.

There was the first tiny awareness of something close to excitement when she went to get the necessary forms to apply for a driving licence. She half expected to find that she didn't have the right documentation but what she'd been issued with passed muster (in fact, it was hardly scrutinised). Booking a few refresher lessons was easy, and the instructor, an amiable middle-aged man, recognised at once that she had driven before.

'Lost your licence, did you?' he said.

If he was waiting for a story about how this had come about, she didn't give him one. Her driving was so smooth and expert he soon gave up directing her and wondered aloud why she'd thought she needed any lessons. Not that I'm complaining, he added, it gives me a holiday.

Maybe it was the exhilaration of driving again that made her careless. The driving instructor dropped her off at the end of her street and she walked briskly down it, her head held high for once. She might even have been humming. Her thoughts were of what sort of second-hand car she would buy. Once she'd had a Ford Escort, then a Fiat, but now she'd try to find a VW Polo, though maybe even a five-year-old Polo might be too expensive. With all this small contentment taking up her mind, it was a shock to discover that her keys were not in her bag. Slowly, trying to be careful and thorough, she put her bag on the windowsill and methodically emptied the contents. There were not many. She unzipped the inner compartment where she kept her money: it was all there. But no keys. She told herself to stay calm and think. The thinking only told her what she'd realised already. The only person who had a key to her house was the landlord and she did not have, in her bag, his telephone number. More thinking, all of it done while she stood absolutely still in front of the house, led to the inevitable conclusion that she would have to break in. This would mean smashing the front window, a rather large piece of glass. The front door was solid wood, no glass panels. What could she do it with? There were no stones lying around, no handy implements. There was no back entrance either: the yard at the rear ended in a wall with a similar yard on the other side. Trying to get into her house that way would mean walking round to the parallel terrace and asking the owners if she could climb over their wall. Even then, she'd have to break a window, though the kitchen had a small one which would be easier to smash. Still she stood there, thinking.

Nancy, watching, waiting, understood at once.

III

'DON'T TELL him,' Nancy said, 'never tell him. It might be against the law.'

Tara started to say that she didn't think having a neighbour's house key could possibly be against any law, but Mrs Armstrong (not yet known by her Christian name) said you couldn't be certain. He, the nephew, the landlord, was a nasty bit of work. No examples of nastiness need be given. Her word should be taken for it. So Tara took it.

It turned out that this key had been in Mrs Armstrong's possession for years and years.

'I was never asked for it back so I never gave it,' she said. 'Nothing wrong with that. That nephew of hers never knew I had it, and she used to have mine. But I saw ahead. Minute Amy fell ill, I got it back. I could see what was coming. Now, don't you touch it. It might be aiding and abetting. I'll do it.'

So the key was produced and fitted into the lock and the door creaked open. It went straight back into Nancy's pocket. Nancy patted it.

'Safe,' she said, 'no harm done.' After that, refreshment most definitely had to be offered.

'Please,' said Tara, 'let me make you a cup of tea. I can't thank you enough. I don't know what I'd have done. Broken a window, I suppose.'

She led the way into the kitchen and put the kettle on, wishing there was somewhere to sit down, but it wasn't that sort of kitchen. It was for cooking and washing dishes and that was all. Mrs Armstrong stood in the doorway, seeming as uncertain as Tara herself.

'Not much change,' she said. 'It's how Amy had it.'

Tara wasn't sure whether this was a criticism or praise. When the tea was made, she said, 'Shall we go and sit down?'

Mrs Armstrong seemed surprised. 'No need for any ceremony,' she said, but followed when the way was led to the living room.

The electric fire was switched on, both bars, but it hardly made any difference to the freezing atmosphere. Gulping her tea, Tara thought longingly of her electric blanket.

Mrs Armstrong didn't appear to be drinking her tea at all. She perched on the edge of her chair, clutching the cup with both hands and looking into its contents as though she were seeing something other than tea there.

'You've been very kind,' Tara said. 'I'm very grateful.'

'He's been in,' Mrs Armstrong said. 'Upstairs too.'

'I beg your pardon?' Tara said.

'The nephew, him, the landlord. He came and poked around.'

'Oh, yes,' Tara said, 'last week. He said he would. He left a note.'

'Did he now?' Mrs Armstrong said, with a strange kind of emphasis on the 'did'.

'Everything was satisfactory apparently,' Tara said.

'Oh, I'm sure it was,' Mrs Armstrong said, nodding in a significant way, though Tara couldn't begin to understand what this significance was.

The fire was beginning to take the worst of the chill off the room, though not enough completely to clear the dull mist on the inside of the window.

'You could write your name on that,' Mrs Armstrong said, pointing to the window. 'No proper heating, in this day and age. The cold killed Amy, that's what I believe. He could've put central heating in, or them storage heaters, but did he bother? No.'

Tara couldn't think of a response, but her silence didn't halt her visitor.

'It'll cost you a fortune,' she went on, 'having to use the electric. The bills! You'd be better off with gas. Have you thought about gas? Getting him to put gas in?'

Tara shook her head.

'Well, you should. I've got gas. Warms the room lovely. Used to the warm, were you?'

'Sorry?' said Tara.

'Where you were, before, you were used to the warm.'

It was said as a statement, not a question. She wondered for a second how to reply to it. Yes, she'd been warm. Nobody suffered from cold temperatures even if from many other things about the conditions. Funny, she hadn't appreciated the warmth, how civilised it was always to be comfortably warm even in the depths of winter. She had a quick flash of the snow falling outside the high, narrow skylight, how pretty it had looked, how it made her long to be outside in the cold and not inside, in the warm. But Mrs Armstrong was waiting, watching her. What had the question, no, the non-question been?

'Yes,' Tara said, 'I was used to rooms being quite warm, but I manage, I don't mind.'

'Thermal underwear,' Mrs Armstrong said, 'that's the way to deal with it. It's pricey, but there's nothing like it, November to May, April if we're lucky. You should get yourself some.'

'Thank you,' Tara said.

How many times had she already thanked this woman? It was so feeble to go on saying it. She should show some interest in Mrs Armstrong, be friendly. Be friendly . . . How was it done? She'd forgotten.

'Have you lived in your house long?' she found herself asking, sounding like the Queen. Hearing herself saying it, feeling quite pleased with how interested it sounded, without being too inquisitive, she repeated a variation. 'I was just wondering if you'd lived in this street a long time.'

'Forty-eight years,' Mrs Armstrong said, with obvious pride.

'Goodness,' Tara said.

A sense of achievement glowed in Mrs Armstrong's face. 'Forty-eight years. 1966, May second. It was raining.'

'Goodness,' Tara said, again, 'that *is* a long time.'

'I'll only leave feet first, in a box.'

Neither 'wow' nor 'goodness' would do in answer to that.

'Not for a long time – years, I hope,' Tara said.

To which Mrs Armstrong replied, 'There's no telling.'

Her tea had only been sipped. Tara could see the cup was still almost full. Oh God, how could she carry on, trying for small talk, exhausted already with the strain. But Mrs Armstrong showed no sign of moving. She sat with her legs slightly apart, her coat buttoned up, her headscarf tightly tied under her chin, staring at Tara. It was, Tara decided, a challenging stare, daring her, but daring her to do what? Come up with another banal query? What? Then she realised that quite likely Mrs Armstrong was waiting for her to tell her something about herself. There should be some sort of exchange, surely. Something to match the revelation that Mrs Armstrong had lived in her house for forty-eight years. She wasn't going to ask directly, but she would be wanting to know why she, Tara – no, Sarah – had come to live here, and how long she was going to stay.

Maybe there was something wrong with the tea.

'Would you like more milk, more sugar?' Tara asked, indicating the undrunk tea.

Mrs Armstrong shook her head. 'You've put a blind up, in the bedroom,' she said.

Did she say it accusingly? Tara wasn't sure.

'Yes,' she said, 'I prefer a blind. It lets in more light.'

'They were good-quality curtains,' Mrs Armstrong said. 'Kept the cold out.'

'Oh, I'm sure,' Tara said.

This could not go on. At the rate the tea was being sipped there would be another half-hour of this torment. Then, suddenly, in a tremendous gulp, the tea vanished down Mrs Armstrong's strong throat.

'I'll have to go, I can't stop,' she said.

Tara was on her feet instantly, full of more thank-yous, endlessly expressing her gratitude, and they were at the front door, and it was over.

She went straight to bed, curling up under the duvet, weak with the effort of trying to be friendly.

Nancy had made sure that she brought the key for Amy's house back with her. She put it in the place she'd always kept it, inside an old box which still smelled of the talcum powder it had once held. Lovely, a lovely faint lavender smell. She put the powder puff on top of it, and then put the box in her dressing-table drawer. Safe, quite safe.

She was a queer one, that Sarah Scott. She looked peaky. Nancy had thought about telling her she looked peaky, and should think about going to a doctor's and asking for a tonic, though probably these days tonics were out of fashion. She was a funny little thing, nothing to her, scared of her own shadow. People like that annoyed Nancy. She found their lack of spirit irritating. No confidence in themselves, always so apologetic. She liked people who looked you in the eye and had a bit of life about them. If you had two legs, two arms, two ears, two eyes, what did you have to look so miserable about? Unless you had some ailment that wasn't obvious. She had to allow for that, she supposed.

She could have asked Sarah Scott where she worked. There would've been no harm in that, but she hadn't been able to think how to word it. She could've said, maybe, 'I notice you leave the house early every weekday,' and then waited. But she had held back from using the word 'notice'. It suggested spying. Better to have said, 'You've settled here, then,' and waited. Something might've come from that. It was an opportunity missed. And the tea was awful. She would show her how to make a proper cup of tea when she came over. This would have to be arranged. Hospitality must be reciprocated, even if Sarah Scott's hospitality had been in return for Nancy's good deed.

She'd done a good deed. Nancy smiled to herself. Oh, she'd certainly been a Good Samaritan, saving Sarah Scott from breaking windows and all sorts of bother. It was a very nice feeling. The beginning of something promising. A proper friendship, maybe.

There was a new routine now, or rather another tiny element added to the existing one. Every morning, as Tara left her house, she saw Mrs Armstrong at her window waving her hand. She appeared to be opening her curtains wider, and this wave was nothing more than a gesture, almost royal the way it was done. Tara raised her own hand in acknowledgement. Now it had to be done every weekday morning. She suddenly remembered Liz waving in that way, the tentative way in which Mrs Armstrong had done. She'd give this little flap of her hand, which could just as well have been swatting away a fly as a wave of greeting. Tara could see her clearly in her head,

Liz rushing through the crowds to meet her, giving this movement of her hand. They were both living in London then. They met sometimes at the Curzon cinema in Shaftesbury Avenue where they had a snack before the film and brought each other up to date on what was happening in their lives. Tara never gave much away, but Liz unloaded the lot. She'd married Mike at nineteen but was having an affair with Alan, a passionate affair apparently. She left no detail out. It then emerged that she was using Tara as her cover.

'But,' said Tara, 'suppose he checked your story out, and I hadn't known you were using me as a cover.'

'Oh,' said Liz, 'he'd never do that, and even if he did, I knew you'd be quick on the uptake and back me up.'

Tara had been quite startled. Would she have understood and backed Liz up?

'Don't tell Molly or Claire,' Liz went on, 'especially not Claire. God knows what she'd do – ring Mike and report me, I expect.'

Yes, Tara had agreed, it was just possible Claire might do that. Then they both laughed.

Oddly, the impulse to send a reply to Claire sprang from this memory of Liz's confession. She found herself thinking about Claire and the letter all day, and as a consequence behaving more like Tara than Sarah Scott. She didn't shuffle along the aisle on the bus but barged her way to the door and was first off when it stopped. On the return journey, in the afternoon, instead of listlessly trailing down the street she almost ran, so eager was she, after a whole day of thinking, in her desire to reply to Claire. She had a point to make. The point was, well, there was a point, to do with loyalty, to do with standing by people and trying to see things from their perspective. There was certainly a point to it. She settled down to write a letter. It was exhilarating writing it until it began to turn into an accusation, full of long-suppressed resentment and bitterness. If the impulse to reply to Claire's invitation was going to be indulged, then it could not take this form. A rant was damaging (to herself). A measured tone was needed. The things she really wanted to express could be implied but not so crudely slapped down. The art was to slip the blade of the dagger in without it being noticed till the pain registered.

Revenge, that was the ugly truth. But revenge for what exactly? There had been no dastardly deed, the sort of thing for which an act of revenge would be appropriate. All that had happened was that friendship, at a crucial time, had been found wanting. It hadn't lived up to expectations. It hadn't survived a true test. But Tara knew she'd got everything out of proportion. There had been a fading away of support, that was all, and she herself was perhaps to blame. She'd pleaded guilty.

Did that not cancel the obligations of friendship? Who would want to go on being friends with a woman who pleaded guilty to *that* deed? And now that this friendship was on offer again, wasn't it understandable? She'd served her time, the slate was clear. She could be a friend again. Wasn't it, after all, impressive to be given another chance? Shouldn't she be grateful, and accept it?

Tara struggled hard to believe this.

She passed the driving test without difficulty, and then began the search for a second-hand car she could afford. Getting the money freed and transferred to Sarah's name and bank account was laborious, involving several meetings with the Woman and then, less pleasantly, the Man again. But finally it was done, and she had £3,000 to spend.

She'd always thought that her money would be forfeited, part of the punishment, but no, it wasn't. She hadn't been convicted of fraud or any financial irregularities, and the money in the bank came from impeccable sources, so there was no problem about it. It had sat there, in a deposit account, all these years, hers to do what she liked with. Knowing this made her feel rich, but until now she'd felt she had no right to spend it. She'd bought an electric blanket, a duvet, a blind and a few other odds and ends, but that was all. What she now earned, the small wage, covered her bills and rent and food and fares, leaving very little over. But this money was there and now was the time to spend half of it. What she bought, from a garage near where she worked, was a little Fiat. Unfortunately it was green, which worried her a little. Green was relatively unusual. It made the car highly distinctive.

She knew Mrs Armstrong would see the car – how could she not? She parked right outside her house, thankful that there was no need, as yet, for a parking permit in the street. There was plenty of room. No one to the right or left of her house appeared to have a car, and on the opposite side neither did Mrs Armstrong or her immediate neighbours. The green car stood out. Coming home from work, she could see it from the end of the street where the bus dropped her off. The sight of it was like a welcome home. Her car. Hers. When for so long she'd had nothing. The significance threatened to overwhelm her. Her first car, hers, after she met Tom (his gift), had had the same effect, a sort of boost to her morale, a lifting of her spirits. The car then had meant all the obvious things: independence, freedom, even the promise of adventure. She'd crashed it. Sarah would never do such a thing.

Sarah was much too cautious and careful. She would treat her car with respect. She wouldn't, as Tara had done, regularly exceed the speed limit and take risks on roundabouts. She would never,

never, get points on her licence. She had learned her lesson (several lessons, in fact) long ago.

'So,' the Woman said, at their next appointment, 'how does it feel to have wheels?'

For a moment, Tara saw herself literally with wheels attached to the soles of her boots, a pleasing cartoon image which made her smile.

'Good,' she said.

'And are you doing much driving? Getting out and about more? Seeing the countryside?'

Tara nodded, but it was a lie. She hadn't yet driven further than the supermarket.

'I'm going to go along the coast this weekend,' she said.

'And will you take a friend?' the Woman asked, watching her keenly. 'Have you a friend yet?'

'Yes,' said Tara, 'I have. My neighbour, Mrs Armstrong.'

'Mrs?' queried the Woman.

'She's very formal,' Tara said hurriedly. 'She prefers to be called Mrs at the moment.'

'Well,' said the Woman, 'that's good. I hope this friendship develops. You need friends, Sarah. It isn't good to go on being so isolated now. Friendship is important, it will do wonders for you.'

A lecture on friendship . . . It was too much. Tara said nothing more after that. Next, the Woman would be asking about her love life and telling her love was important and would do wonders for her. It was so insulting. Rage built up in her, a Tara-like rage, the sort that at one time threatened to rule her life. The trouble was, she'd rarely let it all out. Her habit had been to contain it so that it burned inside her stomach and filled her head with a booming noise. Little whimpers of this rage would escape her clenched lips, but that was all. Her face she knew, because people pointed it out, would flush a deep, dark red. They would ask her if she was all right, whether she suffered from high blood pressure, and she would struggle to smile and say that must be it and she must make an appointment with her GP.

She invited Mrs Armstrong to go with her for a car ride on Sunday.

Once, she and Claire and Liz and Molly had gone for car rides. They couldn't be called anything else except 'car rides'. There was no planned destination, no pretence that they knew where they were going. It was just the fun, the excitement of having the use of a parents' car to drive around in. All of them eighteen and desperate to leave home. Movement was the thing – up, off, away, and who cares where.

It was rescuing that child which brought them together, then bound them, but Tara liked to think that if this incident hadn't happened something else would have drawn them close. It seemed, once they'd become a quartet, that there was a natural affinity between them for all their various differences. What was it? A restlessness? A sense of ambition? What was this friendship based on, what glued it together? Why did they seek each other out years later when they'd all gone their separate ways and it was difficult to meet? Why, when they had all made other friends, and had partners or husbands, why was this particular friendship so deep and special?

History. That must be it. They concluded that what gave their friendship such strength was knowing each other so thoroughly. It was the legacy of lolling around when they were young, talking and drinking the night away, that was what did it. All that *time*, all those hours and hours of droning on to each other, letting slip likes and dislikes, worries, fears, hopes. No friendship afterwards could come near this kind of intimacy. They each had a dossier of emotional confessions on each other, many of them made by mistake and regretted. These were never mentioned in subsequent years, but they were there, in the collective memory of the quartet. And so, when their meetings became much less frequent, they never worried about the time gap, there was never the feeling that they had to get to know each other again. They expected to slip effortlessly, within ten minutes, into the old familiarity.

But Tara remembered how, the last time they'd all met, something like eleven years ago, she'd felt a slight sense of distance from the other three. Maybe, she thought, it was just a matter of how she was ageing differently from them. They were all only in their early thirties but the other three looked older, already on the cusp of middle age in her opinion. Claire's cheekbones had all but disappeared and her hair, now in a stiff bob, made her face look even heavier. She'd taken to dressing in trouser suits which didn't help. And Liz's face was terribly lined for such a young woman, all doubtless due to her disastrous first marriage and the two miscarriages. Molly had put on weight in all the wrong places, but her face was still the same: chubby, cheerful, pink-cheeked. Only her clothes, apart from the new weight she carried, aged her. Fussy blouse, dreary grey skirt, and hideous brown lace-up shoes. She'd studied the three of them saying nothing, but aware that they, too, were aware of the outward difference between them. They might, she recalled thinking, even have envied her. She quite liked that feeling, that they were looking at her and listening to her and being impressed.

She came away from that meeting sensing that there was a new distance between her and Claire, Molly and Liz. She told herself that since their lives were now so radically different they couldn't expect to feel the same connection. But she wanted to. The puzzle was, why did she want to? She had Tom, she didn't need these friends as once she had. They, of course, did not like Tom. They'd only met him two or three times but that, it seemed, had been enough. She was convinced class had a lot to do with it. Tom was clever, he had a better degree than any of them, and he was holding down a high-level job in finance, but he didn't look or sound like a man who was 'something in the City'. His Liverpool accent was thick and his appearance rough. Even in his City suit he looked dishevelled. And his manners . . . She had to admit he did not have the manners of a gentleman. But these things were minor compared to what her friends really held against Tom. They thought he dominated her, and despised them. They were wary, suspicious, uncomfortable in his presence.

'You will look after her, won't you?' Liz had said to him at the wedding.

'She doesn't need looking after,' Tom said.

What was so wrong with that reply? She supposed it was the way he'd said it: contemptuously.

What to wear?

What to wear, for a car ride? On a Sunday? The problem overwhelmed Nancy, threatening to take all the pleasure from the outing. She'd have to wear one of those seat-belt things, and if she wore her coat it might prove uncomfortable. It was a thick coat. But if she just wore a jacket – she had three to choose from, all different weights – she might not be warm enough. Would there be a heater on in this car? There was no way of knowing.

Then there was the matter of where they would be going, whether there was a destination in mind, one where she might be expected to get out of the car and walk about. In which case boots and her thicker stockings would be best. She didn't wear trousers, never had. Everyone else did, a positive fright some of them looked, bulging out all over the place, but she never had. Skirts, dresses, that's what she thought proper. Not always a hat, though. Once, she always wore a hat but often now she resorted to a headscarf, especially if she'd just had her hair set. They didn't do perms any more, or the place she went to didn't and she didn't want to change to a place where they did. Her hair was still good. Thick, a bit of a wave in it, and it responded well to being set every six weeks.

She was ready by ten. The note had said 'about eleven'. She wished people wouldn't be so vague. What on earth did 'about' mean? Five to eleven, five past eleven? And it hadn't been made clear whether she should go across the road at 'about' eleven, or whether Sarah Scott would come and knock for her. Well, either way, she was ready by ten, sitting just to the left of her living-room window so that she could see if Sarah Scott came out of her door. The green car looked odd standing there. The other cars, at the other end of the street, were black or grey. Green stood out. It wasn't, she thought, in very good condition. She could see a bit of rust on the back bumper, and there were one or two dents near the rear door, but maybe they didn't matter. It was the engine that mattered. She felt quite pleased at realising this. She might never have had a car in her life, but she knew it was the engine that mattered.

She didn't like waiting like this, but she was always doing it, getting ready far too early, and then waiting long before it was time. Once, she'd thought this a good habit, one to be proud of having, but now she wasn't so sure. It made time go so slowly, and it made her anxious. Often, when the clock still had twenty minutes to go, she'd be exhausted with all the waiting. She thought about going over at five to eleven, when at last clock and watch both showed that was the time, to knock on Sarah Scott's door, but that might make her look too eager, even though she was. She wanted to seem casual. Not offhand – that would be rude, ungrateful – but casual would be fine. She was going to let Sarah Scott come and get her, and when she did she was going to pretend she had forgotten her scarf – 'Oh, is that the time?' she would say – and keep Sarah Scott waiting just a minute.

Casual.

*

Sarah Scott didn't have a map. Tara would have thought nothing of this, but Sarah knew she would need one. After all, she didn't know the area. She'd chosen it at random and the main attraction was that she didn't know it. All she knew was the bus route to work, and the town centre which she'd walked round. The coast road, which she intended to drive along, was to the west of the town. The bus, at one point, crested a hill from which there was a brief glimpse of the sea. This always lifted her spirits, even on one of the many grey days when the sea was merely a mass of dark matter, still and sullen, not a white wave upon it. She would find that road easily, surely. And Mrs Armstrong would know the way.

At ten-thirty she was on the verge of cancelling the whole outing. The thought of sitting beside Mrs Armstrong for any length of time in a confined space, not knowing where she was going, made her sweat with apprehension. What had got into her, suggesting such a thing? It was madness, folly. She didn't want her neighbour as a friend yet this would be interpreted by her, understandably, as a gesture of friendship. She would be committed ever after to continuing the uneasy relationship. Mrs Armstrong would likely reciprocate, and she would find herself invited to a cup of tea, and she would have to go, and it would trundle on, this 'friendship', and it would all be her own fault. It would be the beginnings of a false friendship, one that would never deepen into anything more than the neighbourly connection it really was. Was she so desperate to prove that Sarah Scott could make, could have, friends, that she was prepared to throw herself at Mrs Armstrong?

But there she was again, comparing Sarah's making of a friend with Tara's. Tara hadn't had to try. Friends had just happened. Friends had been made through people gravitating towards her rather than she to them. Or else they'd been made through events, not all of them dramatic ones like the rescue of the child in the river which had brought Claire, Molly and Liz to her. The sports she played had drawn people to her who went on to become good friends. Especially men. She hadn't met Tom, of course, through tennis – he despised all sport except football – but she'd met several others before him, and had become involved with one of them, become more than a friend.

What was 'more' than a friend? Did the sex, or love, or sex and love, supersede the friend part? Did a man become less of a friend when he became 'more' than a friend? She thought so. Odd, hard to define why, but she thought so. The friendship part became overpowered by the sexual part. Sometimes, she'd wanted the pre-sexual friendship back, that time when she and Tom were finding out about each other, discovering similarities, accommodating differences. He never voted.

That was a big difference, his disinterest in politics. It quite shocked her. She insisted he voted in the first general election after they became friends, telling him that she didn't care who he voted for (though she did) but just that he voted. She said he couldn't be her friend if he did not exercise his democratic right, fulfil his democratic duty, to vote. She was only half joking, though he laughed for ages at her solemn passion. All politicians, he said, were crooks.

Sarah, of course, was older. 'I am Sarah Scott and I am older and it is harder to make friends when one is older. I don't play tennis, or any other game. My workplace is not conducive to making friends.' She tried saying these things to herself but as explanations for her failure to make friends they didn't work. No reason why she couldn't join a tennis club in the summer, or find some other sport, or exercise, she could take up. Physically, she was fit. That was how she'd spent a lot of time in the past years, keeping fit, working out a regime of simple exercises like running on the spot, doing press-ups, avoiding the temptation just to slump. As for work, there were plenty of friendships in existence there. She'd heard women declare that it was the chat, the gossip, the camaraderie that kept them going, the way they all looked out for each other. But she, this new person Sarah, didn't share in this. Why not?

Why not? Because she kept herself to herself for obvious reasons. Sarah couldn't keep herself to herself and at the same time make friends because friendship meant *giving* something of yourself. Giving only a tiny bit was difficult. It led to a demand for more. And then there was the taking bit as well. You had to take as well as give for a friendship to develop and survive, and Sarah emphatically rejected the idea of involving herself in another's life. No, she wouldn't, couldn't, do it. So, could she risk taking Mrs Armstrong for a ride? Too late now. It was five to eleven, and her coat was on, the car keys in her pocket, and she was crossing the street to knock on Mrs Armstrong's door.

Afterwards, once home, Nancy badly needed someone to listen to an account of her Trip (this was how she was already referring to it) but there was no chance of that. So she decided to describe it to herself, making a tale of it, editing and improving it as she went along. She would pretend that she was neither herself nor Sarah Scott but a narrator – that was the right term, wasn't it? – telling a story in which she had no part. Then she could refer to herself as Nancy, or Mrs Armstrong. She loved this idea.

She hummed hymns as she took her coat off and set about making her tea. Then she began her tale. They'd had a cup of tea while they were on the Trip but nothing to eat. It wasn't the sort of café, or the sort of place, she would have chosen to stop at but Sarah Scott had loved it. She gave a little cry of pleasure when they drove through St Bees and she saw, from above, the beach and the cliffs. Nothing special about them that Nancy could see but then she'd been seeing them since she was a child, taken there on Sunday school outings. The beach was vast, the tide well out, and only a few dog walkers were visible marching along, throwing balls for their animals who went mad with joy at all the space. For one awful moment Nancy thought she was going to be asked to accompany Sarah Scott along the beach, and she had all her excuses ready, but no, Sarah Scott wondered if she would mind if she herself had a quick walk and then joined Nancy in the café. Nancy didn't mind the woman having a walk on her own – on her own, thank God – but she did mind sitting in a café on her own, thank you. So she told Sarah Scott she'd just sit in the car and enjoy the view while Sarah walked, and then they could go into the café together. Otherwise she'd have finished her tea and they'd be wanting the table. This made no sense, but was accepted by Sarah who immediately left the car and ran, *ran*, down the steps on to the stones which separated the steps from the sand.

Nancy watched her, startled by her energy. How old was this neighbour of hers? She still didn't know, though she'd laid all kinds of verbal traps for Sarah to fall into and unwittingly reveal her age. Definitely under fifty, but how much under?

Nancy hadn't revealed her own age either, though she was proud of it now, but Sarah had shown no interest in discovering it. She'd shown no interest in anything, come to that. Perfectly polite, and pleasant, but no curiosity. All her life Nancy had been trying to restrain her own devouring curiosity, a trait much frowned on by her mother. Now, watching Sarah stride down the huge beach, right beside the sea, almost in it, Nancy was framing questions in such a way that her inquisitiveness would be disguised and therefore acceptable. 'You're very fit' was a statement, not a question, but ought to lead, with luck, to Sarah saying something like 'Yes, I keep fit, I . . .' and then some revelation about how indeed she kept fit. Nancy nodded with satisfaction at the thought.

The café wasn't busy but that was because it was a cloudy, windy day and it was almost closing time. They sat at a table in front of the window looking at the beach. Sarah went to the toilet, and on the way back stopped to look at a bookcase up against the wall in the corner. It was full of second-hand books donated for sale to raise funds for the lifeboats. She saw Sarah pick out and pay for two of them. They looked in poor condition to Nancy. There was a definite smell of cigarette smoke from one of them and the other had mucky stains on the cover. The titles and names of the authors were in too small a print for Nancy to read upside down and she certainly wasn't going to touch them. Sarah smiled at her. She looked better after her walk, healthier, some colour in her pale face.

'I like to read biographies,' she said.

'Very nice,' Nancy said, knowing it was a meaningless comment, but pleased that at last she'd found out something about Sarah Scott without having to ask: she liked to read biographies. Well!

But no conversation developed from this. They drank their tea. The two women doing the serving started putting chairs, upended, on the empty tables and turning the sign on the glass door to 'Closed'. Sarah took Nancy's arm to help her down the steps which Nancy found thoughtful of her but unnecessary. She didn't like to think she might look as though she needed help. They drove on, down the coast road, mostly in silence. Sarah marvelled at the Lake District hills on the horizon to their left, and said she wanted to explore them another time, leading Nancy to list all the lakes and villages she'd visited. Sarah didn't ask any questions about these places Nancy had mentioned, but then she was concentrating on her driving on a tricky stretch of road and Nancy conceded this might have held her back from talking. They were near Ravenglass by then, passing Sellafield.

'What was here before they built that scary building?' Sarah asked her.

'Farms,' Nancy said, and then, in a rush of speech which was out of her mouth before she thought better of it, 'our farm was one of them. Compulsory purchase, they said. My dad went mad, but it was no good. Lost all his cows.'

They turned round at that point and started back to Workington.

'So you were a farmer's daughter,' Sarah said. 'How lovely being brought up on a farm.'

'Was nothing lovely about it,' Nancy said. 'Cows take a lot of work. I didn't care about the cows going, only the land.'

She'd said too much, given too much away. Now Sarah would pester her with questions, likely. But she didn't. She only asked one, a silly one:

'Were the cows like those?' and she pointed out of the car window at a field full of black cows with broad white stripes across their stomachs.

'No,' said Nancy, 'those are Belted Galloways. Ours were Friesians. They were big enough, though. I used to help Dad measure them.'

'Measure them?' said Sarah, laughing. 'How do you measure a cow? And why?'

So Nancy told her. Sarah listened carefully as Nancy went into detail and found herself repeating the instructions back to Nancy.

'Measure from the shoulder to the second joint on the tail,' Nancy was saying.

'Do tails have joints?' Sarah asked, amazed.

'Of course they do,' said Nancy, sounding bad-tempered now. 'Any road,' she went on, 'multiply five times the length and divide by twenty-one to get the weight.'

'Divide by twenty-one,' Sarah echoed. Her hands gripped the steering wheel even more tightly. 'How to measure a cow,' she kept repeating.

It had annoyed Nancy. Remembering this, as she told the tale of the trip to herself, speaking bits of it aloud, pretending to be Sarah as well as herself, then to be neither, just a narrator. Nancy worried that Sarah had been mocking her. Had she been trying to suppress laughter? But there was nothing funny about measuring a cow. It had been hard. Her father got in a temper doing it. She should've told Sarah that.

She was finished. The day had been gone over, all details about the trip covered. Nancy could find nothing else to add. But of course, she realised, she hadn't included the small, telltale signs her sharp eyes had noticed. These were hard to list. Something about Sarah's expression when she had to halt at a crossing while a child of about ten pushed a woman in a wheelchair over it caught Nancy's attention. It was odd. Sitting beside her, Nancy couldn't see Sarah's full face but from the side she saw her chin go up in a sudden movement and she saw too that Sarah was not looking at either the child or the woman in the wheelchair. She was looking up, almost into the inside of the roof of the car. When the wheelchair was safely across, Sarah didn't drive on. The engine stalled, and she had to restart it.

'Sorry,' she said.

Her hands on the wheel tightened. Nancy had seen the knuckles turn white. Now what had that been about?

This little instance of a peculiar reaction to something ordinary stuck in Nancy's mind. She must, she decided, be extra cautious with Sarah Scott. She was fragile, that was for sure, and tense, never truly relaxed. Had she had a breakdown, one of those nervous ones? Was that why she was here? It put Nancy off the woman. As her mother used to say, we could all have nervous breakdowns if we tried. She didn't want to be involved in one. But then maybe there was nothing wrong with Sarah mentally, maybe how she'd reacted was just to do with some sort of memory. Now, *that* Nancy could relate to. There were plenty of such moments in her own experience when something jolted her memory so violently that for a second or two she was back within it, and she didn't like it. Plenty of memories to make her own lips tremble, if they were suddenly recalled.

But she didn't invite Sarah Scott in immediately for a cup of tea. Best to wait.

IV

TARA BECAME an explorer. Without Nancy Armstrong beside her, she followed whichever road took her fancy once she'd turned from the main roads and headed inland. These roads were empty and she felt as though they'd been kept clear especially for her. They twisted and turned, the hedges either side thick with hawthorn blossom, climbing ever higher. She passed through no villages until she came to a place called Pica, some five miles inland. It was the strangest collection of houses, just one long road, halfway down, at right angles. No shops, no school, no church, only two or three cars. It felt eerie, though it was a sunny day, but Tara liked it. She wondered how these tightly squashed-together houses came to be built here. Was it something to do with mines, at one time? Mrs Armstrong would know. There were no people visible. A ghost village except that the television aerials on every roof, sometimes three of them, indicated otherwise. And at the far end she could see lines of washing pinned to stout ropes, blowing vigorously, giant wooden props holding the lines up.

She drove slowly through the village, then parked half a mile further on. The hills were in front of her, a far-off jagged row of dipping peaks zigzagging along the horizon. She fixed her eyes on them and began to walk. She'd always liked to walk. Her friends had complained about the speed she went at, Molly in particular objecting and asking what was the hurry. She felt strong as she marched along. The smack of her feet on the road was comforting. It told her she was full of energy and now it had somewhere to go. She wondered how far she could get before she had used this energy up but turned back when the calves of her legs began to ache. Her car was so far away she couldn't see it and the houses of Pica looked like distant blurs. The weather was changing. She could see the white wind turbines whirling furiously, and behind them huge, billowing black clouds bunching themselves into a great, ominous mass over the sea. Oh, it was an exhilarating sight, full of power, and though all the muscles in her legs were aching fiercely she began to run, a ponderous, slow run but still she was running. Her body was near to exhausted but her mind was alert and settled. She was Tara again.

It was the end of May. The reunion was to be in late June.

Nancy wished she had a car. Without one, it was impossible to find out where Sarah Scott went to on her, by now, regular outings somewhere. Somewhere . . . but where? Nancy hadn't been invited again to accompany her neighbour. Why not? she wondered (out loud, as usual, wandering about her house, frowning into the living-room mirror above the fireplace, scowling at her reflection in the bathroom mirror). What did I do wrong? It was an insult, not to be invited again. Don't be petty, she told herself but she replied, pretty sharpish, that she was not being petty. She didn't expect to be invited *every* week, good heavens no, and she wouldn't have accepted an invitation if it had been given every week, but occasionally, yes, occasionally, she would have. There was one possible explanation, of course: the failure to reciprocate. Well, she didn't have a car, so how could she? But no, that was letting herself off the hook. Don't be silly, Nancy, she said. There are other ways of returning a favour shown. Tea! A proper tea, with home-made cake and scones, and blackcurrant jam, of which she still had one jar left. She'd put a lace cloth on the little table and set out cups and saucers nicely. Then the two of them could have a proper chat.

She'd waited too long. It was nearly six weeks since the car ride, but Nancy excused herself on the grounds that she'd been expecting another invitation to go for a run in the car and at *that* point she'd been going to ask Sarah Scott to tea. Oh, stop it, Nancy, she said, that doesn't make sense. Just get on with it. Ask her.

Tara sat for a while in her car, looking ahead towards the hills of Scotland across the sea. The silence was intense. She had the windows down, but the only sound was the merest whisper of wind. No human voice. No humans. She felt a sudden burst of happiness, a physical feeling in her chest, and found herself pressing her hands over it, to keep it there. She felt free of Sarah Scott though she knew that for the time being she was on her way back to the dreary woman. She served her purpose, provided a carapace under which her real self could hide until the time was right – but when would that be? A new life was only an external new life. She knew that it should be recognised. But at the moment, physically exhausted by her long walk, she felt free of the burden it imposed. It had been her choice, after all, her choice to recreate herself as someone calm and nice and fury free.

But now she had to find a way out.

Nancy Armstrong came out of her door the moment Tara parked her car. She waved. Tara got out and waved back, trying at the same time to reach her own front door.

'You'll be ready for some tea,' Mrs Armstrong called. 'I've made a cake. I've got the kettle on, come on in.'

I am Sarah Scott, Tara reminded herself. Sarah Scott will go and have tea and cake with her neighbour Mrs Armstrong. Very well. But how she despised this weak woman, this Sarah Scott.

There was always the possibility. Claire said this to Liz and Molly several times. They told her not to be ridiculous, that of course, considering there had been no reply to her letter of several months ago, there was *no* possibility of Tara turning up. But Claire, being Claire, persisted in this stubborn belief and included Tara in all the plans. These 'plans' were hardly extensive or complicated but, Liz and Molly agreed, Claire made a meal of them. She loved organising events, and even if there was not much to organise she created complications, trying to involve the other two in a way they resisted.

'Oh, Claire,' they sighed, 'do what you like. Yes, yes, anything you think appropriate.' Then they left her to it.

But Liz and Molly looked forward to this reunion too. The fact was, the three of them hadn't been together for years. The last time was on Liz's fortieth birthday. They'd phoned each other often, and Liz had met Molly five or six times, for lunch, and they'd each had dates – 'play-dates' as they skittishly called them – with Claire, but they hadn't had a threesome for all that time. Claire was the organiser and she'd been so busy organising umpteen other things that she'd had no time for organising reunions. Liz and Molly never even thought of taking on this not very onerous task themselves. No, no, Claire was the organiser.

'It's always left to me,' Claire complained to her husband Dan, but he didn't bother responding to this. Claire liked to act put-upon but he knew how she relished being relied on, pleased to be doing things for others. Smug? Yes, she was a little smug, but not in an unpleasant way. What she wanted, he knew, was to be admired for her social conscience, her willingness to take the lead in bringing people together and giving them a good time. So long as she was appreciated this smugness did not get out of hand but unless at least one person told her she was a 'treasure' then it could get ugly. He waited for signs of this: '"Do what you like," they say, as if I didn't have enough to do, as if I were forcing them to have a reunion.' He was diplomatic, assured her that Liz and Molly hadn't meant to sound so offhand and that really they had such trust in her organising abilities that they'd meant to say they merely wanted to follow her lead. Grudgingly, Claire accepted this as a possible explanation. Plans went ahead.

But as the day for the celebratory lunch drew near, Claire did wonder why she was feeling a touch apprehensive. This had nothing to do with the meal but with the awareness that Tara might indeed turn up. She'd always hoped she would, but now this hope was tinged with worry. Might there be a scene? Might Tara only turn up to accuse them of betrayal, disloyalty, etc.? And if she did, and in public, how would they deal with it? Claire, for all her practical abilities, had an imaginative side to her nature which sometimes astonished her with its strength. She saw Tara entering the restaurant, she saw herself and Liz and Molly rising from their chairs with cries of welcome, and then she saw Tara stride forward and shout – What? – *and* slap each of their faces. She had to stop herself at this awful point and tell herself not to be so melodramatic and silly. Nevertheless, several versions of this sort of thing played before her eyes and had to be dealt with. She dealt with them, firmly substituting an image of a rather shy Tara hesitantly approaching her friends, unsure of her welcome . . . and oh, how they would rise to *that* occasion, how they would vie with each other to say how glad they were to see her, how they'd thought about her so much and—

And what? This, Claire decided, had to be prepared for. The excuses, the justifications. Best not to give either, because they all knew a test of true friendship had been failed. They had had a meeting at the time. No, not a meeting, a discussion over the phone, first herself with Molly, then with

Liz. They had called each other often at that time, back and forth the calls had gone, all of them speaking for an hour or more about what they'd read, what they'd heard, and most of all about whether it could be true. No, they'd all agreed, it could *not* be true. But nevertheless there it was in the newspapers. Tara Fraser (interestingly, they thought, she'd never taken Tom's surname even though she'd married him) arrested. For murder. *That* was the moment they should have acted, stood by Tara. Immediately, without hesitation. She wasn't allowed bail so it would have meant applying to visit her in prison, and none of them had done that. If Tara came, should any kind of apology be attempted? Or would that at once strike the wrong note? Claire exhausted herself trying to decide, but as June approached the tension became almost unbearable: would Tara come, or not?

The girl – Nancy thought of Sarah Scott as a girl, though not as a lass, the distinction clear in her mind, which was the only mind that mattered – the girl was hungry. She ate two scones, both liberally spread with jam, and needed no urging to have a large piece of Dundee cake. She ate daintily, neatly, no wolfing the food down, and Nancy was pleased to see the linen napkin used to dab the corners of the girl's mouth even though, the jam being blackcurrant, there would now be a stain hard to remove. Nancy ate a scone herself, and talked. She told the girl how she had bought the blackcurrants in the market and made the jam back in July. She told her the exact location of the stall in the market, which was not to be confused with another stall nearby. She recited the recipe for the Dundee cake which she knew off by heart because she'd been making it for more than fifty years even when almonds were scarce. She talked and talked and then, when the girl had finished eating and had declined another piece of cake, Nancy waited for her to talk. And waited. Maybe she needed prompting. Nancy decided the girl, this Sarah Scott, needed help, just as she'd needed it on their outing. This politeness had gone on too long.

'Where you from, then?' Nancy asked, forgetting she'd already asked this when she had that cup of (awful) tea and that this simple enquiry had made Sarah freeze. But it was harmless, wasn't it, asking someone where they hailed from? Course it was. 'Where you from?' she repeated.

'London,' Tara said.

'Big place,' Nancy said. 'There's London and London, isn't there?'

Tara stared at her, the remark apparently worrying her because she frowned, and shook her head, and said, 'Sorry?'

'London,' Nancy repeated. 'I've never been, never wanted to, but I've heard things. There's London and London, folk say – there's

Buckingham Palace and Trafalgar Square and all them bits you see on the television, and then there's bits you don't, unless something bad happens, riots and that.'

'Oh,' Tara said, 'I suppose so.'

It was such a feeble response that Nancy felt entitled to press on.

'What brought you here, then? From London?'

She was watching Sarah closely. Yes, her question had been direct and could be thought cheeky, but they'd had tea, which, in Nancy's opinion, established a degree of intimacy greater than the neighbourliness which had existed before. If she wanted to, Sarah could dodge the question. She could say something evasive – 'I hardly know myself' – and laugh, and move on. But she didn't.

'I stuck a pin in a map,' Tara said.

Nancy knew instantly that this was the truth. Stuck a pin in a map! She was so tickled by this reply that her face creased into a smile the like of which it hadn't known for years. She could feel her cheeks bulging and her eyes widening and her mouth opening in celebration.

'Oh, dear me,' she gasped. 'Stuck a pin in a map!'

Tara was nodding, smiling now herself.

'Have another cup of tea,' Nancy said, wiping away the tears of mirth which had suddenly leaked out.

There were other questions she could ask, but she cautioned herself. It was like betting. Best to stop, at least for the time being, after such a success, unless Sarah herself now opened up and offered more. But she didn't. She finished her tea and got up and said thank you and it had been lovely and she must go. Nancy let her. She saw her to the door and then she went and cleared the tea things away and then she sat down and had a good long think: a woman who came to Workington because she'd stuck a pin in a map. Plenty there to think about.

She'd told the truth. Well, one small truth, nothing too revealing. Tara didn't know whether what she felt was shock or elation. She hadn't dissembled, out it had come, and she'd been believed instantly. Maybe it was that simple: someone asks a question and you just give them the correct answer. But what if her shrewd neighbour had asked a different question? What if she had asked *why* did you stick a pin in a map? Or why did you want to leave London? Or what if she had followed up her enigmatic remark about London – 'There's London and London' – with 'What part of London did you live in?' How easy would the truth be then? So she stopped congratulating herself. She'd been lucky, that was all. A question thrown at her which had not been a real challenge. Nancy – she was Nancy now, permission to use her Christian name given as the cake was cut – Nancy had been amused. There was nothing particularly amusing about sticking a pin in a map but she'd smiled hugely.

It occurred to Tara that she might be able to tell Nancy other things. They were, surely, becoming friends, were they not? Not friends as Claire, Molly and Liz had been her friends, but a new sort of friend. But, strangely, thinking of Nancy as a 'friend' felt too intimate, almost as embarrassing as it would have been if the term 'lover' were used instead. Even calling her by her Christian name felt too personal. Mrs Armstrong, neighbour, was much more comfortable. But there could be no going back.

It was the Woman again. Same meeting place, same routine. The Woman was pleased with her. 'You're doing well, Sarah,' she said. 'Six months now, and you seem settled. Would you agree you're feeling settled?'

Tara, noting that her new name had been stuck to, gave a non-committal nod.

'You don't seem sure. Am I missing something? Work, perhaps? We've always known it is far below your capabilities. Is it becoming frustrating? Do you perhaps need to move on? Are you ready to try to get closer to the work you once did? Sarah?'

The work she once did . . . She could hardly remember it. Lab work. Analysing things. What things? She couldn't remember. Welwyn Garden City, that's where she'd worked for a long time. On cytotoxic drugs. A tiny cog in a complex machine, but she'd needed a degree in chemistry to become that cog. A great career ahead of her, she'd hoped, starting off so lowly, then aspiring to greater things, only the aspiring hadn't got her as far as she'd expected. Meeting Tom interrupted her ambition – that was it. She'd stopped aspiring. She didn't want to go back to being ambitious. Once she'd progressed to being in charge of one small unit, she'd been satisfied.

'No,' she told the Woman, 'I don't want to do the work I used to do. My job is fine. No strain.'

This was the right thing to have said. The Woman nodded.

'Very wise,' she said, 'very sensible, for the time being, if you're happy.'

Tara laughed. It sounded forced, but it wasn't. It always made her laugh when people used the word 'happy' so carelessly. It was ridiculous: happy! Such a silly-sounding little word, covering such a vast array of emotion. Did people go around declaring, 'I am happy'? She didn't think so. Too dangerous. You could get struck down by a bolt of lightning for such daring. The word that could not be spoken or it would surely disintegrate.

'Have I said something funny?' the Woman asked, smiling, but clearly a little offended, suspecting she herself was being laughed at.

'No, no,' Tara said. 'I was just remembering something, you know, that song, that dirge, "If you're happy and you know it clap your hands."'

The Woman looked puzzled, so Tara sang it quietly, lightly clapping her hands.

'Sorry,' she said. 'I can't explain why I laughed. It's complicated. Anyway, yes, thank you, I'm fine.'

She couldn't bring herself to say, as the Woman wanted her to say, that she was happy. Best to change the subject.

'I'm thinking,' she said, hardly able to believe she was about to say what she was going to say, 'I'm thinking of having a holiday. Going away for a weekend soon.'

The Woman said she was pleased to hear this. It showed that Sarah was making significant progress – it really was a very good sign that she was feeling able to do this – and she looked forward to hearing how this planned break went.

It was a long way, something like 300 miles. Tara didn't think she could do it in one day – she'd be too tired. Her concentration wasn't good. She knew that her mind had a habit of drifting if she drove more than an hour or so, and she had to stop and pull herself together before going on.

Why this should be, she didn't know, and she was certainly not going to consult any doctor to try to find out. She'd had enough psychiatric tests of one sort or another in the last ten years and she didn't want any more. Anything the matter with her, if it were not of an obvious physical nature, was always attributed to 'trauma'. It was so lazy, sticking that label on her. She knew what trauma was and she knew she had not been traumatised. To say she had been was an insult to true sufferers.

But there she was, driving to Pica very early on a Saturday morning and her mind wandering in this kind of way so that she hardly saw the tractor coming straight at her, its driver gesticulating imperiously that she should pull up to one side. Hurriedly, just in time, she obeyed, and a herd of cows behind the tractor plodded ahead, filling the narrow road. They were big black-and-white cows, udders full and enormous. They pushed and shoved their way past her car, banging the side, their tails swishing against the bonnet. Behind them came a boy on a bike, a long cane held in one hand. He ignored the car, swerving on his bike to avoid knocking into it, paying no attention to her. It took a full ten minutes for the herd to amble past. In her driving mirror she could see that half a mile behind her they were lurching into a field. But she went on sitting there, the sudden quiet overwhelming her. She knew how to measure those cows. It was the sort of arcane knowledge, utterly useless in normal life, which had always appealed to her. Measure from the shoulder to the second joint on the tail, she murmured to herself. But how would you get one of those hulking animals to stand still? How would she find the second joint in its tail? She wished Nancy Armstrong had demonstrated this art – or science, she wasn't sure which – though the possibility of putting it to the test was beyond remote. She tried to see herself in the field where the cows now stood as she drove slowly back along the road. There was one standing a little apart from the others, chewing away at the grass. But its tail was upright and below it shit poured down.

She would never be able to measure a cow. But she would never need to.

Nancy knew something was up. Sarah was agitated. There was something funny about her all of a sudden. She kept getting into her car, parked right in front of her front door, and just sitting there. Sometimes, she'd sit for a full half-hour without moving. Was it because the engine wouldn't start? Nancy peered and peered from her bedroom window and didn't think that this was the problem. Sarah wasn't pressing any buttons and her foot didn't seem to be in action. She was just sitting. Then, when all this sitting stopped, she got out and stood looking at the car. She walked round it, not touching it. Was she checking for flat tyres? Nancy didn't think so. She, Nancy, had had a squint when Sarah went to work. The tyres were fine. She looked in the car windows too and everything looked neat and tidy. What was going on? Why all this sitting in a trance in a car?

Nancy knew about trances. They were not good news. They meant something was up. Her father used to have trances, after he came back to the farm from the war. Long after he came back from the war, years after. 'Don't make a sound,' her mother would tell her, 'your dad's having a trance, don't go near.' But Nancy did go near. She crept into the room where her father was sitting and she stared at him. He looked all right. It was just that he was very still, hands on his knees, looking straight ahead. A trance didn't seem such a bad thing to be having. It was what followed that was alarming. He would shake his head at the end of it and then give a great sigh and tears would run down his cheeks, tears he made no attempt to mop up. Sometimes he would tremble, and then her mother would come in and say, quite sharply, Nancy thought, 'Enough, John, enough. You're here, you're safe. Now come on, there's work to do.' She didn't hug him or comfort him, so Nancy felt she should try, but at her touch, a mere pat of her little hand, her father would flinch, and say 'Now then' and shake her off.

Of course, years later Nancy heard all about the battle of Loos and what had happened to her father's regiment and how lucky he had been to survive, apparently unscathed. Except for these trances, when he saw things, things he never talked about, or at least not to Nancy. But she picked up, from newspapers and films, that trances, or what she'd been told by her mother were trances, even if that wasn't the proper name for them, were to do with 'emotional disturbance'. She pondered this phrase, when she came across it, for a long time. Her father, such a big, strong man, was never emotional, never, except for the tears and trembling when he came out of a trance. Was that the point, then? Was this him leaking emotion because he was disturbed? It made a sort of sense to her.

Sarah Scott, though. Her trances made no sense. Nancy worried about them. There was no sign, so far as she could tell when she was looking out of a window some distance from the car Sarah sat in, of any emotion. No tears flowed. She could discern no trembling. But there was no doubting the sitting, absolutely still, in a trance-like state. Something was wrong. Nancy, witnessing this peculiar behaviour, felt responsible. Suppose something happened. How would it look, if she, Nancy Armstrong, had noticed trances happening and had done nothing about it? She ought at least to go out, the next time she saw one in progress, and knock on the car window and say are you all right? Ah, but when in a trance, it was best to let the person come out of it by themselves. Who had told her that? Her mother probably. Or she'd read it. Maybe it would be better to mention, casually, the next time she spoke to Sarah, that she'd seen her sitting in the car for ages and had wondered if she, or the car, was OK. What would be wrong with that? Nothing, except it would reveal that she was watching Sarah.

She might not like that.

Tara asked for the Friday and the Monday off, as part of her holiday entitlement. Management said they would prefer that she took a week. A Friday and a Monday was awkward. Tara couldn't see what was awkward about it (for a moment the old Tara flared up again within her) but she gave in. She took a week's leave. The moment this had been decided, an idea began to grow in her mind. She could go south a whole week for the planned reunion and do some checking out. 'Checking out'? What did she mean by that term? Spying. That was what she meant, though she thought that to admit to such a thing was shameful. It was also, she knew, silly. How did ordinary people spy? Skills were surely needed that she didn't have. But she knew where the urge to spy came from: she wanted to give herself an advantage. She wanted to have seen all three of them, in their habitats, before she saw them together, and before they saw her.

She had Claire's address, but Molly and Liz's were old. They might have moved from them long ago. But somehow she thought they would not have done, and even if they had there was a good chance that if she knocked on the door the present owner might know where they had moved to. Anyway, she could count on getting a glimpse of Claire, which was more important than catching sight of the other two. Claire had set this reunion up. She was the one who, by doing so, suggested feelings of guilt about how she'd responded, or rather not responded to what had happened to Tara. Guilt, or perhaps remorse. Tara liked the idea of both, and looming behind that possibility of relishing someone else's guilt or remorse was a malicious delight in making them suffer . . .

Tara rushed out of her house and sat in the car. The car calmed her. Just sitting there, enclosed by its doors and windows, secure in the small space, she felt all these bad thoughts begin to lose their power. What she must tell herself was that a hand of friendship was being extended and if she was going to accept it she must clear away all this resentment and bitterness that she'd harboured over what had happened when this friendship was put under intolerable strain. She must go to the reunion with happy memories, untouched by what had befallen her. It was like trying to leap legs. Keeping oneself to oneself was respected, but not if this tendency went too far. How could it go too far? Easily. Not sharing anything at all in the way of ordinary information, harmless stuff. That was going too far. Not joining in for a cup of tea if invited was going too far. Sarah Scott, it was said, never lingered after work. She never accepted lifts from those with cars who were going her way. She preferred the bus. And she met people who, it was claimed, 'looked like' officials of some sort, in Morrisons café. It was upon these crucial sightings that the rumour hung. She'd been teased about having coffee with a man and the teasing resulted in the colour leaving her face. And her face was quite pale anyway. Nancy dealt with that one scathingly. 'Can't a woman have a cup of coffee with a man in a place like Morrisons café without it being commented on?' she asked.

The suspicion was that Sarah Scott might be on benefits, and the man she saw, and also the woman later on, might be checking up on her. Fraud was in the air. Members of the club were very hot on fraud. It was thought to be rampant these days. But try as they might – and they tried very hard – no one could pin anything definite on Sarah Scott. Nancy was vociferous in her defence. 'She's a decent young woman,' she said, 'and I should know. I've been in her house and she's been in mine and there's nothing wrong with her. She's just shy, quiet, likes to mind her own business as some folk here should be doing.' It was a good line to leave the club on, and Nancy duly left, knowing that the minute she'd gone the rumour would get going again. There was nothing she could do about it. She hadn't seen Sarah with a man in Morrisons café. She'd never set foot in the place. Maybe it was simply a stranger who had sat down at Sarah's table and to whom she'd been polite, that's all. But there were eyes and ears everywhere in a place like this and Sarah somehow stood out as different, suspicious.

Nancy thought about this a lot. Sarah dressed in dull clothes, hardly wore any colour, and drew no attention to herself in that way. She walked with her head down, not seeming to pay any attention to her surroundings. Her voice was low, low enough for people to have to ask her to repeat whatever she said (as Nancy had had to do several times). But in spite of her demeanour, there was something about her that attracted attention. What was it? Nancy pondered and pondered and came to the not-very-satisfactory conclusion that Sarah had some sort of fence around her. No, she didn't mean fence, not a real fence obviously, but a barrier of some kind which gave off a 'Do not approach me' signal. Only determined people like Nancy could penetrate it, caring people. Sarah was also, she decided (though she was self-aware enough to realise she was getting carried away now) like an animal, like a timid cat,

V

THEY MET the week before, at Claire's insistence.

'We need a plan,' she told Molly and Liz, 'we need to be prepared.'

'For what?' asked Liz, annoyed, as ever, by Claire's self-importance.

'For everything,' Claire said, and outlined all the possibilities she'd thought of as to how the reunion with Tara might go.

Molly and Liz stayed silent, enduring Claire's taste for melodrama as patiently as they could. It was all slightly ridiculous. Tara would not come. But they let Claire ramble on, until she started to produce newspaper cuttings.

The first was the one they knew well. They had kept it themselves, though unlike Claire they would not have been able to lay their hands on it. Claire had stuck hers in a scrapbook. Typical. It had hardly faded at all. There they all were, beaming, at the child's bedside, with the mother looking at them, her hands clasped together. Only the fact that the child was yawning slightly spoiled the highly posed picture. Tara stood out. No doubt about it. She wasn't in the centre of the photograph – Claire was – but she stood out because of her great mane of unruly red curly hair. The rest of them had short hair, neatly shaped. Liz had a tidy fringe.

Neither of the other two had cut out and kept Claire's other cuttings. There they were, in another scrapbook. Significantly, it had a black cover whereas the one in which the old rescue cutting was stuck had a brightly patterned flowery cover.

'You kept them,' Liz said, knowing she sounded disapproving.

'Why not?' said Claire.

Liz shrugged.

Claire knew perfectly well why not. It was sick, surely, keeping such dreadful reports of what their friend had allegedly (no, not 'allegedly', she admitted it) done. They were unpleasant cuttings, taken from the lowest of the tabloids.

'How come,' Liz said, noticing this, 'that you got those newspapers?' She knew there was an edge to her voice.

'I went out and bought them,' Claire said, quite composed. 'I wanted to know what the worst was and I knew they'd have it.'

'Heavens,' said Liz.

'Well,' said Claire, 'I wanted to be properly informed.'

'Properly informed,' echoed Molly, 'by the tabloids?'

This black-covered scrapbook lay before them. Claire flicked through it, drawing their attention to one report of the trial which had mentioned how still Tara sat. The reporter commented on the accused's 'serene' expression and her lack of any agitation when certain upsetting details were read out. It wasn't the Tara they had known, they all agreed. She was never serene. She was hyper and volatile, and yet there she was, a different personality entirely.

'We should have been in court,' Claire said, as she had said many times before.

Liz kept quiet.

'Not again,' said Molly. 'We know why none of us could be there.'

'Yes,' said Claire, 'but that's what is going to come up if Tara comes – *why* were we not there, supporting her? We have to have our answers ready.'

'Excuses,' said Liz, 'excuses, not just answers.'

'Oh, don't be ridiculous,' said Molly. 'You really imagine that if Tara comes she is going to sit there and say why were none of you at my trial for murder? She won't want it mentioned, not a word. She'll want to start afresh. If she comes, which she will not.'

Claire closed the scrapbook, stood up, and walked away with it. They heard a drawer being opened and then shut. Molly and Liz made faces at each other. Claire was offended and they'd have to placate her.

'Well,' said Liz, when Claire returned, 'all I know is that I never believed it.'

Molly sighed. 'But Liz, she said she did it. She was quite clear about how she got the drugs, how she administered them, how—'

'Yes,' said Liz, 'I know. I believe her but I don't believe her. And I would never ask her about it. There's no point.'

'Unless Tara herself wants to confide in us,' said Claire.

The other two laughed, not at what she'd said but at the solemn, almost virtuous, expression on her face.

'You may laugh,' said Claire, 'but I was the one she used to confide in, remember?'

'No,' said Molly and Liz, in unison.

'Well, she did,' said Claire, 'but it was confidential and I couldn't tell you.'

Neither of the other two challenged her, either to doubt her again or to compete, though Tara had told each of them, at different times, things she said they were not to tell Claire about or 'she'll never let it go'. In Molly's case, Tara had told her about falsifying her A-level exam results on an application form.

'Can you imagine what Claire would say?' Tara had laughed. 'She'd shop me, even now. Anyway, I should've got A in chemistry, the B was probably a mismarking. What did it matter? They never checked – it was their own fault.'

Molly, at the time, which was long after Tara graduated, years after upgrading herself, didn't think the lie very important. Tara should indeed have got an A. She was good enough. It was all, by then, trivial, who had got what years before in an exam. But Tara was right: Claire wouldn't have thought it trivial. Nothing she would have been able to do about it, but she would have held it over Tara in all sorts of sly ways.

Both Molly and Liz wondered what on earth Tara had confided in Claire, considering how judgemental they knew Tara thought Claire was, but neither of them was prepared to indulge her by asking. Let her keep it secret, as they had each kept Tara's mildly disturbing confidences. But this confiding had had consequences; Tara herself was not confided in. She was simply not trustworthy. Molly and Liz had discussed this often, as long ago as the period straight after the famous rescue of the child, when they all started being friends. They'd noticed, and Claire had too, that Tara embroidered ordinary events so that in her accounts they became colourful and dramatic when really there'd been no drama. Everyone indulged in a certain amount of this kind of exaggeration for effect but Tara did so more than most.

The other three often protested – 'Oh, come off it, Tara, it wasn't like that, I saw it,' one of them would say when she got carried away and described a minor incident like a fullscale opera.

Sometimes, even more peculiar, she painted herself as a cheat when they knew she had *not* cheated. This was what baffled them. Why had she done it? Why would anyone confess to cheating when they had not? What did she hope to gain from this weird behaviour? Their conclusion, then, had been that she was just odd. Odd. Nothing more.

'Well,' said Claire, 'we haven't decided anything. The whole point of this meeting was to plan for every eventuality and we haven't planned anything. We'll all just be caught on the hop.'

'We always would be,' said Liz, 'no planning could avoid that.'

'But it doesn't matter,' said Molly, and repeated yet again that Tara would not turn up.

'Never mind,' said Claire, 'we'll have a nice lunch, and remember her.'

A case went into the green car, on to the back seat, not the boot. Then Sarah came out carrying a raincoat, which also went on to the back seat. After that, there was a lull in activity, and Nancy got tired of slowly watering the plants she had on the windowsill in front of the net curtain. Surely, Sarah would tell her she was going away? She wouldn't just go without a word? An eye needed to be kept on her house, for a start. Surely, she would want to be certain of that? Anyone normal would.

But Sarah didn't come to tell Nancy that she was going away. Instead, a note was put through her letter box very early one June morning. Nancy, who was always awake by 5 a.m. these days, heard the flap shut. It was one of the new-fangled flaps which meant nobody could put their hand through to try to open the door. Nancy had read about these clever flaps in a newspaper and had had one fitted immediately. It made her feel secure, though the disadvantage was that anything coming through the letter box made a noise. When she heard it that morning, Nancy got up and peered out of her bedroom window. Sarah was already in the green car. So sly! Nancy was furious – what a way to behave, sneaking off like this – and was determined not to go immediately to find out whatever it was Sarah had put through her door. If she was not important enough to be told face to face where Sarah was going, and for how long, and maybe exactly why, then her note or card, or whatever it was, was not important enough to be read at once. It could lie there, on the mat, until the proper time for Nancy to get up, which was at 7 a.m. precisely.

It was hard, staying in bed until 7 a.m., but it had to be done. Rules were rules, made for a good reason. Nancy struggled slightly to recall what these rules were, and why they'd been made, and whether she'd made them herself or they'd been handed on to her by her mother. Routine, it was about having a routine, essential on a farm, which got you through the day. In bad times especially, it was essential to Get Through the Day. That was it. Times were not bad for Nancy any more, but if she let her routine go to pot then she'd never reclaim it if bad times returned. Rise at 7 a.m. Essential.

Even then, Nancy ignored the white envelope on the mat. She felt quite triumphant walking down the stairs, seeing the envelope, turning at the foot of the staircase to go into the kitchen without picking it up. Never be too eager, that was another rule. It led invariably to disappointment. She made tea, sipped a little of it, and then, ever so leisurely, she went and picked up the envelope. It was not sealed, and of course had no stamp on it. This rather pleased Nancy. It was a good envelope which could be used for something. Even better was the fact that 'Mrs Armstrong' was written in pencil. It could be rubbed out, leaving the envelope pristine. Not quite as cross as she had been, owing to now possessing a potentially perfect envelope, Nancy took out the piece of paper inside.

There was no 'Dear Mrs Armstrong' or 'Dear Nancy', but the date was written in the top right-hand corner. The message said, 'Just to let you know that I will be away for the next week. Yours, Sarah.' Nancy read it umpteen times, decoding every single word, beginning with 'Just'. Just! What kind of beginning was that? Just? It implied something offhand, something trivial, something the writer of the word could hardly be bothered to communicate. It took Nancy a long time to get past this 'just' and even longer to interpret the whole message properly.

The most wounding thing was that she had not been asked to keep an eye on Sarah's house, and yet surely that had been the point of informing her of Sarah's absence. Why else would she have written this unsatisfactory note? And then there was the other annoying thing: no mention of where Sarah had gone. She was being secretive. She was concealing her destination, not trusting Nancy. Why? What would have been more natural than to say where she was going for this holiday? Even if she'd said, in general terms, that she was going to the seaside, or to stay with a friend, or even to London, maybe.

Something was going on, and Nancy was perturbed.

The further south she travelled, the more unreal the house she'd left behind became. Tara tried to see it in her mind's eye, and couldn't even conjure up the street convincingly. Had she really been living there for months? It was like driving out of fog, all murky and dim, into clear air – the relief! She felt herself become more alert with every mile she drove, and found she didn't need to stop and rest as often as she'd envisaged she might have to. South of Preston, she pulled into a motorway service station and after she'd filled up with petrol she went to the lavatory and undid the band tying back her hair and the clips drawing it severely back from her ears. She brushed her hair and fluffed it out so that it surrounded her face. There. She looked, already, more like Tara than the woebegone Sarah. She smiled at her reflection. She could come back again, she knew she could.

Tara was not quite established again as herself by the time she arrived at the small hotel on the river where she'd booked a room. She was there, pushing to come out, but Sarah held her back. Loosening her hair was one thing, but that was enough for the moment. The clothes were still Sarah's, grey and neat; so was the manner, quiet and hesitant. Better to remain nondescript while she adjusted. But once in her room, she unpacked the dress she'd bought online for the rebirth of Tara and smiled at the sight of it, the colour thrilling her. Tara had always loved red, all the reds, scarlet and crimson and especially the red so near to purple.

She'd loved satin and silk materials too, not the real thing but synthetic versions which looked and felt genuine. This dress was silk, light and pretty, and it came with a little jacket of a thicker, but still silky material, an outfit for a summer's day, worn with a silver necklace which sat beautifully above the neckline of the dress. Really, it was too good for a lunch with old friends. She would be over-dressed, but then that was Tara.

Still in her grey trousers and her paler grey sweater, she went out for a walk. Her legs felt stiff after the long drive and her head ached slightly, but once she got on to the towpath she began to feel better. The river was high and fast flowing with bits of branches being swept along. There must have been a storm recently, as there had been that other June week. Today, there were no children about. She passed a couple of women walking dogs but that was all. Sitting on a stile which led into a field, she thought about the course her life had taken since the rescue of the child. So unpredictable, all the rushing along, heedless of where she was going, always wanting to be different, to stand out, never stopping to consider what this told her about herself. She saw it all clearly now, the restlessness, the impetuous approach to events. She had never given anyone but Tom a chance (and look what he'd done with it); she swept them away with her enthusiasm for whatever it was she had wanted to do. Maybe it had amounted to bullying, but she hadn't seen it like that. She'd had time even before she became Sarah, during all those years of reflection, to realise she had always been a dangerous person. It was not entirely impossible, after all, for her to have done what she had done.

Walking slowly back to the hotel, she pondered the question of whether the old Tara really could emerge again, fully formed, or whether she had gone for ever. No, she hadn't. She wasn't Sarah Scott, she never could be, however well she had played the part so far. Bits of Tara were mixed in there and could be retained and reactivated. The spark spluttered and could ignite but mustn't flare up to a dangerous heat ever again. Control, that was the lesson she'd been obliged to learn. Control: over temper, over passion, over action without thought of consequences. The approaching reunion was a test case. Control over her desire to accuse her friends of betraying the very essence of friendship: loyalty. They had shown no loyalty whatsoever. They had not stood by her at her time of greatest need. But did she want their excuses, their justifications, their explanations all this time afterwards? Tara did, but Sarah realised how pointless it would be to demand these now. There was no point in going to this lunch if all she was going to do was give vent to her disappointment in these friends and pour her scorn and resentment over them. Sarah would not agree to it. Sarah wanted to remain dignified, coolly curious, above any kind of ugly behaviour.

She wanted Claire and Molly and Liz to be very surprised by her exemplary behaviour.

It was almost twenty miles from the hotel where she was staying to where Liz used to live the last time she'd visited. When was that? She couldn't exactly remember, but definitely at least twelve years ago. She parked two roads away, and then walked past Liz's house (if it was still Liz's). What she hoped to gain by this she didn't know, but it felt mildly exciting, a feeling she hadn't experienced for a long time. The colour of the front door was the same. Green. The front garden was the same, a flourishing hydrangea in the centre of an oblong of grass. Proved nothing. She walked on, stopping at the corner shop near the church, where three roads met, surprised to find it still existed, the only evidence that what was now suburbia had once been a village. She stood and looked in the window. There was a board there with notices for various things for sale, rooms to let, gardeners and cleaners wanted. And there it was, Liz's name and number: 'Cleaner wanted two days a week, 9 a.m. – 12 noon. £12 an hour.'

For reasons she couldn't begin to understand this small bit of knowledge satisfied Tara deeply. Liz was still living here, the same sort of life, in all probability, which she'd been living when last they met, years ago. Nothing had shifted. She would know Liz, be able to link straight into her life. It gave her confidence. She decided she didn't need to drive an extra ten miles to lurk outside Molly's house. Molly would not have moved. She and her husband had bought their house in 1994 when they were married, and announced they'd never leave; it was just what they wanted, big enough to house Simon's surgery, and with a lovely view of the river at the back. Molly was stability itself.

Which left Claire's house. She knew exactly where to park so that she could see people coming and going. She saw Claire within ten minutes of parking under a line of trees the other side of the road. Tree-lined, that was Claire's road, broad grass verges, drives to most of the double-fronted houses. Claire looked, as she got out of her car and reached into the boot for several bags, much the same, from the distance that Tara saw her. Heavier, maybe, but still smartly, if boringly, dressed, wearing a trouser suit, the trousers a little too wide for the boxy jacket. Never scruffy, that was Claire. Always formal looking, a business look, though she'd never run a business.

It was enough. Tara felt armed. She drove back to her hotel, ready.

It wasn't, after all, a sunny day. Claire always saw the reunion taking place on a sunny day, with the sun doing what it so often could, lifting the atmosphere with all its light. But it was a grey day, not exactly raining but with an intermittent drizzle depressing everyone. The river looked black and sullen when only the day before it had sparkled in the sun. At least nothing out of doors had been planned, though she'd envisaged them all having a Pimm's in the pub garden first. The table she'd booked was in the far corner of the long dining room, beside a window with a view of the river, though today this view was dreary, the willow trees hanging limp over the damp lawn. But the table itself looked cheerful, with a white tablecloth overlaid with a smaller pink one and in the centre a small jug of tiny roses which had not yet opened out. Pretty. And the table was round, which felt friendlier, less formal . . . Oh, she was fussing, it was silly to fret over tables and weather when none of it mattered. It was just that she wanted everything to be perfect in all the details so that this reunion would have a chance of being a happy occasion.

She had come half an hour early, deliberately, thinking that once she'd checked the booking she'd have a wander round the garden and maybe a little way along the tow path, but the drizzle made this uninviting, so she went into the bar, where coffee was still on offer, and sat reading, but not reading, just flicking through an old magazine someone had left, about cars, in which she had no interest at all. All the time, she was looking at her watch, and then at the clock over the bar. Calculating when Molly was likely to arrive. She was usually, but not always, on time. Liz would be late. She always was. Not very late, but late. And if Tara did come? They might all arrive together, and sitting here in the bar she'd miss them and the whole thing would get off the ground without her. Claire got up and slapped the magazine down on the table so loudly and unnecessarily that it looked like some sort of statement, and the barman stared at her, annoyed.

I am tense, she said to herself, tense when I should be relaxed, and why am I tense? She knew perfectly well why.

Because she was afraid of Tara coming.

It would be a mile walk. Tara was too dressed up. She couldn't totter along the towpath in shoes with delicate heels, even though these were not too high. They'd stick in the mud. So she drove, but didn't park in the pub's car park. Instead, she drew up beneath a tree 100 yards away. She didn't know why. Then she sat in the car for a while, composing herself. No thudding heart. She couldn't bear to have a thudding heart or a queasy stomach. She had to be sure she could be calm or she couldn't go through with this meeting.

She lifted the flap in front of her and looked in the small mirror. Her eyes were quite clear, her eyelashes nicely delineated with mascara which she'd used sparingly. The shadows underneath were still there and, she supposed, would never entirely go, but she hadn't used anything to disguise them. Let them be seen. Let them tell their own tale. Her cheeks had filled out in the last few months, and she didn't look gaunt any more even if she didn't look as Tara used to. This would be expected, it was nothing to feel self-conscious about. She got out of the car, locked it, and began to walk along the road. She was on time, but walked slowly. Claire would be waiting. She was always early just as Liz was always late. Molly varied, so did Tara. Thinking this kind of thing, droning on to herself, steadied her. No thudding heart, but she did after all have a slightly queasy stomach now. She turned the corner and there was the old pub, its front spruced up dramatically – so much white paint, so many window boxes bursting with geraniums, and a new sign with a varnished painting of a bull hanging above the door. Somehow, this transformation of an old, neglected pub into a modern gastropub helped. It made her feel that far from going back in time, to face her younger self and mourn for her, she was walking into a place stripped of memories, a place clear of all associations.

She didn't go into the main entrance, suddenly remembering that there used to be a side door leading into a small bar off the main one. If she entered this way, no one would be able to spot her until she'd seen them. Quietly, she slipped in. The layout was the same. She could see into the main bar, which was busy. She scanned the people and knew none were Claire, Molly or Liz. No matter how much they would have changed, she was quite certain they were not among that throng. So they were either in the lounge or already in the dining room, waiting. It gave her the chance to have a drink. It took a while, but at last she had a glass of white wine in her hand, and sipped it carefully. It was a long time since she'd had any alcohol, though there'd been no reason why she couldn't have bought herself a bottle of wine. Even Sarah could have the occasional drink, couldn't she? But staying teetotal somehow went with being Sarah, so she didn't drink anything but tea or coffee. The wine was delicious, cold and clear, and she savoured every small mouthful. Now she was ready, fortified, and made her way steadily from the bar and along the passage to the dining room. She was smiling.

They stood up, all three of them, Molly catching her skirt in a bit of wickerwork in the side of her chair and struggling to be upright. Sorry, she was saying, sorry, and Liz was freeing the skirt but at the same time almost knocking a glass over. Claire stood up and said, 'Tara!' in far too loud and hearty a voice. She held her arms out but with the table between them it was a pointless gesture, and Tara slipped into the vacant seat quickly so that Claire was left standing. Then a waitress came with menus and though Claire tried to wave them away, saying they weren't ready to order, the others seized them and began reading and suddenly they were quiet, the confusion over. Tara's arrival was disappointingly undramatic.

Orders given, they all stared at Tara, who looked at each of them in turn, and waited.

'Well,' Claire said, with a false little laugh, 'well, here we all are. Twenty-five years, can you believe it?'

'Yes,' said Molly.

'Easily,' said Liz.

Tara said nothing. Her face was beginning to ache with smiling.

'You look well, Tara,' Claire said, and knew at once it was the wrong thing to have said, and it was a lie anyway.

Tara's smile weakened. 'And so do you, Claire,' she said. Her voice sounded throaty, and she cleared it, and repeated what she'd said.

'I've put on such a lot of weight,' Molly said. 'Seeing you, Tara, reminds me I was once as slim as you still are.'

'No, you weren't,' said Liz. 'You were never as slim as Tara, Molly.'

An argument began, a good-natured bickering.

Tara's face was a shock. They had all made up their faces carefully before they came, even Molly who rarely did so, and looked so unlike herself with a fiercely pink mouth. But Tara wore no make-up except for mascara. She was pale, unnaturally pale, an underground-living look. They were reminded of how she looked years ago, when she was twenty-something and in hospital with what turned out to be a ruptured appendix. They'd all visited her, organising a rota so that she wouldn't have more than two days without one of them at her side. The nurses had been impressed – 'Such friends!' they'd said. When she was better, Molly had wanted to take her back and look after her, but Tara wanted to go home to Tom. Except Tom wasn't at home. He was abroad 'on business', as he so often seemed to be. But Molly's offer was still resisted. Tara went back to her flat on her own, and they all felt bad.

But at least the red dress was like the old Tara, dramatic, close fitting, and yet looking odd with the too-white face. She'd always been the gamine type whereas they were all what they liked to think of as 'womanly'. These days, 'womanly' meant fat. Not obese fat, not bulging everywhere fat, but plump fat, controllable, responding well to a discreet compression with the help of some Lycra here and there. And there was Tara, so slender, not an ounce of fat on her, and yet she didn't look frail. They all saw a strength in her, a tension that radiated from her slim frame and made it seem somehow threatening, as though her body was prepared to spring into action if it needed to.

When Liz and Molly stopped talking, the sudden silence was uncomfortable, but they were rescued by the arrival of the food, which released another welcome stream of chatter about who used to cook and who didn't, and what their favourite foods had been twenty-five years ago. Not much wine was drunk. They were all being careful, and not entirely because everyone except Claire would be driving later. It was a pity, this abstemious attitude, Tara thought. Wine, more wine, would have relaxed them all, surely. They'd drunk a lot when they were young, often been hopelessly drunk in each other's company.

Claire made the decision to have coffee in the little snug off the lounge. This area was not exactly private, but near enough. The chairs were comfortable and encouraged sitting back in them, the cushions firm behind them. It would have been easy to fall asleep, but they were all alert. Tara reckoned she had waited long enough. Who should she begin with? Not Claire. Molly, Molly was an easier target. Molly, plump and matronly, just as she'd promised to be in her youth. No surprise there, except perhaps in the hair, grey already though the face was unlined and smooth. How should she start? With some vague question, perhaps. Tara tried to frame a vague question in her head but what came out was not vague at all. It was shockingly direct.

'Molly,' said Tara, turning towards Molly and smiling still, 'Molly, did you read about my trial in a newspaper?' From her tone, she might have been asking if her friend wanted sugar in her coffee.

Molly stared at her, opened her mouth as though about to reply, then closed it again. Slowly, a blush crept up from her neck to cover her face.

'I just wondered,' Tara said, 'that's all. I wondered if you did, if any of you did. That's all.'

With Molly apparently speechless, Claire felt she had to speak for them all. It was her role in the group, or it had been twenty-five years ago and she hadn't knowingly given it up. She'd been expecting some sort of challenge from Tara anyway, whereas the other two thought that Tara, if she came, would not refer in any way to the trial, or the crime, or her time in prison. They were not ready for this question whereas she was.

'Tara,' Claire said, 'of course we read about what happened. We worried about you all the time.'

'Worried?' queried Tara, eyebrows raised.

'Yes. We worried. We didn't know what to think, what to do.'

'Goodness,' said Tara, 'I didn't realise it was so difficult for you all, all that worry, all that not knowing what to do.'

'I was going to write, but . . .' Liz said.

'But?' Tara prompted, taking care not to sound aggressive.

'Well,' Liz said, 'it seemed . . . We hadn't been in touch for a while and . . .'

'And?' Tara prompted again, but Claire interrupted. She had her speech ready, it had been ready for months.

'Tara,' she said, voice low and kind, 'Tara, we all feel awful about not doing what we know we should have done, as friends, old friends. There are no excuses. We didn't support you and were ashamed and we're so glad you've come today so we can all say sorry and we hope we can put the lost years behind us and get back to how we were, good friends again . . .'

'Christ, Claire,' said Liz, her eyes closed, her brow tightly furrowed, 'shut up, for God's sake.'

Molly let out a little moan of embarrassment, and looked anxiously at Tara, who was staring at Claire with an expression on her face which was unreadable.

'More coffee?' Claire suggested, nervous now, taking a great gulp from her own cup.

'I don't think so,' Tara said.

This had to be brought to an end. What was the point of prolonging this awkward reunion, which didn't feel like a reunion at all? It was a meeting of strangers, any connection heavily dependent on memories of the past, though not any 'past' which included Tara's years in prison. This, it was clear, was to be regarded as a blank, something that had not happened. So Tara stood up, and said she must go. She had a long way to drive. All three of the others also stood up.

'Oh, no,' said Claire, 'don't go yet, Tara, we haven't got to know you again. Give us a chance, please.'

'Oh, Claire . . .' wailed Liz.

Molly put her hand on Tara's arm.

'What I want to do, Tara,' she said, 'what I've wanted to do since you walked in is just hug you and say sorry. We've done everything wrong.'

It was, Tara thought, becoming a comedy when really it was a tragedy. All this well-meaning concern with no attempt to tackle what lay behind it: the fear. Fear that she would accuse them of cowardice, fear that she hated them for their desertion at that critical time, fear that if they didn't take great care she would make a scene. She'd come near to it already after Claire patronised her. But she sat down again, and so did they.

'What I want to know,' said Tara, 'is why, after the court case, after I'd pleaded guilty and was imprisoned, none of you held out a hand. You let me drop. You were no longer friends. It was as though all those years we'd had together were wiped out by what I'd done. And even now, today, you're scared to be with me. God knows what you thought this reunion was to be about, but it's not what I thought it would be about. And I'm beginning to wonder if I feel anything for you, for any of you. I look at you three and I can't believe there was ever any kind of closeness between us.'

There was a silence then, a stillness. Molly thought she might cry.

'Tara,' said Liz, 'what do you want us to do? We can't go back and act differently. We can't say sorry over and over. You don't want us to confess our shame at how we kept away, do you? Tell us.'

'I want,' said Tara, 'to be friends again, but I don't think we can be.'

'Of course we can!' said Claire, far too heartily. 'We're friends again already, just by meeting here. It's a beginning, isn't it?'

'No,' said Tara, 'it isn't. It feels like an ending. I never really imagined it would work, and now I know it won't. You aren't friends, you're memories, good ones for years and then one big bad one.'

'Oh, Tara,' said Liz softly, 'we have memories of you, too, and they ended with one big shock. It was no good us saying you couldn't have done it when you said you did and all the evidence was there. But you hadn't turned to us for help, had you? While all that stuff before, with Tom, was going on, you turned us away. You didn't return phone calls, you didn't reply to letters. You gave us one clear message – back off. And we did.'

Molly looked shocked, Claire bewildered. Liz, Tara thought, had always been more astute than the other two. There was truth in what she'd said. She had indeed kept her friends away once she'd decided what she was going to do. She didn't want her resolution weakened, she didn't want arguments, and most of all she didn't want to involve them even in the most indirect way. But none of them had tried to bridge the gap she'd created then, or had they? She struggled to remember, but Liz already had.

'I rang you, the week before Christmas that year, the millennium year, when I hadn't seen you for ages. I rang you to suggest that we all meet up in the New Year, do something together. Your phone was always on answerphone and eventually I left a message. You never called back.'

Tara did remember. It was true. And Claire sent her an invitation to a New Year's Eve party – odd, that she hadn't rushed to mention this, or that she alone had written before the trial. It wasn't like Claire not to show off her concern.

Tara nodded at Liz.

'Yes,' she said, 'I remember. But that doesn't alter the fact that when I obviously needed support you didn't come forward.'

'Obviously?' said Liz. 'There was nothing obvious about it. What were we meant to do? Say we didn't believe for one moment that you were a murderer? Say that, when you'd admitted guilt straight away?'

'You could have shown some interest,' Tara said.

'How do you know we didn't?' said Liz. 'We talked about it non-stop on the phone for weeks, fretting about what the newspapers were saying, hardly able to believe it all, and yet we had to. We thought about applying for a visiting permit or whatever they call it—'

'But you didn't,' Tara said. 'That's the point we come back to again and again, isn't it? You did nothing.'

The waitress came to ask if they wanted more coffee, and to clear away the cups and saucers when they said no. The clatter of the crockery was welcome.

'Tara,' Molly said, in a whisper, 'how are you? How has it been for you?'

'She won't want to talk about that, Molly,' said Claire, quite sharply.

'Oh, but I do,' said Tara. 'I'd quite like you to know how I am and how it's been for me. I'm glad you at least, Molly, are interested.'

She settled more comfortably into her chair, but at that moment two more people came to the doorway and looked into the room, eyeing the two remaining chairs and then deciding to come and sit in them.

'Let's go to my room,' Claire (who was staying that night) said. 'It's quite big.'

So they all got up, collected their things and followed Claire upstairs in complete silence. Her room was indeed large, with a good view over the river. There was a double bed and, in front of the window, a small sofa as well as an upright chair beside the bed. Molly took it.

'Better for my back to sit upright,' she said.

Liz flung herself on the bed.

'Better for mine lying down,' she said. 'God, I could go to sleep in an instant.'

This left Tara and Claire to share the sofa, but Tara didn't care for this. She sat on the floor, nicely carpeted, and leaned against the bed, closing her eyes.

Nobody said anything for a while, then Tara began to speak.

'This is what happened,' she began. 'I'll tell you that first, then I'll tell you how it was for me and how I am now.'

It was almost dark when she drove back to where she was staying. Claire had urged her to remain, saying she was in no fit state to drive – they'd had room service later on and two bottles of wine – but Tara said she was fine and she wanted to go. There were kisses and hugs all round. Tara enjoyed them. It was a long time since she'd had that sort of physical contact with anyone and it felt comforting. They used to kiss and hug a lot when they were young. It was the time when everyone their age started behaving in this un-English way, to the embarrassment of the older generation. They were always flinging their arms round each other and saying 'Love you', only half mocking. But now, leaving them, she saw the difference twenty-five years had made. None of them could trill 'Love you' in the same way. Hugs were serious. There was no exaggerated embracing, only an uncertain, diffident pressure from body to body, a slight squeezing of the arms and then a quick release. Still, it meant something, though quite what she hadn't yet worked out.

Alone in her hotel room, Tara found herself thinking about Nancy Armstrong. Claire, Molly, Liz . . . then Nancy Armstrong, oh God. Sarah Scott's only friend, and the friendship so pallid, so timid, so unlikely ever to flourish. It had no history, no depth to it, and never could have. Their ages were wrong, their backgrounds unfathomable to each other. Their tentative friendship rested on proximity – that was all.

Claire was on the phone as soon as she got home next morning, to first Molly, then Liz, ostensibly to check that they had got home safely, and then to plunge into the credibility of the tale Tara told them. 'Do you believe it?' she asked each of them. 'All of it, I mean?' Molly said she saw no reason not to, incredible as it seemed. She just found it sad. But Liz had some hesitation about accepting certain parts of Tara's story.

'There's a gap,' Liz said, 'something still missing, something she hasn't told us. I don't quite trust it. It's too hard to believe that she went from adoring Tom to this vicious hatred all in a flash.'

'It wasn't in a flash,' Claire protested.

'Comparatively speaking,' Liz said wearily.

'Personally,' Claire went on, 'I think she was always afraid of him but she would never admit it, she would never admit she was afraid of anything or anyone.'

'No,' said Liz, 'it wasn't just fear. There must have been something else. And in any case, why didn't she just leave him? Why didn't she get the hell out?'

'Anyway,' said Liz, 'I'm depressed by it all. But it's her life now that worries me. The waste,' she said, 'when she's so clever. I mean, whatever was she thinking of, exiling herself like this.'

'It's a sort of penance,' said Claire, 'a sackcloth-and-ashes thing.'

'Oh, don't be so ridiculous,' said Liz. 'She's done the penance bit. Ten years in prison – that's penance enough.'

'I thought she seemed quite, well, quite lively.'

'That's because she was angry,' Liz said. 'Anyway, Claire, I've got to go, we'll discuss it later.'

Tara had given them her mobile number, but not her address. This seemed highly significant to Claire. Clearly, it meant that she didn't want to be visited. She wanted her new life to remain secret. And yet, at the same time, she'd agreed that she'd like to stay in contact and perhaps meet again soon. But how soon? When was she going back to this town she wouldn't disclose to them? She hadn't said.

Always, with Tara, the need to be mysterious.

VI

It was dangerous. Tara knew it was dangerous, but the necessity of doing it overrode any danger. She needed to be there again, in the area, in the road. Not in the house though. She understood that would be impossible.

There was a Pizza Express next to the Belsize Park tube station, still there. This pleased her. She went in and sat at a table for two, near the front window, and ordered a pizza. It was a good place to eat alone. Nobody was the least bit interested in her. She enjoyed looking across to the cinema, where they used to go so often, and the bookshop. The pavements here were wide, with benches now and again. She tried to analyse the difference between this scene and any street scene in Workington, but she couldn't. Was it the buildings? Was it the people? Was it the general air of prosperity compared to one of austerity?

Whatever it was, this difference was marked. This, a long time ago, had been her place, her slot, and she'd lost it, and couldn't get it back. Not the way it had been, anyway.

She crossed the road and walked down Belsize Lane to what was called the village, a small open space where all the Belsize roads met. It was, in fact, quite like a village in feel, though nothing like the Cumbrian villages she now was acquainted with. Slowly, she crossed it and began walking down Belsize Park Gardens. The houses were huge, proper mansions, most long since divided into flats. But they were all in good condition, plenty of fresh paint around. Her heart was thudding as she neared their old home, their first home. She walked past the house, then crossed the road and walked back past it again, looking up at the two top windows which had been theirs. They'd had such a view over the gardens at the back. Tom had said one day he would buy the whole house, which had made her laugh. What on earth would they do with such a huge house? He said they'd rent it out, make a fortune. She didn't take him seriously. She told him the thought of a fortune didn't attract her. It was his turn to laugh. Everyone wants a fortune, he told her, and he didn't believe anyone who said they didn't. That was their first row, the first time she glimpsed another Tom.

It irritated her how much store Tom set by the visible signs of wealth. With the exception of clothes, which didn't interest him, though he wore good suits for work, Tom valued 'the best' in everything else. He bought things Tara thought ridiculously flash, like a Rolex watch worth £20,000, and of course there was his veneration for top-of-the-range cars. It appalled Tara. She struggled to decide what all this meant about Tom, why flaunting the evidence of materialistic success was so important to him. Was he, she wondered, reacting to some impoverished background she knew nothing about? They never talked about their respective upbringings. They'd agreed on that when they first met: their lives began then, and what had taken place before was irrelevant. Except, more and more, she was coming to believe, it wasn't.

He never bought the rest of the house, of course. They were in that apartment only two years, the two happiest years of her life. Then Tom came home one day announcing that he'd bought a new place, without consulting her, in Chelsea. He said she'd love it, and in a way she did. It was in a terrace, quite a small house like a cottage, painted pink, but she missed their old flat, missed the size of the rooms there, and the views. She felt she was playing at something, though she didn't know what. She tried to talk to Tom about this odd feeling but he just said good, playing is good, everyone is playing at something. So she asked him what he was playing at and he said winning the game of life, which annoyed her. She wanted him to be serious, and to take her seriously, but he didn't seem to want to. He got cross when she got serious. He said he thought he'd married a wild, fun girl, and where was she now?

Her mind full of these disturbing flashes of memory, she sat on a bench opposite their first home, looking up at its windows, struggling to reclaim her time there. Young, happy, busy, with so much to look forward to, or so she'd believed. She couldn't do it. It was better to let those two years fade. She was being morbid coming back to this road. Abruptly, she got up, and began to walk briskly to where she'd left her car. She would drive back to her hotel, and tomorrow go north again, take up Sarah Scott's dull life. It was no good hankering after the time before anything bad happened, before she began to realise what Tom's 'game' was. She had to get on with the new life she'd chosen and this time not mess it up. Before she left, though, she was going to meet Liz, on her own. Claire and Molly had both urged her to come and visit them but she'd accepted only Liz's suggestion that they should meet in a café they used to frequent years ago.

Why Liz? She didn't exactly know, but it had something to do with Liz having no patience with either sentiment or hypocrisy.

*

Nancy Armstrong watched Sarah Scott's house all the time. There was nothing to watch but she did it all the same, checking that the bedroom blind was still half drawn, checking that the curtains in the front window were not quite closed. There was a gap of approximately six inches between them. Nancy approved of that. Leave curtains wide open and, come night time, it looks suspicious; close them completely and during the day it looks equally suspicious. She kept an eye on the letter box, too. The postman, that young Mark, was careless. He didn't always bother to shove larger envelopes through the flap and left them sticking out. But Sarah Scott got no mail while she was away.

It would be nice to get a postcard from wherever Sarah had gone. A view of the sea, perhaps, though there was no knowing if she'd gone to the sea. A few words would do, 'Having a nice time, weather good', that sort of thing. Most of the postcards Nancy received over the years had that sort of message. Nothing else was expected. Her mother sent her a postcard once from Blackpool which said, 'Lodgings fair to middling, h. & c. in room.' Nancy was staying with her aunt at the time and her mother was in Blackpool for a holiday on her own after she'd been ill. Nancy couldn't understand what h. & c. meant. Her aunt said it meant there was hot and cold running water in the bedroom where her mother was staying. Nancy kept that postcard. She kept every postcard, and had a stock of them in a drawer. Someone at the club told her old postcards could fetch a fortune, but she doubted it.

Anyway, no postcard from Sarah Scott. Nancy tried not to mind. But she missed the young woman. Well, she wasn't young exactly, but compared to Nancy she was. Youngish and unhappy, Nancy thought. But she could get nothing out of her. Close as a clam. It would take time, that was all. Sarah Scott would need to be summered and wintered and summered again before anything might be revealed. Nancy understood that. She approved. You had to really get to know people before personal things could be confided. That was what friendship was for, to provide a safe place for perhaps painful information. When she was young herself, after they had to leave the farm, she had friends like that, two of them. They lived in the same street, went to the same school, started work together at the factory. Then boyfriends happened, to the other two but not to Nancy. She could no longer share their secrets. They whispered together, excluding her, because they said she wouldn't know what they were talking about. She made other friends, in time, but it was not the same. No confiding went on. And then, when she met Martin and got married, she had different sorts of 'friends', some of whom she didn't really like. Martin was her only true friend, and though she could tell him anything, and did, even if she knew he didn't really listen and he didn't reciprocate. When he died after only three years of marriage, she decided she was done with friendship. Having some company, at places like the club, would do.

Yet she found she was missing Sarah Scott. She couldn't claim that Sarah was a real friend but by now she was more than just a neighbour, surely. She warned herself not to get carried away, though.

Liz came straight to the point.

'This new life,' she said. 'Tell me about it. You didn't tell us a thing.'

Tara said there was very little to tell. She lived in a quiet street in a Cumbrian town – no, she was not going to say which one – and she worked in a factory, doing a simple job making boxes.

'Oh, Tara!' said Liz. 'This is ridiculous. What on earth are you thinking of?'

Tara smiled.

'I'm thinking of being a blank,' she said. 'I want to be just a blank. It's such a relief, doing what I'm asked to do, doing it automatically. It's easy, once you've got the knack.'

'But the boredom,' said Liz, 'for someone with your brain.'

'Boredom is lovely,' said Tara. 'Really, it is.'

Liz stared at her, silent for a minute.

'And outside working hours? Is that boring too?'

Tara hesitated.

'Not exactly. I drive along the coast and around the countryside. I walk along beaches. I like getting to know the area.'

'On your own?'

'Usually. Well, always, except for Mrs Armstrong, my neighbour. An elderly woman, about seventy – maybe eighty – something. I sometimes take her. She's told me how to measure a cow. It's fascinating. I mean, not just the idea of it – I kept seeing her, in my mind's eye, standing with a tape measure, asking someone to hold the cow's tail straight – but the *need* for it. Why measure a cow? And I asked her, and she got cross, started talking about working out the weight and how important that was. "You know nothing," she said, when she'd finished. I sat there nodding foolishly and thinking she's right, I knew nothing, and now at least I know how to measure a cow.'

It was easy to tell how disturbed Liz was after hearing all this. She laughed at the cow story, but then she frowned ferociously over her coffee, drinking it in two noisy gulps before banging the cup down on its saucer. She seemed, to Tara, to be trying to control her anger which, with an obvious struggle, she did.

'But,' she suddenly said, 'you left your blissfully boring life to come to the reunion. Now, what does that tell me?'

'I don't know,' said Tara. 'What does it tell you?'

'That you might be bored with boredom. That you aren't altogether satisfied with pretending to be this Sarah Scott.'

'Wrong,' said Tara. 'I came because I wanted to embarrass you all. I couldn't resist it.'

'Liar,' said Liz, and smiled. 'You came because this Mrs Armstrong isn't enough. You need us.'

Tara paused.

'Well, then,' she said, 'if that's true it's sad, isn't it? Because none of you need me.'

Liz played with a teaspoon, tapping it gently on the table.

'I've something to tell you,' she said, 'something Claire and Molly don't know. Don't ask me why I never told them, because I don't know the answer myself. I came to your trial, the first day. I didn't know if you would be able to see me or not, so I sat at the very back and I wore a hat with a big brim so that even if you could see everyone watching you wouldn't be able to identify me. I was behind a tall man, two tall men actually, so I was more or less screened from view. But I could see you, in the dock.'

Tara began to say something, but Liz leaned over and pressed her hand.

'No, let me finish. I only went that one day because I couldn't bear to go again after I'd seen you there. "Guilty," you said, loud and clear, absolutely definite and without shame. You didn't smile, but my God, you looked near to doing so. Your head was held so high, you looked so strong and sure. And it made me want to cry. I knew, I just knew, this was all wrong, but there you were, with your "guilty". I wanted to shout out that what you were guilty of was delusion – why hadn't the psychiatrists seen it? You must have been seen by a psychiatrist, I knew that, so maybe it was going to emerge that it was a nonsense for you to claim to be guilty. But I couldn't go again. I was afraid I'd shout something out. And I didn't know by then what to think, I mean, when all the details came out in the papers about what Tom had been involved in and how he'd treated you. I was so shocked, I couldn't think straight.'

Neither of them spoke for a long time. Liz scrutinised Tara's expression, unable to interpret it. Was there defiance there? But if so, what might she be defiant about? Or did her face reveal a different truth – regret? There was a certain worried look in her eyes, almost pleading, even if otherwise she looked so controlled, her mouth set, lips clamped tightly shut.

Liz risked putting her hand across the table to touch Tara's. She patted it experimentally, waiting to have it snatched away. But it wasn't.

Tara opened her fingers and grasped Liz's. They squeezed each other's hand, and then both withdrew at the same time. There was now a light air of embarrassment.

'He deserved it,' Tara said, 'he really did.' Then she shook her head. 'Enough,' she said. 'I never want to talk about Tom, never.'

'Tara,' said Liz, 'it isn't enough, it doesn't even begin to be enough.'

'Liz, you read the newspapers, you said, so you know it all. That's enough. It's irrelevant, all that. I have a new life, and I don't have to think about what happened any more. So. Enough. You tell me about yourself, your life. Go on.'

Twenty minutes later, after Liz had described the dire state of her marriage, they left the café.

'Why don't you leave him, if it's as bad as you say?' Tara asked.

Liz shrugged.

'I didn't say it was *bad*. I just said he bores me more and more. Boredom isn't grounds for leaving the children. There's only two or three years to go and then they'll be off and I can leave then. Maybe.'

Tara shrugged.

'I'd leave him,' she said.

They were almost at their cars, parked one in front of the other across the road.

'But Tara,' said Liz, 'that's the point. You didn't leave Tom. You should know how hard it is to walk out of a marriage, and you didn't even have children to complicate things.'

'It was different,' Tara said.

'Oh,' said Liz, 'it's always different, every case is different, we all think we're different. Will I see you again, or is this it?'

'I'm going back north today,' said Tara, 'but you've got my mobile number, for chats, if you like.'

Liz laughed.

'Chats?' she said. 'Is it likely, Tara? What would we chat about when you're in hiding?'

'I am *not* in hiding,' protested Tara. 'I just have a new life.'

Liz didn't bother replying; she simply made a face and got into her car.

Tara waved as Liz drove off. She didn't get into her own car. Instead, she began walking along the road. She remembered a park somewhere nearby which in spring was full of white blossom, pear and plum trees lining the main pathway. It was summer now, but the trees would still be there, their leaves almost touching from tree to tree giving shade on this hot day. She, Claire, Molly and Liz had had picnics there, simple picnics, no more than sandwiches and cans of fizzy stuff. She could see herself quite clearly in a yellow dress, short skirted, sleeveless, and Liz in a none-too-clean white T-shirt and black shorts which were knee length, showing off her legs. Sweet. The image was sweet. But even then . . . She pulled herself up sharply, turned round, walked rapidly back to her car, got in, and drove back to her hotel. She hadn't come here to do a memory-lane tour.

She was Sarah Scott and she was going back to where she now belonged.

This couldn't be called 'going home'. All the way up the M6, Tara was reminding Sarah that, like it or not, Workington was home. That squashed terraced house in that dreary street was home. It was unlike any other she had ever known, devoid of memories or ties of any kind: an anonymous home for an anonymous person, very fitting.

She drove through the Lake District, the scenic route, putting off the arrival. There was at least some pleasure, once she was past the tourist traps, of thinking that Cumbria was also her home now. She was a resident of Cumbria. That felt good. She didn't have to stay in Workington. She could move to some beauty spot, near a lake, and find other work. She felt a faint sense of excitement at this thought, but then wondered if it would be wise. It might drain her energy, make her feel faint and weak again, unable to manage life. It was too soon. She, Sarah, must stay put longer, keep the dull life she led wrapped round her. She'd been to the reunion, and that was a victory she'd never thought she would achieve. Best be content with that.

But contentment was the last thing she felt as she pulled up outside her house. Instead, a great dread filled her. She was afraid of the emptiness inside this house, the lack of any feeling, of any connection to herself. It was hard getting out of the car when what she wanted to do was drive straight on, quite aimlessly. She clutched the key to the front door so hard it dug into the skin of her hand and the more it hurt the harder she pressed until the metal made a small tear in the skin on her palm. That helped. It forced her out of the car, helped her take the two or three steps to the door and insert the key. Once inside, back against the door, she breathed deeply, eyes closed. There was an odd smell, not unpleasant, but she couldn't identify it. Maybe just the smell of a house shut up for a week. Steadier, she moved into the kitchen, just as there was a knock on the front door. She wanted to ignore it, to hide, to pretend she was still away, but a voice was shouting through the letter box, 'Hello, hello,' and she knew who it was.

'I knew you'd have nothing in,' Nancy said, 'coming back from holiday, so I brought you some bread and milk, semi-skimmed, that's what they say is good for us these days.'

'How kind,' murmured Tara. 'Thank you.'

They were still standing in the narrow hallway, Nancy proffering a plastic bag. She took it and let it hang from her wrist.

'You look done in,' said Nancy. 'Shall I put the kettle on? Have you had a long drive? I'll put the kettle on and make you some tea, shall I, eh?'

The words 'shall I' sounded in Tara's ears like a hiss. She didn't reply, but Nancy needed none. She was already in the tiny kitchen filling the kettle and switching it on.

'Won't be a minute,' she said. 'Give me that milk, you sit down, I can manage.'

Tara sat. The tea was produced, and Nancy was gratified.

'Nothing like a cup of tea, eh?'

Tara thought she might scream, but all that came out of her mouth was an 'oh' which seemed to go on for ever.

'Did you have a good time?' Nancy was asking, peering closely at her. 'You haven't got a tan, any road,' she said. 'You're as pale as ever, looks as if you've never been out in all this sun we've been having. Mind you, these days they say it gives you cancer, so maybe it's just as well you kept out of the sun, being so fair-skinned.'

On and on it went, Nancy needing no response to the drone of all her banalities, quite happy merely to have Tara captive, saying nothing. She is being kind, Tara told herself, kind, but this kindness felt like a weight being lowered on to her. It had to stop.

'Bed,' she said. 'I'm sorry, I have to go and lie down on my bed.'

'You go then,' Nancy said, 'and I'll just finish my tea and wash the cups, and I'll pull the door behind me, you don't need to worry. I said you looked done in, didn't I? Off you go.'

Tara went. Nancy hummed as she scrupulously washed the cups and set them on the draining board. She'd wondered whether she should come over when she saw Sarah pull up in her car, but she knew now that it had been the right thing. This holiday had done the poor girl no good at all. She looked worse, not better. And different. But what was different? Nancy, gently closing Sarah's front door behind her, couldn't decide. Was it the girl's hair? Yes, that was it. Her hair was now loose and curly. It had always been scraped back from her face and tied tightly on the nape of her neck. But today it was loose and bounced around her face changing it entirely. Her face, Nancy realised, might still be very thin and drawn but this loose hair, this thick, good hair, made her almost pretty. How, all these months, had Sarah managed to squash her hair into that knot she compressed it into?

Back in her own house, Nancy pondered this question. Some sort of oil, or similar, must have been used, or conditioner. Sarah must have doused her curls in it, but why? It came to Nancy that there could only be one answer: to make her look different. But no one knew her here, so why would she want to look different? Nancy became exasperated with herself, getting so obsessed with such an unimportant detail. It was what she did, get worked up over nothing. Nobody else she'd ever known did this. Her mother, her old childhood friends, even Martin had all looked at her as though she were mad when she picked on some trivial point and went on and on about it even when, quite obviously, there was no answer or no explanation to what she was seeing as a problem. Why Sarah Scott had had her hair flattened down and tied back, and then had let it free, was of no significance at all. She'd been on holiday. On holiday, she liked it to hang free. She'd worn it tied back because it was tidier for work. Simple.

But to Nancy, it was not simple. There was some meaning there which she was failing to grasp. It bothered her so much that she was going to have to ask Sarah a direct question about her hair, to bring herself peace of mind.

Grey again: grey trousers, grey sweater. The grey lady. There was no need for it, but Tara went back to grey the next day, when she returned to work. She slipped into her place without speaking to the women either side. They didn't speak to her, or even appear to notice her. When her break came and she went into the canteen to have a cup of coffee from the machine there, nobody spoke to her, though a few looked up from their coffees as she came in. She took her drink over to the window and stood looking down on the huge car park. Behind her, someone gave a melodramatic sigh, and said, 'Jesus!' and someone else laughed. Fifteen minutes, that was what she had. Fifteen minutes to look at the car park and count the cars as she drank her coffee.

She would give in her notice.

It was the Woman again, thank God.

'I gather, Sarah,' she said, her voice low, 'that you've given in your notice?'

'Yes,' said Tara, knowing that she sounded defiant. 'I have. It was too . . . the job was too . . . it just suddenly seemed ridiculous.'

'Ridiculous?'

'To be doing what I was doing when I can do other things.'

'But it was what you wanted,' the Woman said, voice still low and gentle, though there was such a hubbub in the café that there was no danger of anyone hearing her except for Tara.

'I know it was what I wanted, what I needed, but I don't need this, this blankness any longer. I want out of it. I want to go back into my old job.'

The Woman sighed.

'That's going to be difficult,' she said, 'maybe impossible. You know why.'

'But I would never do it again,' Tara said.

'That's not the point,' the Woman said. 'You did do it, and you knew how to do it, and employers only have to look at the cunning you showed for them not even to think about trusting you in a laboratory. Come on, Sarah, you know that.'

'Well, then,' said Tara, 'some other work, something that means I have to use my brain.'

The Woman studied her for a while, and then she said, 'It was your trip down south that brought this on, wasn't it?'

Tara nodded.

'Do you want to go back to London, then, is that it?'

'No,' said Tara, 'not yet. It's the job. I can't do it any more. I'm not . . . I'm not blank now, I wanted to be, but I'm not. I'm coming back to my real self, I feel more normal.'

She thought the Woman might congratulate her, say that was good, this feeling normal, but she didn't. For a minute, Tara wondered if, instead, she might dare to say, 'But, Sarah, Tara, you were never normal, you know that', but she didn't.

'There are not many jobs of the sort you want up here,' the Woman said. 'In fact, there are not many jobs of any sort. And any possible employer would have to be fully briefed about you. You're not going to be anyone's first choice.'

'I know that,' Tara said, spitting the words out.

'Well, then,' said the Woman, 'have a go yourself, and report back to me.'

Tara stared at her.

'Is that all?' she asked. 'Is that all you're going to say? Is that all the help I get?'

'Yes,' said the Woman, her voice rising now. 'You've had a great deal of help. There have been cuts, you must know that, and our services are stretched. You're lucky still to have our time.'

Nancy didn't really like going to the works pensioners' club, but it was a habit hard to break, one she really didn't want to break even though she didn't enjoy keeping it any more. At least she liked the bus ride there and the feeling of going somewhere. It took her half an hour. She liked to arrive fairly early, before the seats near the windows were all taken. There was a good view from these seats, right over the whole town beyond. If she was really bored with whoever came and sat beside her, as she often was, Nancy could just look out of the window until they took the hint. Mostly, she knew all the women who came week after week, as she did, but occasionally a newly retired one would appear. A fuss was made of these newcomers, this new blood. Everyone else rushed to introduce herself and plied the new arrival with tea and biscuits. Nancy never did. She watched the new member closely, sizing her up, and waited. You could tell a lot from such scrutiny. Sometimes she knew straight away that a fresh face was not to her taste. There would be something about it she was suspicious of, and as far as Nancy was concerned, that was that.

Two weeks after Sarah Scott returned from her mysterious holiday, a woman Nancy had never noticed arriving came and sat beside her. She didn't speak at first, which gave her full marks in Nancy's opinion, just drank her tea. There was a flower-arranging demonstration going on at the time, two women doing what Nancy thought were daft things with various flowers, piling them up, supported by thin wire, into animal shapes. Ridiculous. All you needed to do with flowers was stick them in a jug. Without realising it, Nancy was clicking her tongue in annoyance.

'Those poor flowers,' the woman murmured next to her.

Nancy didn't respond. The newcomer wasn't directly addressing her, after all, but she then said, 'Do they do this sort of thing often here?' and that was a direct question.

'No,' said Nancy, 'it's a new thing. Won't last.'

'I don't really know why I've come,' the woman said. 'I just thought it would be company. I'm going to miss the company at work. Not the work, mind, the company.'

'You get used to it,' Nancy said, and then, as an afterthought, 'the tea is good.'

'Yes,' the woman said, finishing her cup, 'it is.'

And so a connection was formed, or so Nancy felt. Would it develop into a friendship? Only time would tell. She was enjoying this thought when another woman she knew well, and detested, came over.

'I've been meaning to mention something to you, Nancy Armstrong,' she said, 'about that lass living opposite you, know who I mean?'

Nancy frowned.

'Lass?' she repeated, as though she had no idea what a lass was.

'Sarah Scott,' this woman, Ivy Robinson, said.

'Oh, yes,' Nancy said, trying to cut Ivy off from continuing, just by the tone of her voice, which she was careful to make sure betrayed no curiosity whatsoever.

'Yes,' Ivy said, 'our Gillian has worked beside her these last few months. She says she's a strange one.'

Nancy did not reply, but looked pointedly out of the window.

'Speaks to nobody,' Ivy said. 'She's not popular, carries keeping to herself too far.'

Again, Nancy remained silent while inwardly raging at this criticism of Sarah.

'Any road,' Ivy said, 'she's given notice. No loss, Gillian says.'

'Given notice.' All the way home, Nancy repeated the words to herself until they ran into each other and became a strange word she didn't know. Why would Sarah give notice? Where was she going? Did it mean she was leaving the town? Had that nephew of Amy's given *her* notice, to leave the house? She tried to answer her own questions but her answers were not satisfactory. There might be a simple explanation: Sarah was just bored with the job and wanted to have another. Simple. But Nancy was not in the habit of accepting simplicity. Her mind thrived on complications, real or imaginary. Until she'd spoken to Sarah nothing could be known for sure. Ivy Robinson could have got everything wrong.

Nancy watched the front door of Sarah's house the next day. She'd been watching it since fifteen minutes before Sarah usually left for work. The front door stayed shut. By 9 a.m., when it was still shut, Nancy went into action. She'd made a fruit cake the day before. Half of it was now wrapped in tinfoil, ready to give to Sarah, who had expressed a liking for it when she came for tea. Over the road Nancy went, the half-cake in one hand, her shopping bag in the other, though she'd no intention of going shopping. The bag was just part of her armour, her everyday protection from looking as though she was just wandering about. She knocked on Sarah's door, imitating the kind of knock she'd heard the postman give, a rat-a-tat with the knocker. Silence. Well, Sarah might be in the bath. Give her time. Nancy gave her time, and then knocked again, and heard movement inside. She expected that Sarah would be in a dressing gown, since she wasn't going to work and would surely be taking

'Talk!' repeated Tara, and laughed. 'About me giving my notice in? Sounds very grand, that, doesn't it? Actually, you don't need to "give notice" to leave a job like that, do you? You just say you're quitting.'

Nancy cleared her throat.

'Well, then,' she said, wishing she could think of something else to say.

But Sarah didn't seem to mind that Nancy was so inarticulate all of a sudden. She'd made tea and brought the two mugs in and told Nancy to have a seat. Then she went back to the kitchen and reappeared with a plate and a knife and proceeded to cut the cake. She took a huge mouthful and as she ate gave little moans of pleasure. Nancy was a bit shocked. Fancy eating fruit cake at nine in the morning. Sarah was laughing again.

'You look shocked, Mrs Armstrong, I mean Nancy. Don't you ever have cake for breakfast?'

'No,' said Nancy.

'Well, you should try it.' They were sitting opposite each other, Nancy still with her coat on, regarding Sarah with fascination. It wasn't just the clothes, it wasn't just the smiling and laughing, it wasn't even the eating of fruit cake for breakfast. It was that something was in the air in Amy's house that hadn't been there before. Nancy couldn't define what it was and didn't know how, or what, to ask Sarah. So she waited, sipping her tea, and feeling a little tense. She wondered if it would be all right to ask the one question she could think of, and decided it was. It was normal, if someone left a job, to ask if they had another to go to, wasn't it? Or was it pushing friendship too far? The sort of friendship they had, that is. But Sarah saved her the trouble.

'I haven't tried to get another job yet,' she said. 'It's just that I got fed up, you know?'

Nancy nodded. She knew. But she knew, too, that even if you were fed up rent had to be paid and bills.

'How will you manage in the meantime?' she asked.

'Oh, I'll manage,' Sarah said, 'don't you worry.'

She put her head on one side, looking at Nancy as though sizing her up.

'I used to be . . .' she said, very slowly, pausing. And then, 'What do you think I used to be, Nancy? Guess.'

Nancy did not approve of guessing, or rather in confessing to guessing.

'I'm sure you could have been anything,' she said. 'You've got the brains.'

'Have I?' said Tara. 'How do you know?'

Nancy was silent. How *did* she know Sarah had brains? She had no satisfactory answer. She didn't even know why she'd said Sarah had brains.

'I'd better be going,' she said. 'The window cleaner is coming.'

'Oh, now, Nancy,' Tara said, 'I've offended you. I'm sorry. I just really wanted to know why you would think I was clever when you can't have seen any signs of it. You've only seen me being stupid, a little dullard trotting off to a monotonous job, hiding in her dreary little house when not at work, speaking to no one unless she had to – what was clever about all that, Nancy?'

Nancy was lost. Something was going on, and it alarmed her. She was being played with, she was sure she was. But why? All kinds of explanations were running through her mind, some of them frightening. Best to get out.

'Well, I'm glad you like the cake,' she said. 'I'll be seeing you,' and she got up and walked towards the door, but Sarah was on her feet too, and rushed ahead, barring the way.

'Don't go, Nancy,' she said.

'I have to,' Nancy said. 'The window cleaner is coming. It's nearly twelve weeks since he came, the windows are a disgrace, I can't manage them myself, see.'

She lunged at the front door, grabbing the handle before Sarah got to it, and pulled it forward so that the door sprang open. Once in the fresh air, Nancy felt better, but she was aware of Sarah close behind her and stepped quickly out on to the pavement. Only then did she turn round.

'Sorry,' Tara said, 'sorry, Nancy.'

'Nothing to be sorry for,' said Nancy, but she was pleased. Sarah's behaviour, and her change in appearance, was odd. That's all there was to it. But all the same, she was glad an apology was offered even if she had no idea exactly what it was for.

The Woman was right. There were few jobs available in Workington that Tara could apply for with any hope of the work being interesting. She would have been happy to go back to being a lowly laboratory assistant, but there were no laboratories anywhere near. She thought Sellafield might be a possibility. She was a scientist, she had a degree in chemistry, surely that qualified her for some sort of job there, but the posts available all seemed to be administrative. And of course should she get an interview her CV had a big gap, and any checking up would instantly reveal her record.

Money was not yet a problem. She didn't worry about it too much. She wasn't greedy, she wasn't materialistic, and she knew how to budget. There were no shops in Workington which tempted her to buy new clothes, except for the dress she'd worn for the reunion, though she would have liked some. What she did was haunt the charity shops where she bought things she could put together or alter, mixing different styles and colours. She liked sewing, though it was frustrating that she had no sewing machine so everything had to be done by hand. She was finishing the armholes of a jacket from which she had just cut the sleeves, to make a waistcoat, when her landlord arrived without any warning. She stared at him, not knowing who he was, and he had to introduce himself. She saw Nancy's curtain twitch as she invited him in and closed the door.

'I thought I'd come in person,' he said, 'to explain.'

The explanation was simple and could easily have been made in two minutes, but he droned on until Tara wanted to jab the scissors she'd been using into his hand. She could see herself doing it, see the cut appear, the blood leak. She could hear his 'My God!' and his rage. He'd yell at her, and she'd just sit still and smile.

'Fine,' she said, when at last he seemed to have got to the end of his explanation. 'I understand.'

He seemed relieved, and relaxed in his chair.

'How have you been getting on?' he asked. 'No problems? No unpleasantness?'

She stared at him. It would amuse her, she decided, to push him to define 'problems' and 'unpleasantness'.

'I don't know what you mean,' she said, eyes conveying, she hoped, indignation.

'Well, I just meant . . . Well, they keep themselves to themselves up here, but they find things out somehow.'

Her eyes really wouldn't go any wider or her eyebrows higher.

'Things?' she repeated. But he was on his feet, not willing to play the game which he knew he would lose.

'Right,' he said, 'so you've got six weeks left. Good luck with finding somewhere.'

She gave him a big smile as he left. What a ridiculous man. He was welcome to his horrid little house, and his insinuations.

VII

NANCY SAW the nephew arriving, and leaving. She timed him: eleven minutes inside. Come to inspect the house again, see how Sarah Scott was keeping it? Unlikely. He'd already been, already knew. Could he be going to sell it? Quite likely. So, if he did, where would Sarah go?

'None of your business,' Nancy said, aloud. She was quite shocked at herself. Sarah was now a friend, or well on the way to becoming one. Shouldn't a friend be offered temporary shelter? 'Certainly not. Don't get ideas,' Nancy heard herself say, and was instantly ashamed at her own vehemence. Friends should offer help when it was needed. They stood by you, through thick and thin. Nancy nodded her head in tribute to this saying. There crept into her mind the memory of an occasion when she had been grateful for the support of friends. It was all a misunderstanding but it hadn't seemed so to the shop's manageress. Nancy had had to appear in court, utterly mortified. She'd looked up at Martin, sitting there, winking at her, and when the case was dismissed he stuck his thumb up. It had taken her weeks and weeks to get over the whole shocking business. People were funny with her. Nobody said anything, but they'd undoubtedly read the small paragraph in the local paper. She felt their suspicion, the 'no smoke without fire' reaction, in spite of the magistrate's decision. But two friends had spoken up for her. The awful thing was that she now couldn't remember their names. She had married Martin soon afterwards and they moved to Workington, and she never saw these friends again. Now whose fault was that?

Nancy banged the kitchen door closed. Stop rambling, she scolded herself, stop all this muttering. Do something, if you're so bothered. Don't be so damned hesitant, don't let yourself off by claiming you don't want to be nosy. You *do* want to be nosy. There's nothing wrong with wanting to know what is happening to a friend. She could just cross the street and knock on Sarah's door and say how are you? Simple. Friendly. No need for excuses like offering half a cake. But it would be such a huge break with a lifetime of reticence that Nancy couldn't quite manage it, and so, when, agitated by all these indecisions, she stood at her front window and saw Sarah Scott crossing the road to her she felt quite faint with relief.

She had the front door open before Sarah could knock.

'I saw him,' Nancy said. 'The nephew. Bringing trouble, was he? Come in, you look worried.'

But Sarah wouldn't come in. She stood on the doorstep, saying that no, she wasn't worried, she was excited.

'Excited?' Nancy queried.

She didn't like the sound of this. Excitement was not good. Then Sarah told her why she was excited.

'He's selling my house,' she said, 'and I'll have to move, so I've been ringing estate agents and I've got a whole list of houses to look at, but I don't know any of the places they're in, so will you help me? There's a good-sounding one in Cleator Moor, but where's Cleator Moor?'

'A place you don't want to bother with,' Nancy said firmly. 'Are you off there now?'

Yes, Sarah was proposing to set off house hunting immediately, if Nancy would accompany her and act as her guide. It was one of the afternoons she went to the club, but Nancy didn't hesitate.

'I'll get my coat,' she said.

They met at Molly's house. Nothing from Tara. They'd all sent text messages over the last month but there'd been no response.

'She just wants to disappear again,' Claire said to Liz and Molly.

'It's obvious. You would have thought old friends reunited would count for something, but no, apparently not.'

'Reunited?' said Liz. 'Don't be silly, Claire. We met for one lunch. That's not reunited.'

She didn't mention her own later meeting with Tara. Claire would be jealous, Molly disappointed, that neither of them had had a tête-à-tête with Tara.

'Anyway,' Liz said, 'I don't know why it upsets you so much. If Tara wants privacy, that's her affair.'

'But I *care* about her,' Claire said. 'I can't get her face out of my mind again.'

'Oh, Claire, for God's sake!' said Liz. 'You've managed very well without any contact with Tara for the past ten years, so don't talk rubbish. The "reunion" as you call it was a failure. It was a well-meaning gesture and it failed. Enough said.'

'I don't *want* to fail,' said Claire, her voice loud. 'I don't like failure.'

'We already failed Tara, Claire,' said Molly. 'That's the explanation for why that reunion didn't work. It was never going to. Tara will have new friends. She doesn't need old ones, the ones who were not there when she did need them.'

'But old friends, friends you've known since you were at school, they have to mean something.'

'Why?' said Liz.

'Because they are like foundations,' said Claire.

Liz immediately laughed.

'Foundation garments, do you mean, or foundations for a building?' and she laughed again.

'You may mock and sneer,' Claire said. 'You always did. But you know perfectly well what I mean.'

'Really?' said Liz. 'And what's that?'

But Claire glared at her and would not reply.

Molly was tired of them both. Claire ever self-righteous, Liz sharp and caustic. She knew how they'd all come together at such a young age, but the puzzle was how this friendship had survived. It hadn't exactly flourished in the last decade but it was significant surely that it was still there in some shape or form, when they'd had so little in common for so long. All they talked about when they met, or on the phone, was their own history full of do-you-remembers and then often quarrelling over what was remembered. Tara obviously didn't want that. She'd said her bit, had her moment, and as far as she was concerned, that was it. Why Claire would not accept this, Molly couldn't understand. She herself found that she didn't care if she never saw Tara again. What was so awful about that? But if she said it aloud, Claire would be shocked. Friends old and new were important to Claire in a way Molly knew they were not so important to her. Nice to have good friends, yes, and she had plenty, but more important, she had her children and she had Simon. But Claire rated people according to how many friends of long standing they had. To say of some woman 'I don't think she has many friends' was the ultimate indictment.

'Anyway,' Claire said, 'I don't think Tara has many friends, from what she was saying.'

'You haven't the faintest idea if that's true,' said Liz, 'and even if it is, it's her own choice and there's nothing wrong with that.'

'Yes, there is!' said Claire, emphatic as usual, but the other two sighed and refused to go on with the subject.

This meeting had not been a great success. Still, there was always a sort of comfort in being together, however far apart they'd become, though they quite often bored each other with detailed accounts of their own children's progress. It was odd, Liz had often thought, that on their rare meetings all together they never discussed current affairs. The state of the country, the state of the world, was shut out. They seemed only concerned with their own world, with their personal lives. Self-centred, Liz decided. We're all self-centred.

'I thought maybe Pica,' Tara said. 'There are three houses for rent there, and they're so cheap.'

'I'm not surprised,' said Nancy. 'Pica! Back of beyond, no shops, no transport. No wonder the rents are cheap. You'd be stuck, if you went to Pica.'

'I have a car,' protested Tara. 'I wouldn't be stuck.'

'What about work, though?' Nancy asked. 'There's no work in Pica. You'd always be travelling. No, get Pica out of your head. Dear me. What about Egremont? Now that's a nice place, bound to be something there to suit you.'

So Tara drove along the coast road to Egremont. Beside her Nancy was humming, thoroughly enjoying the drive. Tara thought she could risk some direct questions without offending her.

'Nancy,' she said, 'you wear a wedding ring but you never mention your husband. Has he been dead a long time?'

Nancy stopped humming, and fidgeted slightly in her seat.

'Nearly forty-five years,' she said.

'What did he die of?'

'A stroke,' Nancy said. And then, after a pause which Tara did not like to interrupt, 'He was a good man.'

'Mine wasn't,' Tara said. 'I thought he was when I married him, but he wasn't.'

Nancy stared ahead and tried to think this information through. What did you say when a woman told you her husband wasn't a good man? She tried to separate what she wanted to know from what it might be cheeky to ask but got tangled up in her own confusion. She coughed, took a mint from her bag and popped it into her mouth.

'Would you like one?' she asked. Tara shook her head.

Nancy sucked the mint for a bit, and coughed again, and then said, 'I didn't know you'd been married.'

'No,' said Tara, 'I took my ring off as soon as I was free.'

'Divorced?' queried Nancy.

'No.'

'He passed away?' Nancy asked.

'In a manner of speaking,' Tara said, and laughed.

Laughed! And 'in a manner of speaking'. What did that mean? But at that point they arrived in Egremont and Sarah was expressing agreeable surprise. The main street was broad with small, attractive-looking shops lining it. Everything looked newly painted and fresh. A woman walked past the car as they parked, and smiled and nodded as she went behind to cross the street. She was carrying a basket with a gingham cover over it.

Sarah said, 'A basket! I thought wickerwork baskets were long gone, it's all carrier bags now.'

'Nothing like a decent basket for wear and tear,' said Nancy, 'but they're heavy, mind.'

'Let's have some lunch,' Sarah said, 'my treat.'

It was easy to find a café, settle themselves in comfortable, well-padded chairs at a small table covered in a startlingly clean pink cloth.

'This is nice,' Nancy said.

She was, Tara noticed, quite flushed with pleasure. They ordered the home-made soup and rolls, and Tara thought of Liz and that other café.

Nancy knew nothing about her. That was the beauty of being with her. And she had risked spoiling this by volunteering the news that she had been married and that her husband had not been a very nice man. Nancy, it was easy to tell, was shocked at being told Sarah's husband had not been a good man, but she hadn't gone on to ask why, or in what way, he hadn't been good, or exactly how he died. It was against Nancy's own personal code. That, Tara suddenly realised, was the attraction of Nancy for her. She wouldn't prod and poke and drag out any history. She would listen and, on the whole, simply accept what she was told. It was such a relief realising this. Tara's heart began to beat a little faster as a strange kind of excitement took over. How far was she prepared to go? What was she going to dare to tell Nancy? Why the urge to tell her any more than she had already done? Oh, do be careful, she said to herself, don't spoil things . . .

The soup came and was delicious. Nancy was surprised. Soup in cafés was, in her limited experience, never any good. Home-made usually meant out of a tin with something added. But this was a thick broth, the vegetables clearly identifiable, carrots and potato and onion and a whole lot of others. She remarked on how good it was, but Sarah said nothing. She had a funny expression on her face, a sort of half-smile which was not a proper smile, and her lips were compressed in an uncomfortable-looking way, as though inside her mouth she was biting her tongue. She hadn't touched her soup.

'You haven't touched your soup,' Nancy said. 'Go on, taste it, it's really good. Taste it, it'll get cold, go on. It'll do you good.'

Slowly, Tara dipped her spoon into the broth, but as it neared her mouth she suddenly put it down again, slightly spilling what had been on it.

'Oh, dear,' Nancy said. 'Here, dab it with this tissue,' and she pointed to the tiny stain on the pink tablecloth. 'It'll come out in the wash,' she said. 'Don't fret.'

It was as though she was speaking to a child. Nobody, Tara thought, aware that tears were coming into her eyes and only rapid blinking was stopping them from falling, has ever told me not to fret when I've done something wrong. Dropping a tiny bit of soup on to a tablecloth wasn't 'wrong' but her foster mother would have reprimanded her sharply. She would never have said, 'Don't fret.' No excuses, no comfort, only blame: that had been her foster mother, and then, eventually, Tom.

'My mother,' she began, and then stopped.

Nancy looked uncomfortable. Tara could see that what Nancy dreaded was A Scene in a Public Place, and she, to Nancy, must be looking as though she was on the edge of causing one.

'Sorry,' she said, and lowered her head, eating more of the soup and not spilling any.

'There now,' Nancy said, pleased, 'you'll feel better for that.'

Nancy relaxed – thank God, the girl wasn't going to cry. She wondered if maybe the young woman had had a nervous breakdown in the recent past. It would explain a lot. She couldn't ask her, of course, but silently tried to think of ways in which she could obliquely bring the subject up. None presented themselves to her at the moment.

'Should we be getting on?' she said, the soup finished.

There was no reply.

'Are you all right?' Nancy asked.

They'd be in a fine pickle if Sarah wasn't fit to drive. Who could I call, Nancy wondered, what will I do? She wished this had happened in Workington.

But Sarah had recovered.

'Yes,' she said, 'let's get on, you're right.'

Nancy loved looking at the houses to let on Sarah's list. On each doorstep, as the front door opened (all the houses were occupied at the moment) Sarah introduced herself, brandishing the estate agent's details, and then said, 'This is my friend Mrs Armstrong.' This pleased Nancy inordinately. She didn't want to be on Christian-name terms with strangers and Sarah had deduced that and shown respect. While Sarah talked to the householder, Nancy's eyes darted round the rooms, taking in the damp patch on the ceiling and the signs of woodworm on the skirting board and the state of the kitchen sink. Two of the houses were so untidy she was embarrassed for the occupiers, unable as she was to believe people could live with dirty dishes piled high and waste bins overflowing, not to mention bathrooms with tide marks engrained on the porcelain and lavatories that hadn't been bleached in weeks, if ever.

Once back in the car, she exclaimed over what she had seen but Sarah didn't seem shocked.

'Oh,' she said, 'we used to live like that when we were young.'

'Who?' Nancy asked, before she could stop herself.

'My friends and I,' Sarah said. 'We once shared a flat, just for a year, four of us. We were such slatterns except for Claire, and she couldn't control us.'

Nancy was silent. She tried to build up an image of Sarah as part of a quartet of slatterns.

'Well,' she said, after a long pause, 'you've changed. You keep your house tidy and clean now.'

'That's because I'm not me any more. I'm not Tara,' she said, 'I'm Sarah.'

Nancy frowned. She repeated the words to herself in her head: 'I'm not me any more. I'm not Tara, I'm Sarah.' What was going on? Was Sarah being funny? People were always telling her that they were 'only being funny' when she didn't understand something. But it hadn't sounded funny. It had sounded despairing, bitter. Nancy struggled with an urgent need to ask a whole list of questions but asked none of them. Best not to pry. She cleared her throat.

'Which house did you like best?' she asked, pleased at how innocuous her enquiry was.

'None of them,' Sarah said. 'They all made me want to scream.'

Scream. Here was another conundrum: what was there to scream about? They were just ordinary houses, *nothing* to scream about. Nancy realised she must have made some sort of sound that betrayed her surprise because Sarah/Tara, whatever she was called, then said, 'Scream with horror at the ordinariness, the way it closed round us, strangling us.'

This was getting ridiculous. The girl was away with the fairies.

'Nothing wrong with being ordinary,' Nancy said, rather grimly. She wanted to add, 'I don't know what you mean with this fancy, daft talk,' but she didn't. Best not to fall out, especially as Sarah/Tara, whatever, was driving and needed to concentrate.

'Oh, I can't bear ordinariness, dreariness,' Tara said, 'and now I'm ordinary too, looking at ordinary places to live and hating them all. I want to go back, and I can't.'

Now, Nancy wondered, which question can I ask first? What would be safe, innocent? 'Go back to where?' she dared to ask.

'My life,' said Tara.

Nancy really could not take that in. Sarah/Tara was talking as though she had died. This sort of silliness, Nancy decided, should not be encouraged, so she said nothing, just shifted in her seat and fiddled with her seat belt. There was silence, though not a comfortable one, for several miles.

Then Sarah/Tara said, 'You like your own life, don't you, Nancy?'

Here we go again, Nancy thought, exasperated. 'Of course I like my life,' she said irritably. 'I only have one, don't I? You make the best of it, that's all. It isn't a matter of liking it. Goodness me.'

That was as far as she was prepared to go. If she said anything else she'd regret it.

They were on their way now to Cockermouth, where there were quite a few houses to rent. Sarah/Tara took to Cockermouth straight away, though Nancy didn't care for it, never felt comfortable there. It was 'too county' she told Sarah/Tara, who didn't understand what she meant, and Nancy couldn't explain. It was several years since she'd been to Cockermouth and she had to admit that since the floods in 2010 the main street had been prettified with the shop signs different and the buildings freshly painted. They were looking for a house in Waterloo Street behind the main street.

'Oh, no,' Nancy said, even before they went in. 'Look, it's too near the river. It might flood again, and anyway there'd be all that damp all the time, coming off the river.'

'I like a bit of danger,' Tara said dreamily.

Nancy clicked her teeth in annoyance. At times, she wanted to give Sarah/Tara a slap. They found the house, and Tara announced that she loved it even before the door was opened. Nancy saw nothing to love. It was a stone house, probably very old, and old houses caused all kinds of problems. Inside it was rather dark except for the kitchen at the back which overlooked the garden sloping slightly down to the river, currently rather high, the water gushing along at a great rate. Nancy shuddered, but Tara was in ecstasies.

'I love it,' she said to the estate agent, who'd met them outside. 'I'll take it.'

Nancy was so shocked, words failed her.

Tara wanted to wander around the little town and maybe have something to eat later, but Nancy said she had to get back.

'Why?' asked Tara. 'What's the rush? What do you have to get back for?'

This was outrageous. 'I have to get back' should never be questioned. It was a well-known euphemism and Tara was deliberately not understanding it. She was, instead, seeking to emphasise that Nancy had nothing to get back for, no husband coming home from work and needing his tea, no children coming home from school, no dog, no cat, only an empty house and – Nancy felt – an empty life.

'I'll get a bus,' she said, 'you stay as long as you like.'

She knew the bus service to Workington these days hardly existed, but she didn't care. She wanted to emphasise to Sarah Scott – she'd always be Sarah Scott to her – that she was independent and had always been independent and always would be. Her face, she knew, she could feel it, was red with anger and Tara could see it and if she didn't recognise what 'I have to get back' meant she would certainly interpret Nancy's flush correctly. And she did.

'I'm sorry, Nancy,' she said. 'Let's go.'

They drove back in silence, with Nancy only relaxing when the grey street that was hers was turned into. It comforted her, just seeing the familiar houses, the narrow pavements, the tarmac-covered road with potholes in it at regular intervals. She could see that some might find it a depressing scene, but it did not depress her. Leaving this street would make her feel cast adrift. She saw, quite clearly, that this Sarah Scott, who wasn't Sarah Scott, had never belonged here. Well, she'd thought that from the beginning, but she'd imagined the woman would adapt, and she'd thought she had, to a certain extent, over the last few months. But no. She hadn't. This was going to be a promising friendship which would never mature. It was a shame, but nothing could be done about it. As usual, acknowledging that 'nothing could be done' about something made Nancy feel almost triumphant.

'Thanks for coming with me,' Tara said, as she pulled up outside her house.

'I enjoyed the drive,' Nancy said. She wasn't going to say that she enjoyed anything else.

'Will you come in and let me make you a cup of tea?' Tara said.

'No, thanks, I have to get home,' Nancy said.

If Sarah asked why, she might let fly, but she didn't ask.

'Sorry,' she said, as Nancy started to open the car door. 'Sorry, Nancy, if I, you know, if . . .'

'Nothing to be sorry about,' said Nancy.

'Oh, but there is,' Tara said. 'I'm full of lies, and I'm sorry.'

Here we go again, Nancy thought, another peculiar statement, but she wasn't going to ask what Sarah – it was no good, she couldn't call her Tara – meant by saying she was full of lies. It was too childish. Once she was in her own house, though, having her own tea in her own kitchen, and soothed by the familiarity, she naturally pondered what these lies could be. Clearly, *something* had brought Sarah Scott here, to a place where she did not belong, but how was a lie, or a whole lot of lies, involved? If she, Nancy, had responded with 'What lies?' would Sarah have started confessing them? Nancy shuddered. Always a mistake, letting someone confess to you. Lies should be kept quiet. The urge to share them was in itself a dangerous sign. She nodded to herself. She'd done the right thing by sidestepping Sarah's invitation to hear about the lies she'd apparently told.

But all that evening, she speculated.

The house she'd taken in Cockermouth would be vacant in three weeks. And there was a job she'd applied for at the community hospital there as a receptionist, though she was pretty certain that checks on her application might be too thorough and she'd be ruled out. She'd made up the references needed, and then tore them up. Much too risky. Instead, she portrayed herself as never having had a job before owing to the ill health of her now deceased husband. She said she felt the experience she'd had with doctors and hospitals on his account made her aware of the skills a receptionist needed, balancing efficiency with sympathy. She was rather pleased with that bit. There was another job going, in Carlisle, in the pharmacy at the infirmary, but she didn't dare apply for it. Checks there would be extensive, and she no longer had the Woman or even the Man to help her. But she had to have a reference of some sort, and there was no one in Workington except Nancy Armstrong who could give one. She couldn't give the factory charge-hand as a reference because she was saying she'd never worked before. What a tangled web, etc. – a whole new network of complications.

Inevitably, she thought of her old friends, in particular of Claire. All she'd be asking her to do was write a letter saying she had known 'Sarah Scott' for twenty-five years and could vouch for . . . for what? What on earth could she ask Claire to vouch for? Intelligence? Certainly. Claire would have no problem with the truth of that. Efficiency? That should be OK. Dependability? Probably not. 'Caring nature?' Oh, God, no. But did employers bother about all these qualities when the job was only a receptionist's? She hoped not. Claire could make her reference as short as she liked. The thing to do was to represent it to her, obliquely of course, as an opportunity to make up for letting Tara down at a crucial time. But she'd have to give her address, if what she wanted was a letter, headed notepaper and all. Well, that wouldn't be dangerous because she was moving soon.

Then there was Nancy. She would have to ask Nancy, who'd known her some months but who didn't know her at all. This would be an asset. She could truthfully write that Sarah Scott had been her neighbour this past ten months and she had found her quiet, dutiful and helpful. (Did taking Nancy for car rides count as being 'helpful'?) Nancy, though, probably didn't write anything regularly. She might see writing a reference as beyond her ability. But the minute she'd considered this, Tara scolded herself for being patronising. Nancy might well be in the habit of writing letters frequently to friends or relations Tara knew nothing about. She might even be flattered at being asked to give a reference.

She was not. When Tara explained, over the inevitable cup of tea and shortbread biscuits, that she was going to apply for a job as a doctor's receptionist, and needed someone to write her a short reference, Nancy said:

'Who will you ask? No one knows you, except me and those you worked with, and you don't even seem to know their names, from what you told me.'

'Exactly,' Tara said. 'That's why I want you to do it, just a couple of sentences saying how long you've known me and that I'm, oh, I don't know, respectable, that sort of thing. I'd be very grateful, Nancy.'

Nancy broke a biscuit in two and pondered long before selecting one of the halves and eating it. She munched slowly, though it was a very small fragment of biscuit.

'I don't know that I'm the right person to oblige,' she finally said.

'You're the only person,' Tara said. 'I don't know anyone else.'

She wasn't going to go into why she couldn't ask for a reference from her previous employer. Nancy would think her reasons suspicious (and of course they were).

Nancy drank some tea, and then said, 'There's nothing I could write. Best ask someone else.' She got up, saying, as she inevitably did, 'Oh, look at the time, I've got to get back.'

Tara let a few tears appear in her eyes. (She'd always been able to turn on tears easily, a formidable talent she'd made great use of in her life.)

Nancy saw them, as she was intended to, and said, 'It's nothing to get upset about, goodness me.'

'But I am upset,' Tara said. 'I was counting on you.'

'Well, you shouldn't,' Nancy said, quite sharply. 'No good counting on people you hardly know. Leads to trouble.'

Tara realised she'd made a terrible mistake: tears were not going to soften Nancy. Tears disgusted her. Tears were for dying children and other tragedies. Tears, because a reference was being withheld, were daft.

'I'm sorry,' Tara said. 'I was being stupid, you're quite right. But I need this job, Nancy.'

Nancy was already at the front door.

'Good luck, then,' she said, and was out without a backward look, walking briskly across the road to her own house. Tara thought she closed her door with unnecessary force, quite a decided bang as she went in.

So that was that. Then, suddenly, she thought of her landlord, 'the nephew' Nancy hated so much. He might give her a reference, along the lines of excellent tenant, orderly, neat, rent always on time. He even, in a way, owed her a favour, for giving her notice long before the time he'd promised she could rent the house. He wouldn't care tuppence that he didn't know her at all. A short reference from him and another, she hoped, from Claire, and that should suffice.

She didn't need Nancy Armstrong.

So much was revealed in Tara's short letter that Claire took a while to absorb it. Tara's address, and her new name, felt sort of exciting to see. 'Sarah Scott', and the town in Cumbria, such a long way away. And a letter was wanted, on headed notepaper, 'your usual impressive stuff'. Claire frowned over that. What was 'impressive' about headed notepaper? Was Tara mocking her? Surely not, when, after all, she was asking a favour, one she made sound simple but which was not simple at all. Claire got the message. She realised Tara was exerting a kind of emotional blackmail, along the lines of this being her chance to make up for having, so many years ago, let Tara down. But Tara had been guilty. Why should she have expected her friends to stand by her after she'd admitted her guilt? A question they'd never asked her when they'd had the chance.

It was hard to get into Tara's mind, but then it always had been. She did such odd things, reacted to events in such a strange way. You could never count on her, the way you could on Liz and Molly. Unpredictable, that was what she'd always been. It made her fascinating, just trying to guess what she would say, or do. And now she wanted a reference, concentrating, she said, on the number of years Claire had known her and emphasising her kind nature and pleasant manner and reliability. 'Kind', when she'd done what she did? And 'pleasant' wasn't exactly true either. Tara *could* be pleasant, but it was not her outstanding feature. 'Reliability' was a problem too. Tara, in Claire's memory, was always late for any appointment and not too apologetic about it when she did arrive. Writing a reference in which she did not perjure herself would be tricky, and that was if she wrote one at all.

She expected that Liz and Molly would have been asked too, but no, they hadn't, and they were a touch offended, though they tried to hide it (but Claire knew them too well).

'I expect it's the lack of headed notepaper,' Liz joked. 'In fact, I don't think I've got any paper except plain A4 stuff.'

Molly said it was a relief that she hadn't been asked. 'I'd have tied myself in knots trying to write a reference,' she said. 'I'm not good with words, as Tara knows. Poor you, Claire, picking on you. What will you write?'

An hour of discussion on the phone with each of them followed, resulting in Claire deciding, with their encouragement, that saying Tara was 'reliable' was out of the question but 'pleasant' was permissible.

'I'll have to think of other words, other qualities,' Claire said, 'like her quick thinking, her adaptability, those kind of qualities.'

'Good luck,' the others said, 'and don't overdo it. She's got quite a cheek asking.' Claire thought so too, but then Tara had always been cheeky.

She struggled over the reference for days, to the irritation of Dan. Every meal they had, Claire went over and over the difficulties of writing it, the battle with her conscience and yet wanting to help Tara.

'I want to make up for not standing by her when she needed me,' she said, making him sigh with exasperation.

'We've been through that millions of times,' he said. 'Look, Tara was a friend and now she's hardly someone you could call a friend at all. You're trying to pretend you actually still know her and you do not. End of.'

'We were so close once,' Claire murmured.

'Oh, for God's sake, Claire, grow up. You're just indulging in sentimental rubbish, drooling over the past. Send a reference if you want to, but don't turn it into a bloody drama.'

'You don't have friends,' Claire said, 'so you don't understand the link.'

'I said, don't turn this into a drama,' repeated Dan. And then, bad-temperedly, 'Of course I have friends.'

'It's not the same.'

'Well, I'm glad it isn't,' said Dan, 'if having friends like your friends is the result.'

'You're jealous,' Claire said.

Dan's laughter, she assured herself, was forced.

It was a week before she managed to write a reference which, she told herself, did not compromise her principles.

Nancy was hurt. It took a while for her to admit this, but finally she acknowledged that this was the reason she could hardly drag herself out of bed and had a struggle following her daily routine. She was suffering from unfulfilled expectations. How that phrase came to her was a mystery, but it did – 'unfulfilled expectations'. And of what? Friendship, of course. With Sarah Scott. She'd thought it had been growing nicely, slowly, as true friendships should, but no, it had withered on the vine. That was another expression that startled her, popping into her mind quite abruptly, and very satisfying to find lodged there.

Maybe she shouldn't have taken umbrage at Sarah asking her to provide a reference. She didn't quite grasp why she had refused to do so. It wasn't that she couldn't have written one – good heavens, she wasn't illiterate, though it was a long time since she'd had cause to set pen to paper. It wasn't that. No, it was that she felt she was in some way being exploited by Sarah. Used. All day she rattled around her house doing unnecessary things like emptying out perfectly tidy drawers and putting the contents back again in almost exactly the same order. Her conversations with herself got increasingly heated. What on earth did you want from the girl, she asked, what was wrong with your contact with her? What did you want from her? Nothing, she answered herself and immediately scoffed at this reply. What you wanted, Nancy my girl, was to know her, to get to really know Sarah Scott, without her – ah, this was the point – *without her really getting to know you*. But Sarah wouldn't give. Hints thrown out, but nothing revealed. And whose fault was that, who hadn't taken up these hints? You, Nancy. Afraid of getting involved. And now Sarah Scott was moving away and that would be that. She'd get someone else to give her a reference.

Nancy went to the club that afternoon simply because it was Wednesday and one of her club days. She was fuming with a rage she didn't understand and knew there was an unpleasant scowl on her face. As usual, she took a seat near the window but she didn't survey the room, seeing who she might pass a bit of time with. Instead, she looked fixedly out of the window, regretting already that she'd come. It was that Ivy Robinson, of course, who came up to her and plonked herself down beside Nancy. Ivy could sense distress of one sort or another. She was attracted to it like a cat to the smell of fish. There was no pussyfooting around, though.

'What's the matter with you?' Ivy asked. 'You've got a face like thunder, it'd turn the milk sour.'

Nancy picked up her cup and drank her tea without giving Ivy the satisfaction of any sort of reply. Rude? Yes, but Ivy had been rude. Ivy wasn't in the least put out.

'Saw you on Friday,' she said, 'in the car, with that woman, what's-her-name, the one used to work beside our Gillian and got the sack.'

'She did not!' said Nancy, and regretted saying anything at all. It only encouraged Ivy. Silence was the best weapon to use against her sort, a dignified silence, of course, not a sulky one. But she'd spoken and could not take her few words back.

'That's what they say, any road,' Ivy said. 'That, and more. There's things being said about that woman I wouldn't like to repeat.'

Nancy kept her face impassive, or so she hoped, but a little thrill went through her, like an electric shock. Ivy knew something that she was longing to divulge and whatever it was it would be unpleasant. She had that look in her eyes that Nancy knew only too well, a look that was both triumphant and nasty. All she needed was the slightest of reactions, and out it would all pour, the gossip she'd heard, the hints, the guesses transformed, in her mind, into facts.

Nancy got up, carrying her cup and saucer over to the serving hatch. Her hand trembled slightly as she put it down, the cup faintly rattling against the saucer. Ivy had followed her, placing her own crockery down beside Nancy's.

'Well,' she said, 'if you don't want to know I'm not telling you.'

Nancy was tempted to snap that she had no wish to listen to anything Ivy had to say, but she controlled herself.

'Just you ask your new pal where she was before she landed here,' Ivy said. 'Just you ask her. You might have more in common than you know, you two.'

Ivy smiled, and asked for more tea. Nancy moved out of the way, turning her back because she knew her face was red. 'More in common . . .' The words repeated themselves in her head. 'More in common . . .' But, really, she had nothing in common with Sarah Scott, except that they lived in the same street, and soon not even that would be true. She knew she was falling victim to Ivy's mischief but she couldn't control the hot rush of curiosity now coursing through her. If she couldn't ask Ivy, and she couldn't, who else could tell her what she allegedly had in common with Sarah Scott?

Nancy went home, confused and upset. Really, it was best to keep yourself to yourself, as she'd always done since she'd stopped being a girl, when friendship had meant companionship and not much more. And yet she acknowledged to herself that she had wanted friendship from Sarah, wanted something deeper than companionship, but all the time, these past few months, she had been wary, suspicious of yielding to this longing. Let Sarah take the lead, she'd said to herself, but when Sarah did, or tried to, when she'd made tentative moves towards confidences, Nancy knew she had drawn back. And now she had lost her chance, it seemed. Sarah was moving away, and the vague friendship they had would not survive this moving, and now Ivy had made things worse by claiming that she and Sarah had 'something in common'.

Her house didn't seem comforting at all when Nancy returned to it. She closed the front door and stood with her back to it. She had to *do* something before it really was too late. She had to make an effort before Sarah moved away. But she never made efforts of this sort. They were foreign to her nature.

Her nature would have to change. Quickly.

*

Tara tore Claire's reference up the moment it arrived. It was not at all what she had asked for. Typical Claire, the pompous tone of it sounding unconvincing, full of weasel words which could be taken in different ways. She'd drawn a blank with the landlord, too. He simply didn't reply.

That left only Nancy Armstrong, who hadn't actually refused to write a reference but instead had sidestepped a decision, or that was how Tara was persuading herself to interpret Nancy's reaction. It was familiar Nancy behaviour, always to be cautious and suspicious and never to reveal what she really thought. Tara had noticed this behaviour, too, in the women she'd worked with. Maybe Cumbrians, as a massive generalisation, were cautious and suspicious by nature. It was just their way. So she'd set about asking Nancy much too directly. Better to have introduced the subject of perhaps giving a reference in an oblique fashion.

'I don't know what I can do,' she might have said. 'I need someone to vouch that I'm respectable and I've no one to ask.' Might Nancy then have said she'd do the vouching? But this scenario didn't ring quite true.

She could forge a reference, of course, banking on no one checking it out, but she'd promised herself she wouldn't, in her new life, do that any more. No lying, no deceit of any kind. Instead, she would invite Nancy for a 'last' cup of tea, not delivering the invitation by note or telephone but by knocking on her door. It would be harder, she reckoned, for Nancy to shut the door in her face than to put the phone down or ignore the note. She practised her expression in front of the mirror before she went over the road. It must be worried/slightly distressed/pleading. Voice should be low, but not whiny. So over she went and stood in front of Nancy's door, knocking gently with the brass knocker. She waited. The lace curtain twitched. She waited again, knowing Nancy had seen her from the living-room window. After a couple of minutes, she knocked again, longer this time, and flapped the letter box.

'I'm busy,' Nancy called, 'can't answer the door at the moment,' and then a Hoover started up.

Tara stayed there, waiting till the sound stopped, and then she lifted the flap of the letter box and shouted:

'Nancy, it's me, Tara. Sorry to bother you, so sorry.'

There was a pause, and then the door was opened cautiously, not quite to its full width.

'I'm busy,' Nancy said.

'Yes, I know, I'm sorry to interrupt you, but I wanted to ask you if you would please, please, come round for a last cup of tea before I go?'

'When's that?' Nancy asked.

Her face, Sarah thought, had softened slightly.

'Next Friday,' Tara said, 'so come any other day, except Thursday when I'll be packing?'

VIII

CLAIRE WAS a great one for 'signs', for things being 'meant'. Mocking her did no good, so her husband didn't even try, though he was astonished at the 'meaning' she saw in his visit to Sellafield. Claire was going to come with him to see Tara. Workington was near Sellafield, and the opportunity too good to miss. The fact that Tara wanted privacy was irrelevant. Dan pointed out that Tara might be furious if Claire turned up on her doorstep, but Claire rubbished this idea. So Dan gave in. He'd be staying near Sellafield for two days while he carried out his inspection, so Claire could drive herself to and from Workington while he was working. Claire beamed.

She bought maps. She loved maps, loved plotting routes and scorned sat navs. All she lacked was a street map for Workington but she would pick one up when she got there. Workington couldn't be like London so it should be easy to find Tara's street, her house. She told Liz and Molly her plan on the phone. Liz said nothing, but Molly sounded anxious and said:

'Oh, Claire, is this wise?'

As neither of them had been asked to provide a reference, she thought their disappointing reaction to her plan might be because they were jealous. Claire knew people were often jealous of her but there was nothing she could do about it. But, disappointingly, neither Liz nor Molly showed any signs of envy.

The drive to Cumbria was long, with heavy traffic all the way. Dan was a careful driver, never exceeding sixty miles an hour. Claire knew it would be foolish to complain, so she tried to concentrate on looking out of the window. The countryside surprised her. Somehow, never having been north, she'd imagined something along the lines of dark satanic mills, forgetting that the M1 and M6 would obviously avoid cities and towns. What she saw was a green and pleasant land, field after field of hay amidst others of bright yellow and sharpest emerald green. Even the verges were lush with wild flowers and hawthorn, gold and white interlaced together. And the trees – she hadn't reckoned on the masses of trees suddenly appearing at regular intervals. Then the hills came into view and far-off mountains all grey-blue and hazy in the sun. It made Berkshire, where she'd spent nearly all her life, seem cramped and tame. Maybe, she thought, Tara had done a clever thing in choosing to come here. Maybe Workington was going to turn out to be a charming, pretty town.

It wasn't. Driving to it was pretty – more than pretty – the views of the Solway Firth dazzling in the sun, but the town itself bewildered her. There seemed to be no centre, or none that she could find, blundering round the streets, so she parked outside Marks & Spencer's and set off to buy a street map and a guide book. It was absurd, but she felt she was in a foreign land, though all the shops were familiar and everyone spoke English. She'd never thought of herself as having a posh accent, but here she felt she did and was embarrassed by it. It marked her out as a stranger. But nobody seemed curious about her; nobody asked, as she sat studying the street map, if she wanted any help. She was ignored, and suddenly felt lost and strange. She tried to think of Tara arriving here, a place completely unfamiliar. She must surely have been disorientated, wandering around trying to find somewhere to live, but maybe the choice had been made for her.

Street map in hand, Claire crossed the main road opposite Marks & Spencer's and began climbing a hill. Below, the traffic thundered along, skirting the town, and she longed to get away from it. But somehow she must have misread the map and ended up back on this noisy main road, further along. She realised that in any case Tara's street must be the other side of the road, and a good way down it. She thought, briefly, of going back for her car but decided not to. Instead, she trudged along the road, deafened by the roar of the lorries, desperately consulting her map again and again. The wind was in her face, blowing dust from the dirty pavement straight at her. She bowed her head against it and wished herself back home. Almost at the point of giving up, she finally found Tara's street. It shocked her. The houses were so close together, their bricks blackened, the narrow pavements either side hemming them in. It was not a cold day but smoke was coming out of some of the chimneys. She could see only two cars parked in the street, though there were no notices restricting parking. It was two o'clock in the afternoon and absolutely silent. The main road she'd longed to escape now seemed less alarming than this dreary street. Slowly, Claire walked along it, searching for number 18. The windows of the houses, one ground-floor window each, were so close that it was an effort to be polite and not stare into them, though she noticed they were mostly shrouded in net curtains, and little could be seen.

In front of number 18 she hesitated. She'd expected some visible sign that Tara lived here, something different about this house from the others. But there was no difference. There were net curtains covering the window just as they covered the other windows. Looking around her, up and down the street, knowing she looked furtive, Claire pressed her face against the glass, searching beyond the net for some splash of colour, some painting on a wall, that would indicate Tara did live here. Nothing, except for a bit of material, red and white, over the back of a chair. Claire took a step back and looked up. There was a blind on the top window, pulled down. Was Tara in bed, at two in the afternoon? Unlikely. Though in fact, why had she come at this time? It was silly. She should've come in the evening.

There was no bell, only a knocker. She knocked, recoiling lightly from the dull thud it produced. Should she leave a note? No, she should do the sensible thing and either ring or text Tara and arrange a meeting. Relief at deciding this made her feel dizzy. She'd wanted to see where Tara lived, where she was hiding, and now she wished it had remained a mystery. This was too pathetic, too not-Tara. She felt so upset that, as she set off back down the street, crossing to the other side to avoid a puddle lying greasily in a pothole in the tarmac, she almost bumped into a woman coming out of her house. Apologising, all she got in return was a glare, and then the woman walked off. She was slow, and Claire was obliged to continue walking on the road in order to pass her. She was almost running before she got to the end of the street and then she turned the wrong way and didn't recognise the landmarks she'd carefully noted on her way to Tara's address. She began to panic, though she knew there was no need to. All she had to do was ask the way back to Marks & Spencer's. But when she looked around, the road she was now on was empty of people except for the woman she'd passed on Tara's street, just turning into the main road.

'Excuse me!' Claire called out, but the woman carried on walking, the plastic bag she was carrying fluttering in the wind. She ran to catch her up, and said again, 'Excuse me!' but was ignored. 'Please,' she said, 'I'm lost. I need to get to my car. I've left it at Marks & Spencer's.'

The woman stopped, a strange expression on her face, half contempt, half a sort of amusement. She said nothing, merely pointed ahead, and then did an odd half-turn with her hand, to the left.

'Straight ahead, then left?' Claire said.

She got a nod in return, and that was that.

It was more than straight ahead and then left. Claire had to ask again, but was luckier with those she asked. One woman insisted on walking her all the way to the end of a street, though it was in the opposite direction from the one she herself was going in, and another woman gave her, in great detail, a way of taking a shortcut which completely disorientated Claire. Eventually, she got back to her car, and sat for a while to calm down. Why she was agitated bothered her. Nothing had gone seriously wrong – she'd merely been momentarily lost – but it felt as though it had. She'd panicked, not because she was lost, but because of Tara's address, because of the feeling she had about the street and what it must have been like for Tara arriving here, to this no-man's-land. How had she sunk herself into it? How would she get out?

She tried later to discuss it with Dan, but the whole subject of Tara and her strange ways bored him.

'What was wrong with this street?' he said. 'Sounds a perfectly ordinary street in a perfectly ordinary town.'

'But that's the point,' Claire said. 'Tara isn't ordinary, she's just trying to make herself so.'

'And?' said Dan.

'And . . .' began Claire, and stopped. 'Never mind,' she said. 'You wouldn't understand. I can't explain, but I was frightened for her.'

Dan made a face. 'Tara can look after herself,' he said. 'She always could. I don't know why you seemed to think she was so wonderful. She was the most selfish person I ever met, all me, me, me, spouting all that nonsense she did.'

'What nonsense?'

'Oh, the tree-hugging thing, for one. She didn't give a damn about trees. She just wanted her picture in the papers. And those rallies, marches, whatever you want to call them. She hadn't the faintest idea of the politics involved, she just liked the excitement.'

'That's not true,' said Claire, 'she *cared* about those causes.'

'Rubbish,' said Dan. 'Anyway, I've had a long day and I'm tired. The last thing I want to do is talk about your silly friend. Goodnight,' and he went to bed.

Claire lay awake for hours, walking Tara's street again, thinking about Tara living there. She tried to see it as Dan would – a perfectly ordinary street – but couldn't.

It seemed to her there'd been something more than just depressing about it, something there to pull Tara down. But, as Dan would say, she was getting carried away again. She wondered if she should visit the house again, at a different time, but phoned instead. There was no reply, and it didn't switch on to answerphone.

The visit didn't begin well. Tara noticed that Nancy had dressed up, a bad sign. She was, as usual, wearing a skirt but instead of one of her usual checked affairs, it was a plain pleated grey. Usually she wore a blouse and a cardigan but today she had on a bright blue twinset which looked as though it had never been worn.

'Goodness,' Tara said, 'you look smart.'

Nancy didn't like that. Tara suddenly understood the meaning of 'bridled'.

'I mean,' she said, 'I like your twinset.'

Again, the wrong thing to say. Comments on clothes should not be made, apparently.

'I'm on my way out,' Nancy said. Tara wasn't foolish enough to ask where she was going.

Tea was made, offered, accepted. Tea, as ever, helped a bit.

'When are you off?' Nancy asked, though she already knew the answer. 'You won't be sorry to leave,' she added. 'Cockermouth is more your kind of place, I expect.'

She sniffed as she said this, and though Tara interpreted the sniff correctly, she did not react to it. Very quietly, she put her cup down and said:

'I'm sorry to be leaving you, Nancy, though I hope we'll still keep in touch.'

Nancy took a noisy gulp of tea, and then coughed.

'There are things I've never told you,' Tara said, 'about why I came here, what I was doing here. Haven't you ever wondered, Nancy?'

'I don't pry,' Nancy said. 'I mind my own business.'

'True,' Tara said, 'and I respect that, I really do, but still, you must've wondered, no? I always meant to tell you about myself but it was never the right time. I never felt we got to know each other well enough.'

Nancy shifted uneasily in her chair and said, 'I have to go soon,' but even as she was saying this one part of her was shouting in her head, 'Let the girl speak.'

'I know you do,' Tara was saying. 'I know you don't want any messy confessions from me, but it would explain so much and might make sense to you, so I thought, before I moved, I should tell you about myself, as a sort of apology for being, perhaps, a bit strange. What do you think? Would you listen?'

The most Nancy could manage to do was shrug, and even that took an effort, full as she was of embarrassment at any hint of personal revelations.

So Tara plunged in. 'For a start, as I told you before, my name isn't Sarah Scott. It's Tara Fraser.'

No response from Nancy, not a flicker of astonishment or surprise in her tight face.

'And I've been in prison. For a long time, ten years.'

Now there was a reaction Nancy couldn't control, and her lips disappeared, so complete was their compression. She didn't ask what Tara had been in prison for.

'Well,' she said, after a long pause, 'well, then.'

'I was here to make a new life,' Tara said, 'so I took a new name, and I tried not to think about the old me. You were an important part of my new life.'

Nancy looked startled.

'Not me,' she said, before she could stop herself, without thinking what these two words might mean. 'I've nothing to do with you,' she added, knowing she was making things worse. 'I don't want to be involved, I don't want any trouble, I don't want to be mixed up in anything.'

Tara stayed calm. No good saying how disappointed she was. She'd anticipated this, and prepared for it.

'Do you remember, Nancy,' she said, 'when I went away for a week, in June? I went back to see three old friends of mine, friends since we were seventeen. They invited me to a reunion, and I went. But what I went for was to make them ashamed because they didn't stand by me when I needed them. It didn't work, really. They had perfectly believable excuses, reasons. I wished I hadn't gone. I wished I'd stuck to my new life, to being Sarah, living in this street opposite you. You steadied me, Nancy.'

Nancy got to her feet.

'I have to go,' she said, 'all this daft talk, it doesn't make sense. Steadied you? What does that mean? I haven't touched you. Now, where's my coat?' She knew she was red in the face with sheer exasperation – 'steadied' indeed.

'I'm sorry,' Tara said. 'I just wanted to be straight with you before I left. I felt I owed it to you.'

Nancy walked to the door, but Tara was quicker. She stood with her back to the door, and said: 'Sit down, Nancy, please.'

She didn't shout, nor was there anything threatening in her tone of voice, but Nancy felt alarmed.

People didn't *do* things like this. She was more astonished at this woman's impudence than anything else – what a way to behave.

'I'm leaving,' she said. 'Get out of my way.'

'No,' said Tara. 'I won't. I can't let you leave like this. You haven't understood what I was trying to tell you.'

'I don't care about that,' Nancy said. 'I don't want to hear any more. Now let me out, I have to go.'

Still Tara stood there.

Nancy went closer. She hesitated, unsure whether she could bring herself to touch Sarah, shove her to one side, but a horror at the thought of the tussle that might follow held her back. Two women fighting? Shocking thought, like something which happened on the tougher council estates. Amy would be turning in her grave at the thought of such a thing happening in her house.

Furious, Nancy turned and went towards a wooden chair, an old-fashioned dining-room chair, and not towards the armchair she'd just vacated. She perched on it uncomfortably, saying nothing, her handbag on her knees, held securely in her hands. Tara didn't move.

'I was trying,' she began, 'to explain about why I was so odd, and how much it meant to me that you helped me. I thought you were a friend, a new kind of friend for me. I didn't mean to upset you.'

'Well, you did,' snapped Nancy, though she had vowed not to speak at all.

'Then I'm sorry,' Tara said, 'truly sorry. Can we at least part friends, even if you never want to see me again?'

'We were neighbours,' Nancy said. 'That's the point.'

Tara frowned, then slowly moved away from the door. There were tears beginning to trickle down her cheeks as she gestured towards Nancy, indicating that she could open the door and leave.

Shocked, Nancy said, 'Sit down now. I'll make some more tea.'

Tara said nothing, just stood in front of the armchair. Nancy took hold of her shoulders, though she hadn't wanted to touch her, and gently pushed Tara into the seat.

'There,' she said, 'stay there.'

The whole simple business of making fresh tea was a relief. Nancy stood beside the kettle, suddenly loving its shiny chrome surface, Amy's old kettle still in use. The teapot was another relic, never used, so far as she knew, by Sarah, Tara, whatever she was called. It was a pleasure to rinse it out with hot water, and would have been an even greater pleasure to put real, loose tea in it, but she could only find teabags. She knew making this tea was simply a diversion, a cliché, one used on all kinds of occasions to calm things down, to treat shock. Well, she was shocked, had been shocked. The melodrama of this woman barring the door! It was a wonder she hadn't passed out.

Tara was still weeping when Nancy took the tea through. She made no sound, no movement, but the tears streamed on.

'Dear me,' Nancy said, 'dear, dear me,' and she took a handkerchief from her pocket and cautiously attempted to dab Tara's face. 'Now, that's enough, it's enough.'

Tara's eyes were so huge. Nancy wondered why she had never really noticed this before. How could she not have registered the size of these doe-like blue/grey eyes, now still pools of tears? It was like treating a child, making soothing noises and dab, dabbing away till the handkerchief was sodden.

'I've made such a mess,' Tara then said. 'I always do, I mess things up.'

'The only mess,' said Nancy, 'is your face. Here, blow your nose,' and she produced another handkerchief. (There was one in the right-hand pocket of her coat as well as in the left, and tissues in her handbag. At all times.)

Ten minutes later, with no tea drunk, and Sarah/Tara silent, though the tears had stopped, Nancy wondered if it was safe to leave. Might Sarah/Tara do something? She looked as if she was going to stay for ever slumped in that chair, eyes now closed, but what if, the minute Nancy left, she took some pills, or picked up a knife to harm herself? Nancy wasn't used to not knowing what to do. She'd always been decisive, good in an emergency people said (though she knew fine well that she'd never been involved in a real emergency). Eventually, after a good deal of thinking, she said, 'I don't like to leave you like this, but I have to go, I'm meeting a friend.' At the word 'friend' Tara's tears started again. Nancy sighed, and sat down.

Tara finally controlled herself but sat, listless, with her eyes closed.

'Now then,' Nancy said, 'that's better. No point in upsetting yourself.' She thought about patting Tara's hand but decided not to. She cleared her throat. 'You should get away from here,' she said. 'Isn't there somewhere you can go for a while? Family, maybe?'

Tara shook her head. Nancy wasn't sure whether that meant she had no family, or that she didn't want to go to them.

'Friends?' she queried. 'One of those friends you mentioned? Down south, are they? I'm sure they'd be glad to see you, make up for letting you down, eh?'

No response.

'Well,' Nancy went on, 'we all get let down.' She paused. 'And we do our share of letting down.'

She felt herself flushing, appalled at how she was talking, what on earth had got into her. But Tara had opened her eyes.

'Have you been let down, Nancy?' she said.

The most Nancy could manage was a nod. There'd be questions now and she didn't want questions.

But Tara didn't ask any.

'I tried,' she said. 'I really tried, and I'm still trying.'

Nancy thought she would just keep quiet.

'I thought I could make a new life here, and be a new, contented, unadventurous person, working at a dull job, taking pleasure in routine, enjoying simple things like the countryside, the views, minding my own business, like you mind yours, Nancy. I took my lead from you. I wanted to be you – no, honestly, I did.'

'Well, you shouldn't have,' Nancy said, 'it was daft, a young woman like you. It's a waste.'

'Of what?' Tara asked. 'What would I be wasting, trying to be like you?'

'Oh, you're off again,' Nancy said, 'twisting things, it's silly. You know what I mean. You're bright, you're clever underneath, all that butter-wouldn't-melt-in-your-mouth look. I don't know much about you but I know you were educated, sticks out a mile, and you probably had a career, I don't know what, and you can't wipe those out. And it's daft – I've said it already and I'll say it again – it's daft to think you could be like me or anyone like me. Who'd want to be me? You don't know what goes on in my head. And don't start – I'm not going to tell you. Now, get up, wash your face, and go for a walk or something. I'm going to the club. I'll see you before you go.'

And with that, Nancy left the house. Could Tara have killed her husband, or someone else, to be put away so long? Probably, if she'd been in prison ten years, then the sentence was bound to have been longer. Nancy felt sick thinking of Tara being a murderer. Why had she done it? What had this husband, who she described as 'not a good man', done to her? Maybe he hadn't done anything to her. Maybe it was what he'd done to others. Tara had wanted to tell her, but she'd been too embarrassed to listen. Embarrassed! How could she have been *embarrassed*? Yet that had been her reaction. To run away, escape from the awful atmosphere which had built up in that confined space. Why did people have to *tell* things, why not keep things to themselves and deal with it? But, she reminded herself, Tara had tried to deal with it, and it hadn't worked. She, Nancy Armstrong, had resisted it working.

She wished the woman, Sarah/Tara, would just go away. Quickly. Quietly. She should never have got involved with her in the first place.

'It was such a depressing street,' Claire told Molly. 'Grey houses, all squashed together. I just couldn't imagine Tara in one of them all this time. I mean, there are some lovely streets there, but she chose this dreary one near an industrial estate. What do you think it was, a penance, or something?'

'She wanted to disappear, I expect,' said Molly, 'and where better to do it than the street you've described?'

'But she'd stand out,' Claire said.

'No,' said Molly, 'she wouldn't, not as this Sarah Scott. Tara's an actress, don't forget, she loves new parts. I bet she loved changing everything about herself, especially how she dressed. Can't you see her, doing a little "Miss Mouse" impersonation? Who would see through it? But then, when it was too successful, the old Tara would start peeping through, don't you think? It would have got boring. She'd want a new script, a new part.'

'Do you suppose,' Claire said, 'she's made any new friends up there? Or is she acting this "new part" as you put it, all alone?'

'Well,' Molly said, 'she had a job, or so she said. She'll be in contact with people that way. And neighbours – she's bound to have neighbours, especially in the sort of street you describe.'

'Not her sort,' Molly said.

'And men?' Claire asked. 'What about men? How on earth will she meet any men, in her new role?'

'Maybe she doesn't want to,' Molly said. 'Anyway, you shouldn't worry about her, Claire. You're not her mother, and she's made it clear enough that she doesn't want any of us in her new life. Accept it.'

But Claire couldn't. Thoughts of Tara nagged at her all the time. She should have knocked on her door, or left a note saying she was nearby, just for two days. What was the point of having gone to Workington if not to see Tara? And now that she was home again, more than 300 miles away, she couldn't recreate the feeling that had come over her in that street, the panic she'd felt. She couldn't follow Molly's advice. No, she wasn't Tara's mother but her concern felt maternal. It always had done. That had been *her* role in her old friendship with Tara. Tara didn't have a real mother when Claire became her friend. It was a gap she filled, or tried to. It made her friendship with Tara different from her friendship with Molly and Liz.

Tara's mother, or lack of a mother, had been a mystery. Was she dead? Nobody knew. All Tara had said was that she didn't have a mother and no amount of prying made her say anything else. Liz guessed that she simply didn't know anything. She had a foster mother, though; she'd had the same foster mother since she was three, she told Claire. Did she like her? Was this woman kind to her? A shrug. She was OK. To Claire, deep in her settled, relation-rich, middle-class family, Tara's situation was the stuff of fairy tales. Everyone else's family background was ordinary, Tara's mysterious. Claire, at seventeen, couldn't understand how she could be calm about it. To the question, 'Will you try to find your real mother?' Tara said, 'Why?' as though it had never occurred to her, but surely it must have done.

Claire knew she was like her own mother, both in appearance and personality. So was Molly, the similarity to her mother even more marked. Liz, though, was nothing like her mother, which she professed to find a relief. But at least they all knew their mothers, and could see, and feel, what they'd inherited from them. Tara couldn't. These rages she sometimes flew into: was her mother the same? The lying, the taste for dramatic outbursts: could her mother have told her that she, too, had gone through this phase and come out of it? The trouble was, Tara had no pattern to follow, or reject, when it came to her mother. And as for her father, the same applied but somehow, to Claire, this didn't seem to matter so much. All this troubled Claire greatly, and made her excuse Tara almost anything. She was always hoping Tara's mother would one day turn up, though as time went on this grew less and less likely.

Liz's theory was that Tara knew she had been abandoned and would never forgive her mother (though in fact she was convinced Tara's mother was dead). Molly thought that when Tara had children of her own she'd change her mind about not wanting to find out if her mother was still alive. But Tara never did have children. Said she didn't want them. Tom didn't either. When, over the years, she came to visit Claire, Molly and

Liz, all three breeding busily for a whole decade, she ignored their offspring. None of their babies was picked up and cuddled by Tara, no toddler played with. It had been quite hurtful, really. And then, when the children were older, towards the end of Tara's regular visits, things improved a bit. Tara liked their surliness, their rudeness, the hostility some of them directed towards their mothers. It amused her. She championed them, and it was annoying. She even once told Liz's bolshy elder daughter that if she wanted to leave home, when she became a teenager, she could come and live with her in London. Liz, who knew Tara didn't for one minute mean this, was furious. The daughter in question might well go on to take the offer seriously, only to be met with Tara saying it had only been a joke.

Tara, Claire reckoned, had always needed her mother. She just didn't realise it.

Nancy, when she left Tara, went to the club. It was not her regular day, but too bad. She was in a state, but she had nowhere else to go and needed some kind of distraction. It would settle her. She knew she was still red-faced – she could feel the heat in her cheeks – but walking would cool her down. She tried, as she walked, to sort out the scene she'd just been involved in. That was the right word. 'Don't make a scene,' her mother had always been warning her, and as a child the word puzzled her.

Scenes were in plays, they were labelled as Scene 1, Act 1 in books of plays at school. But she wasn't in a play. She was in real life, so what did 'scene' mean? Later, when she absorbed the meaning in her mother's phrase, she liked it. 'Making a scene' was creating a disturbance, drawing attention to yourself in some way, doubly reprehensible if this was in public.

Tara, who had been Sarah, had made a scene. One hell of a scene. Nancy quickened her step as she went over it, checking what part she herself had played. Had she been too harsh, too unsympathetic? Well, she'd been shocked with all the carry-on, the tears, the barring of the door. Good heavens, what a scene. Thank God no one had heard or seen it. She wouldn't tell anyone about it, of course. There was no one she could tell, in any case. Keeping yourself to yourself meant there was never anyone to whom confidences could be given. Nancy understood that very well. The relief, even the thrill, of describing scenes of the sort she'd just been part of could not be hers. She knew she would go over and over it in her own head until the memory faded.

Arriving at the club, Nancy made straight for the tea. She was so thirsty that she stood and drank a cup at the counter where it was served and then refilled it before moving to her usual seat by the window. Settled there, it helped to have something to watch. The street below was not a hive of activity but there were enough people coming and going to distract her slightly from replaying the scene at Tara's house. Tara. She thought about the name. Fanciful. She'd never known anyone called Tara. Where did it come from? Sarah was a much better name. Down in the street she suddenly spotted a Sarah she knew, Sarah Vickers. She'd known her because she bought tomatoes from her stall when she first came to Workington. The stall had long since gone, but when they met in the street they always said hello. She was an acquaintance, Nancy decided. Not a friend but an acquaintance, through habit. Her life, she reflected, was rich in such people. She might have no one she could truly describe as a friend since Amy died, but she had tons of acquaintances. This realisation comforted her, so she was in a happier state of mind when Mrs Curwen sat down beside her.

Mrs Curwen was always addressed as Mrs Curwen. Nobody was familiar enough to call her by her Christian name. Indeed, no one at the club seemed too sure what it was. Asked her name, Mrs Curwen said, 'Mrs Curwen,' and that was that. Quite what she was doing at the club nobody was certain. Had she worked at the factory or in the office? She didn't look as if she had done either, with her posh air, but if she hadn't then what was she doing at the club? She didn't come often, only about once every six weeks, but when she did her entry caused a slight hiatus in conversations going on. She got stared at, and seemed to enjoy these stares, smiling and nodding like the old Queen Mother used to do. Slowly, she would circulate the room, teacup in hand, and then invariably sit by one of the windows, or, if no seat was available there, simply stand near the fireplace, leaning on the shelf above it. It was an ancient fireplace, never used, with elaborate Victorian tiles round the grate, and a set of splendid tongs and pokers resting in front of it. Mrs Curwen looked striking, leaning there, as though she might be the hostess of the gathering before her.

Nancy had never spoken to her, or been spoken to by her, but today Mrs Curwen came and sat in the spare chair next to her. 'May I?' she asked, but sat down before Nancy could say a word. It was a daft question anyway – 'May I?' What did the woman mean? She didn't need to ask permission to sit on an empty chair which had nobody's handbag on it and no teacup on the little table in front of it. Nancy sniffed. Mrs Curwen raised her eyebrows and said:

'You were keeping this chair for a friend, perhaps?'

Nancy shook her head.

'Good. I just wanted to be sure. I'm so glad to be able to sit down. My legs are exhausted, it's been such a tiring day. Do you know what I mean? One of those tiring, tiring days.'

Nancy stared, and sniffed again. Clearly, Mrs Curwen wanted to be asked why her day had been so tiring. She didn't look as if she knew what a tiring day was. Some of these women in the club could have told her. When they were young, with several children, working shifts in the factory before coming home to clean and do the washing and cook – those were tiring days. Nancy knew that although she'd worked hard herself she'd had it easy compared to the common lot in her youth ('youth' went up to forty-five in Nancy's opinion). She looked at Mrs Curwen's hands. Smooth, unused to rough work. Mrs Curwen saw her looking, but said nothing. They both drank their tea, and then just as Nancy thought she would leave Mrs Curwen said:

'You're Mrs Armstrong, aren't you?'

'I am,' Nancy said. She wanted to add, 'So?' but rudeness was rudeness.

'You were Mrs Taylor's neighbour, weren't you?'

'Friend,' Nancy said sternly. 'I wasn't just a neighbour.'

'Oh, quite,' said Mrs Curwen. 'Neighbour and friend. I'm thinking of buying her house for a granddaughter of mine. It's for sale, you know.'

'Yes,' Nancy said, 'I do know.'

'There's apparently been a rather odd person renting it, or so Mrs Taylor's nephew, the owner, tells me. Something hush-hush about her, about her past, though I've no idea what.'

Nancy was momentarily speechless. Did Mrs Curwen know about Sarah being in prison? Automatically, she wanted to protest at the spreading of such gossip but she didn't want to give Mrs Curwen the satisfaction. So, instead, she simply got up and walked away, taking her cup and saucer to the hatch. But now all the good that sitting quietly by the window had done her had disappeared.

She was as agitated when she left as she had been when she arrived. But she had come to a decision.

There wasn't much to pack. The sum total of what she'd accumulated during her months in Workington didn't even fill the boot of her car. And she hardly needed to clean anything, so sparing had she been in the use of the oven, the kitchen surfaces and so on. She hoovered all the rooms and the stairs, though there was little need to, and she hung the curtains back up in the bedroom though she didn't take down the blind. It all looked pretty much as it had done when she arrived: colourless, tidy, worn, depressing. Exactly what she had thought she needed.

There was a knock at the front door just as Tara was zipping up the last of the bags with her clothes in. Nancy stood on the threshold when the door was opened.

'Can I come in?' she said, immediately stepping inside and almost brushing against Tara in her hurry to lead the way into the living room. 'I've something to say,' she said, 'something I should've said long ago.' She was huffing and puffing with embarrassment.

'Sit down, please,' said Tara, and sat down herself.

'You wanted to tell me things and I wouldn't listen,' Nancy said. 'I wanted to, but . . . but, well, I'm not used to it.'

Tara, not at all sure what it was that Nancy was not used to, kept quiet, merely smiling and nodding in encouragement.

'Prison,' Nancy gasped. 'You said you'd been in prison, and I didn't let you tell me why. I wanted to know but . . . I'm not used to it, it doesn't come easy, asking questions, so I clam up.'

Tara thought she should offer tea, a calming gesture which Nancy would recognise as such and accept, but she was sick of tea. Somehow, it would belittle Nancy's outburst, make it seem merely something to brush aside. Instead she stayed still, and said:

'Thank you, Nancy, you're a good friend, whatever you think.'

Nancy registered the present tense: no mention of 'you were' or 'you have been' a good friend. It was stated as a fact, this friendship, and it pleased her.

'Well, then,' she said, and that was all, but Tara hadn't finished.

'I did want to talk to you about prison, and why I was there, and why I came here, but it doesn't matter now. Least said, soonest mended, eh?'

Nancy sighed, the tension she'd felt all day seeping away.

'If you're sure,' she said.

'You'll come and see me in my new place, won't you?' Tara said. 'Come on the bus and I'll bring you back. Or I could pick you up too, if you like.'

'Oh, I'll come on the bus,' Nancy said eagerly. She liked bus rides of that length, Workington to Cockermouth, only half an hour or so.

It was arranged before Tara departed. Nancy watched while Tara wrote down the day and time. It made the proposed visit seem official. She went home, put a red circle round the date on her kitchen calendar and wrote within it 'Visit to Sarah', then crossed out 'Sarah' and put 'Tara'. It looked good, next to the black ticks marking club days and doctor's appointments, and other mundane things.

Maybe it would become a regular date.

IX

LEAVING WORKINGTON early on a wet afternoon, with the road shining blackly ahead and great arcs of spray rising as cars passed each other, Tara felt a strange kind of excitement. She was on the move again, sprung from the deadly routine she'd once thought would be the making of her. This hopeful feeling lay somewhere in the pit of her stomach, pulsing almost rhythmically, like a steady heartbeat. She had to quieten it down or it would take over and make her panic. Panic, obviously, was not good. Panic made her do silly things, dangerous things.

She was gripping the steering wheel too tightly. The windscreen wipers were working overtime and seeing clearly was difficult. This was the coast road, but she could hardly glimpse the sea. Once, she peered into the little mirror, stuck into the flap which hung down over the driving seat. How she'd changed! Quickly, she pushed the flap back into position. She didn't want to look at herself. How, when had she begun to look so different? It was this *look* that struck her as weird. She wondered how her features could possibly have changed so much without recourse to plastic surgery. Her face had surely once been almost fox-like, narrow, cheekbones sharp. And then, later, early in her marriage to Tom, the happy years, her face had filled out, her eyes becoming not so dominant. Her body had not put on weight, she'd remained slim, but something happened to her face, her *look*. Then, she wasn't quite sure when, the tight-face returned. Was it at the time she first began to suspect what Tom was doing, where his money came from? Or maybe it was when she was given that research project at work, and had her own team, and though she loved what she was doing the stress was considerable.

'Give it up,' Tom said. 'You don't need to do it.'

But she did need to. Once, he'd understood that.

What do you do if you don't like your own face? Well, make-up could change a lot, but not enough. She was, she reckoned, still quite attractive. The last vestiges of prettiness were still there, just. She'd done such damage to her look through being Sarah Scott. There must be no more head down, shoulders hunched. She must throw it off, hold her head up, square her shoulders, smile, let all that vitality within her come through. It would be like lighting a fire from a bed of ash with a couple of twigs. It would splutter and smoke and then a flame, a little one, would leap up. Her old challenging look would return, her don't-mess-with-me defiance which Tom once said was what had attracted him in the first place.

The crash happened while she was still thinking of what she must do in yet another 'new' life, the car coming towards her swerving, herself swerving, and then the impact, the roar, her own screaming.

'Hello?' a voice said. 'Hello, can you hear me?'

Tara could hear the voice, but didn't recognise it. She tried to say something, but only a grunt came out. Her hand was patted.

'You've had an accident. We need to find out where you're injured so that we can treat you.'

Tara closed her eyes. She was on some sort of trolley which was now being wheeled along. She heard doors opening and slamming shut. An accident. She struggled to think about this. An accident. Where? How? Her face, she remembered looking at her face, in the car . . . So it was a car accident. Her head began to throb.

Nancy's telephone so rarely rang late in the evening that the shrill sound shocked her. She was on her way to bed, clutching a hot-water bottle, and paused on the stairs. A wrong number, almost certainly, or what they said was 'a cold call'. It happened. Who would be ringing her at nearly ten o'clock? And if she answered it, she wouldn't be nicely settled in bed ready for the news on her radio. But nevertheless, she put the hot-water bottle down, turned, and carefully went back downstairs, holding the banister firmly. A telephone ringing was not going to make her hurry and slip on the stairs and break a hip and be done for.

'Yes!' she shouted into the receiver as she picked it up. She knew she sounded angry, but then she was.

'Good evening, madam,' a calm, male voice said. 'Am I speaking to Mrs Nancy Armstrong?'

'Who wants to know?' Nancy said. She was on the alert now, ready for this to be some sort of trickster.

'The police,' the voice said. 'I'm PC Mike Pattinson, and I'm calling with regard to a friend of yours who has had an accident and is in the hospital.'

For a moment, Nancy was silent, taking these words in.

'A friend?' What did this mean? Why would she be rung up because someone who said they were her friend – *said* – was in hospital? She wasn't next of kin to anyone. Expressing neither curiosity nor concern about the state of this 'friend's' health, she said:

'How do I know you're a policeman?'

'Because I've told you I am,' the voice of this Pattinson man said.

This did not seem at all satisfactory to Nancy, but the man's tone had been stern.

'Well, then,' she said, 'what are you bothering me for at nearly ten o'clock at night?'

'I am bothering you,' said the man, 'because your name and address and telephone number were found in the pocket of a woman who is currently in a serious condition in Cumberland Infirmary after a car crash on the A66 road between Workington and Cockermouth.'

Nancy hadn't missed the edge of irritation in how the policeman had pronounced 'bothering you'. He thought she was heartless, unfeeling.

'Hello?' he was saying. 'Are you still there, Mrs Armstrong?'

Nancy managed to gasp that she was.

'I'll have to sit down,' she said.

'Good idea,' the policeman, whose name she'd already forgotten, said.

But there was no seat where she kept the telephone. The nearest seat would be on the stairs and the cord of the phone wouldn't reach that far.

'Oh,' she repeated, 'I'll have to sit down. You'll have to wait while I sit down.'

She let the phone dangle on its cord and went and sat on the bottom step. Accident. Car crash. Hospital. Slowly, her mind made sense of the words. It must be Sarah Scott who was in hospital (why Carlisle, why not Hensingham?) and had had a car crash. That, at least, was clear. But what about this note in her pocket? Why was that there? Hesitantly, she got up again and took hold of the phone. There was a lot of noise in the background but she could distinguish the policeman's voice.

'Hello?' she said. 'Hello, hello, hello, I'm here again, hello . . .'

And at last she was answered. She meant to apologise, for being 'short', but somehow she didn't. She just said, 'What happened? How is my . . . my friend?'

Early next morning, a policewoman came to take Nancy to Cumberland Infirmary. It was a matter of identification, they said. The only clue they had, as yet, was this piece of paper with Mrs Armstrong's name on it, and a date a week ahead. The car was a write-off, though the registration number was being traced and some items salvaged. But the woman hadn't spoken, and since she was seriously ill her relatives should be informed as soon as possible. Nancy's help was vital. Eventually, documents from the car, however badly damaged, would reveal a name, but Nancy could give that information quicker, if she were willing. Nancy had agreed to go and look at this injured woman though, as she'd explained to the policeman, she didn't need to. It could only be Sarah Scott. The minute she said the name, she corrected herself.

'I mean Tara, Tara somebody, I forget the surname.'

The policewoman was interested in this.

'Two names?' she said.

'She changed it,' Nancy said. 'I don't know why.'

A lie, but she wasn't going to tell the police that Tara had been in prison. They could find that out for themselves. All the thirty or so miles to Carlisle, Nancy was fretting about what she'd already said. Tara might not be pleased to have Sarah mentioned. She should have kept her mouth shut. The policewoman driving her tried to chat to her, perfectly pleasantly, but Nancy ignored her except for a grunt or two. She was feeling uncomfortable wearing, as she was, her best skirt which for some time now she'd known perfectly well was too tight for her expanding waistline. And her jumper was too warm, and itched, and her jacket made things worse but she didn't want to take it off. The policewoman had offered her the seat next to her but Nancy had elected to sit in the back. It was a foolish decision. She could see now that the two front seats were better upholstered, and also of course she would have been able to see more without having to turn her head. She ended up spending a lot of the journey with her eyes shut, trying to prepare herself. She'd seen lots of medical programmes on the television so she knew what an intensive-care ward would look like, and what the doctors and nurses would likely be wearing, so none of that would surprise or overawe her. But what she didn't know was how Tara would look, and that scared her.

The policewoman went into the hospital with her, to Nancy's relief. She wouldn't have found her way anywhere, so confusing were the signs and so endless the corridors. Her heart began to beat uncomfortably rapidly as they reached the intensive-care unit. It was as eerie as she'd expected, with some machine bleeping but otherwise silence, the nurses moving about without making any noise at all, seeming to glide between patients. There were four there, all with their eyes either closed, or their eyelids flickering, and two with tubes in their mouths. Sarah – no, Tara, Tara, she mustn't call her Sarah now – had no tube. Nancy was beckoned closer by a nurse. Lord, what a mess. Stitched cuts all over her face and half her hair shaved off. But Nancy recognised her.

'Yes,' she said, 'that was my neighbour. Sarah Scott. My friend.'

Adding 'my friend' choked her. She'd never said it before. Sarah – no, Tara, Tara – was such a new friend. And she'd said the wrong name. Oh, God. The nurse had already written it down, and was now saying it, gently, to Sarah.

'Hello, Sarah,' she said. 'Can you hear me, Sarah? Your friend is here, Nancy your friend is here.'

Tara heard these words clearly. She wasn't Sarah any more. Being Sarah was an experiment that had failed.

'Tara,' she said, 'Tara.'

The nurse frowned, whispered to Nancy, 'She's confused.'

'No,' Nancy said, 'she's just telling you her real name. She was only pretending to be a Sarah Scott.'

The nurse raised her eyebrows, then wrote something down, and motioned to Nancy to leave the room. Before she did, Nancy lightly touched the side of Tara's damaged face, stroked it gently. Tara's eyes filled with tears.

It was all so upsetting. Nancy could hardly compose herself on the way back to Workington. She felt she'd done everything wrong. She'd let that poor woman down. The policewoman, whose name Nancy didn't seem able to grasp though she'd been told it often enough, had questioned her closely about Tara, alias Sarah. How long had she known her, what did she know about her, who were her other friends, who were her relatives? They had stuff from the car by then, documents, driving licence and suchlike, and they were all in the name of Sarah Scott, but there was no clue as to background. Why was she driving on the A66, did Nancy know? The Cockermouth address was duly noted – she was asked what else she knew about the injured woman.

'Nothing,' said Nancy. 'She was quiet, went to work, kept herself to herself, never mentioned relatives.'

'And friends, besides yourself?' the policewoman prompted.

'I don't know them. They were down south,' Nancy said. 'Old friends, she had old friends down there.'

She was still not going to mention anything about prison. Keeping quiet about that was the least she could do.

The dreams were long and vivid. Tara went in and out of them all the time, sometimes even when she was awake. These dreams slipped in and out of her mind, plaguing her, tormenting her because in them she was so happy, so full of vitality, and out of them she could hardly raise her head or move a limb. Claire, Liz and Molly, young again, were all around her, their faces alight with laughter, their bodies moving feverishly around her, round and round, an endless mad dance, and herself in the centre, screaming.

But sometimes Tom was there too, shoving the girls aside and enclosing her tightly, too tightly, in his arms, and then she struggled and pushed and a nurse would appear because she'd been shouting, and she'd be given another pill. But then, slowly, these dreams, which were more like hallucinations, began to lessen, and there were periods of calm when she was able to work out where she was and what seemed to have happened. She still had no memory of this, but the policewoman who came to her bedside several times filled her in. Nobody had been killed, that was the important thing, and it had not been her fault. She'd been caught between two speeding cars, one overtaking her, one coming round a bend too far into the centre of the road. That was all she needed to know, all she wanted to know. She couldn't, yet, take in information about insurance claims and so forth.

Repeatedly, she was asked if there was anyone she would like the police to contact. A social worker – or someone she assumed was a social worker, though she failed to take in either the woman's name or proper title – also came to make the same offer.

'You'll need help when you're out of hospital,' the woman said. 'Is there someone who could come and stay for a while?'

Tara shook her head. She was Sarah Scott again, timid and alone in the world, except for Nancy Armstrong. But no, she'd promised herself, no more Sarah Scott. Of course Tara had friends. And she had Nancy, who appeared at her bedside a week after she came out of intensive care, bearing a tin of shortbread. She was just there when Tara opened her eyes one afternoon, sitting there with her handbag clasped tightly on her knee and a solemn expression on her lined face.

'Nancy!' Tara said.

'Oh, you've come to,' Nancy said. 'I thought I was going to have had a wasted journey, with you asleep, and the bus goes at half-four and I can't miss it.'

Tara smiled, but smiling still hurt, with her right cheek in the shape it was, so she also winced.

'My, you're in a state,' Nancy said. 'What a to-do. Who'd have thought it'd come to this. Well, you're mending. They say you're mending. Take it easy, though, don't let them turn you out afore you're good and ready.'

'Nancy,' Tara whispered, 'could you do me a favour?'

'Why d'you think I'm here?' Nancy said. 'Of course I'll do you a favour so long as it doesn't mean too much walking – my knee's playing up.'

Tara said it didn't mean any walking. It meant writing down a few telephone numbers and ringing people up.

'I haven't got a pencil,' Nancy said, 'else I'd do it.'

Tara gestured to her bedside table. She'd been provided with a biro and writing paper as well as other things.

'You'll have to go slowly,' Nancy said. 'I've got stiff fingers.'

So Tara went slowly, giving her the three phone numbers.

'And what am I to say?' Nancy asked. 'I'll need to know, and I'll have to write it down or I'll forget. It's nearly four o'clock, we'll need to get a move on.'

Tara, when finally Nancy left, after she'd put the piece of paper in her bag and shut the clasp so tightly that the sound was magnified to a loud bang in Tara's ears, was exhausted.

Claire listened to the answerphone message three times. The voice was northern, the tone loud. No name was given, either at the beginning or the end, but Claire dialled 1471 before the caller's number could be replaced by another. As she expected, it was a Cumbrian code. Then she sat down and pondered what the message said: 'Tara has had a car crash, she is in hospital in Carlisle, she just thought you would want to know.' Now, what, Claire asked herself, did those last words mean? Did they amount to that cliché 'a cry for help'? How could they not – but what sort of help? Was Tara expecting her to go to Carlisle and visit her?

Naturally, she rang Liz and Molly, and yes, they too had had the same message but Molly had actually spoken to the caller whereas Liz had only the same recorded message as Claire.

'She's called Mrs Armstrong,' said Molly, 'and she lives opposite Tara. I asked her exactly what had happened and she said all she knew was that on her way to Cockermouth – she was apparently moving to a house there – she'd had a car crash, not her fault, and had a lot wrong with her. Those were Mrs Armstrong's words, "a lot wrong with her". She said she'd visited her in hospital but it was a long bus ride and her legs were bad and she didn't know how often she'd be able to manage it.'

'How did she sound?' Claire asked.

'Quite cross, gruff,' Molly said, 'and a bit breathless.'

'Old, then?'

'I should think so.'

'Well,' Claire said, 'what are we going to do?'

The past, Tara lay thinking, is a menace. She was tired of it, exhausted with going over it, worn out with the repetitious cycle of old memories. She wanted nothing to do with the past, her past, anyone's past. Yet the future was hardly more attractive. She couldn't see anything in it, only a white blur filling her head. They were bothering her now that she was improving, asking her where she could go to convalesce, who could help look after her, apart from what social services would offer, the Meals on Wheels, the twice-daily visits. She had no answer. 'Have you got friends you can call on?' She didn't tell them about asking Nancy to make those phone calls.

She was able now, on two crutches, to walk a few steps without too much pain. Limping across to a window, she looked down on a packed car park and beyond it rows of houses. It was all meaningless. She was in a hospital in a city she'd never been to, where she could identify no one and nothing. But this was what she'd wanted: anonymity, a new start, removed from everything she'd known. She'd been going to develop an entirely new personality, not so much a reformed character as a completely remade one. And she had failed. Abysmally. What had she to show for that attempt? Nothing, save for her odd friendship with Nancy Armstrong, and there was no depth to that. Poor Nancy saddled now with a sense of duty to her, visiting her because she felt she ought to. Tara had seen it in her expression, resentment struggling with compassion. Nancy was sorry for her, but wanted free of her.

Back in her bed, Tara realised it was no good hating the past. Only drawing something out of the past would help her, but first she would need to humiliate herself.

'Dad?' Tara said.

There was no reply, but the phone was not put down.

'Dad?'

Her voice was weak, not like her own voice at all. It was barely above a whisper, and she knew it sounded frightened. Not a good idea.

'Dad,' she said for the third time, dropping the interrogative lilt, 'I need help. I've had an accident, a car crash, not my fault.'

Still silence. She knew he'd be on the edge of hanging up.

Then he said, 'Money, is it?'

'No,' she said, relieved he was speaking at all, 'not money. I need a place to go, someone to help me get over this. Not for long. A couple of weeks, maybe.'

'Begging, are you?' he said, but there was a hint of sarcasm in his tone.

'I'm begging, yes,' she said.

He'd been at her trial. She'd seen him quite clearly, sitting at the end of a row, arms folded, one leg stuck out into the aisle. She'd been surprised, hadn't thought he'd come. She imagined there would have been newspaper reporters bothering him. Probably he hadn't said much. A man who kept his own counsel. But she knew he was capable of real fury because she'd been at the receiving end of it. Livid, he'd been, on more than one occasion, when she'd come home in the early hours 'wasted' as he put it. He'd accused her of taking drugs, but she never had. Alcohol, yes, cigarettes, yes, but drugs, no. It was something she was proud of, the fact that she'd never even sampled cannabis. It made Tom laugh. He said she should try a little bit of hash, it would relax her, but she refused. When she was eighteen, she'd been told the truth about her mother but she'd sensed it anyway. She'd found the information among documents in her foster parents' possession during a stage when she enjoyed rifling through the contents of every drawer in the house searching for God knows what. She didn't tell any of her friends, and she didn't tell Tom. It troubled her that she hadn't told Tom, but later she was glad.

It came out at the trial, all the stuff about her mother, the drug addiction, the baby born with traces of heroin in her body. She, Tara, had been lucky that this was dealt with immediately and she recovered quickly. Her mother died, though. She didn't know why this had to be told. She didn't want anyone to know about her mother. She was going to plead guilty and so-called mitigating circumstances had nothing to do with anything. She felt shamed by having these details read out in open court. Her foster father's account, given to the police she supposed, was not as painful, strangely enough. He wasn't called as a witness, for which she was grateful. Everything he'd told the police was true. She had, from the beginning, been a troubled child, though with no recollection of what had gone on in her first three years she hadn't known she was 'troubled'. She had apparently spent her first two years with the Frasers having violent tantrums, nightmares, spells of not eating. Even later on, when she was said to have settled down, she was capable of acting strangely. His wife, her father said, had been made sick with worry when Tara stole things, when she smashed crockery in a rage, when she threw paint at the newly papered wall. There was such violence lurking there and they'd struggled to deal with it. But he'd said he'd always known she was clever. It was no surprise to him that she did so well at school. Then, he'd been proud of her, but all the same he couldn't forgive her for being so cold and horrible to his wife. There was no excuse for that.

He visited her in prison, the first prison. That was a surprise. She hadn't expected him to. She thought, as he would put it, that he'd have 'washed his hands' of her. But there he was, sitting grim faced, arms folded as usual when he was angry, as though he was restraining himself. They stared at each other a long time. She wasn't going to speak first.

Eventually he said, 'What a mess.'

She didn't reply. The mess was over. Everything was tidy now.

'What did he do to you?' he asked. 'You said nothing about that. You only talked about the drugs, what he was doing, but not what he did to you. They couldn't draw you out. Why?'

'I'm not, ever, going to talk about Tom,' Tara said, 'so you can leave now, if that's all you've come for.'

She hated people prying, all in the course, they said, of 'understanding' her crime. Over and over she was asked, 'What did he *do* to you?' They wanted her to say he had beaten her, abused her, tortured her in some physical way. Then all would be, if not forgiven, 'understood'. But Tom had done none of those things. His tyranny was of a different sort. He scared her not with blows but silence. He could fill the house with such a menacing silence that he made her talk faster and louder to try and break it down. Then he would pick her up and put her in a room and lock the door and leave her for hours. How could she possibly convey what this harmless-sounding behaviour had done to her?

But her father was speaking. 'I've come,' he said, 'because I'm your father. I have a right to know.'

'No,' said Tara, 'you don't. You have no right. You cared more about your wife than you did about me.'

'Well,' he said, 'that's how it should be.'

She'd smiled at that.

'Find that funny, do you?' he said.

'No,' Tara said, 'I find it tragic. Just go away. We're done with each other.'

And now there she was, ringing him up, pleading.

'You can't come here,' he said, 'so get that out of your head. There's only Barney's place, it's empty for a month. You could go there, on certain conditions.'

Barney was his brother, and his 'place' was a flat which her father owned and let out now that he was dead.

'All right,' Tara said, 'thanks.'

'There's no one there to look after you, mind,' he said. 'You'll have to arrange a nurse or someone. Can't you do that wherever you are? Haven't you got a friend up there, 'stead of trailing back down here? What's the point?'

The point was Claire, Molly and Liz, but she didn't tell him that. He asked practical questions, such as how she was going to get to Barney's place if she had no car and couldn't drive anyway if, as she told him, she had a broken leg as well as other injuries. 'Stay where you are,' he said, but when she insisted he agreed to post the keys to Cumberland Infirmary. Once that was settled, there was no need to go on talking, but it was he who prolonged the phone call.

'How've you been?' he asked. 'Not a word from you all this time.'

'Sorry,' she said.

'You're always sorry,' he said. 'Lot of good it does. Sorry too late, that's you. You could've made something of yourself. I don't know what went wrong, what we did.'

'You know you did everything you could,' Tara said. 'It was me, just me.'

'Wilful,' he said.

'Yes,' she said.

There was plenty of help provided. She was driven to Carlisle station and helped on to the train, and at Euston she was met with a wheelchair and taken to the next station and the next train, and put on it. Everything was arranged for her, involving at least three voluntary organisations. The only tricky bit was getting off the last train. She had to rely on Claire being there with a wheelchair and on someone on the train opening the door and helping her out. But when the time came, there was no one in her carriage. She had to manage her crutches and her bags and she couldn't do both. The train, she knew, wouldn't stop for long, so ahead of time she lurched along to a door, trying to drag her bags, two of them, with the tip of one crutch. She made the door just in time to press the button and make it open, and then pushed the bags out. Getting herself out was harder, but she knew the train wouldn't start again so long as she was in the doorway. She was perspiring profusely, and felt dizzy, before she was at last on the platform. It was empty, except for one man sitting reading a newspaper. There was no sign of Claire.

Nancy was more upset than she would admit, even to herself, in the privacy of her own home. She held Tara's letter in her hand and read the few words on it over and over. Yes, the phrase 'Thanks for everything' was there, and so was 'You've been a good friend' and 'I'll be in touch'. But they made no difference to Nancy's growing conviction that she'd been made a fool of and should have known better. Tara, Sarah-Scott-as-was, had gone.

Done a flit – well, in a manner of speaking that was what it amounted to. Nancy had turned up at the hospital, all that way again in the bus, her knees paining her, and there she'd been given this letter. Tara had gone, that very morning, and the letter was to be posted if Nancy did not turn up. Why hadn't she phoned and said she was going? Nancy said this to the nurse, who shrugged and said she expected Tara hadn't thought Nancy would be visiting again. Feeble excuse. And there was no address or phone number given for where she was going. Nancy crumpled the letter up and stuffed it in her bag. Now she had the long bus journey back, and all for nothing. All the way to Workington she felt hot with rage, rage mostly because she had enough sense to realise it was a manufactured rage. She let herself get into these states and then she had to haul herself out.

It was nearly five-thirty before she got off the bus, her knees sore and her back stiff from sitting bolt upright on the not very well padded bus seats. She didn't feel like going home, knowing that being on her own while she felt so upset and cross would only make her worse. First, she needed a cup of tea, and to be among people just for a short while. The club would do. She didn't have to speak to anyone. All that was required was to be among others while she calmed down. It was nearly closing time so there were not many women there when she arrived, and none she knew very well. It was easy to get her tea and sit in her usual seat. Better, she felt better. She was able to tell herself that she'd been silly, getting worked up about nothing. Sarah/Tara was nothing to her. A bird of passage, that's all the woman was. Mixed up. Didn't know what she wanted or who she was. To be pitied. Well rid of her. Nancy nodded as each thought occurred to her. A warning, it was.

Once home, she took the offending letter out of her bag, smoothed the creased paper, and read it again. Then she took a match and held the paper over the sink, and burned it. Made a mess of the sink, but easily cleaned up. There. It was over.

Tara was in a small room, opening off the hall in Claire's spacious house. It had been a cloakroom in the days when people had cloaks but it was now converted into a spare room. Claire's house had plenty of spare rooms, five bedrooms upstairs with only one in permanent use now that the last of her three children was at university and hardly came home at all, even in the holidays. But on account of the broken leg Claire thought Tara would need to be on the ground floor and so here she was. Claire had put flowers on the bedside table, and there was a pretty patchwork cover on the bed. Tara knew Claire would have made it herself.

It was a perfectly adequate room. Small, yes, but neat. The window was narrow and didn't let in much light and there was no view because the panes were semi-opaque. Dan was not home yet, which was a relief. Tara knew, with absolute certainty, that he would have strongly objected to his wife letting her stay for the night. He'd never liked her, and Tara did not like him. She hadn't actually seen him for so long that she was mildly interested in how he would have aged. She warned herself not to make any comment if Dan now had a paunch and had lost his hair, but she rather hoped both of these changes had taken place. Smug bastard, so aware of his own good looks, always smoothing his thick blond hair down. She'd seen him, many times, pulling a comb out when he thought no one was looking and combing his hair lovingly. So unmanly, so unlike Tom.

Tom had no personal vanity. He knew he was not good-looking. He didn't care much about signs that he was developing a bald patch. His pride was in his physical strength, his muscles, his strong legs and broad back. He could take anyone on in a fight, he said. She believed him. He must, she thought, intimidate his colleagues though she had only ever seen one of them, Clive, at their wedding. It never occurred to her that one day he might intimidate her. On the contrary, she'd felt protected by his strength. It had attracted her, though she would never have admitted this, not even to Liz who she knew suspected this was the case.

'What do you see in this Tom?' Liz had asked. 'Just give me a hint?' etc.

'What do you see in Alan?' she'd snapped back. 'He's boring.'

'No, he isn't,' said Liz. 'He's quiet. That doesn't make him boring to me. Quiet, dependable, agreeable—'

'Oh, shut up,' she'd said, but Liz wouldn't.

'Give me a list of three things that attract you to Tom. Go on, any three. You can't, can you? Because there's only one. You're attracted to him sexually. You think he's a wild, dangerous man. Maybe he is, Tara, but that's not enough.'

'Have you finished?' she'd said, and at last the subject was dropped.

Now, Claire was still flustered and had gone off to her kitchen to make coffee. Her car, with the wheelchair in it, broke down on the way to the station, which was why she hadn't been on the platform when Tara arrived. Claire wasn't at fault. She couldn't help her car breaking down, but Tara understood very well that Claire *would* regard this as her fault, in some weird way. She was full of sorry, sorry, sorry, and how awful, how awful, and oh, you poor thing, and there was no stopping the apologies. This was how it would be, this is how Claire was, wonderful, kind, but there was a price to pay. Succumbing to being bossed around, that was the price. And being grateful, loudly grateful and appreciative, that was essential. Imposing on

Molly or Liz would have been preferable but neither of them had rushed to offer to have her until Claire had already done so.

'What are friends for!' Claire exclaimed (trying to sound mocking, but failing), when she extended her invitation. Solidarity, that was the thing. You'd have done the same for me, she gushed, knowing that Tara would not have done, not ever, but she said yes, that's it exactly, of course I would, if I could. Maybe Claire missed the implication in that last bit: I am not in a position to help anyone whatever their need. I am the needy one, down on her luck, the one who's had bad times and bad luck, whereas you, Claire, you're in clover, well off, husband of twenty years or however many it is, three healthy children, big house, it's easy for you to be lady bountiful.

What a bitch I am, Tara thought. What a bitter attitude, how unfair such a description of Claire is. I am making her pay for once, only once, letting me down. And I am enjoying it.

Molly and Liz came, at considerable inconvenience, to help Tara settle into Barney's place. Molly cancelled a hospital appointment and Liz didn't go to a school concert where her youngest was playing a clarinet solo. Neither of them mentioned these things to Tara, of course, not wanting to seem virtuous. They told Claire, though, and Claire said she could have managed to ferry Tara to Barney's place, and see her installed properly, on her own.

'We're sure you could,' Liz said, the edge of sarcasm in her tone missed by Claire.

They were all familiar with Barney's place. That was where they gathered, in their last year at school, when Barney used to give Tara the key and pay her a fiver to go in and clean the place when he was away. That was where they drank vodka and tried smoking (only Tara got the hang of it, and continued) and where the boys came, not always by invitation. It was all harmless, though. These gatherings never got out of hand, nothing awful ever happened there, and they all helped Tara clean the flat up each time before Barney returned. It was exciting, at their age, to have somewhere to go apart from their respective homes. They all felt free, not worried about a parent or a sibling spoiling things. The very words 'Barney's place' thrilled them.

It was not in the least thrilling returning to it twenty-five years later. The whole house, with Barney's flat at the top, looked like a condemned building: the steps up to the front door were cracked and moss covered, and the door itself bore only the faintest indication of once having been painted red. Silently, they padded up the steep, narrow stairs, remembering how they'd all giggled and shushed each other as they passed the door of the middle flat where an old woman lived who might complain about them to the landlord. (It was ages before they found out that she was completely deaf.) When they got to the top flat, there was a lock on the door, a padlock round the handle. The key Tara had didn't fit.

'We can't break and enter,' Claire said.

'Oh, yes, we can,' Tara said, but in the end there was no need.

Liz, examining the lock carefully, discovered it was a fake. One twist, and it gave way. Triumphant, they all trooped in, Tara on the point of collapse. The stairs had almost defeated her and she'd ended up being half carried by Claire and Molly.

There was nothing there to remind them of past good times. The flat was poky, the two main rooms far, far smaller than they recalled. How had they fitted sometimes forty teenagers in here? How had they once had a live band playing? It was inconceivable. Tara lay on the one bed, and closed her eyes. The comfort of Claire's spare room the last week seemed the height of luxury.

'There doesn't seem to be any hot water,' Claire said, 'and the bath and shower need a good going over.'

'The fridge has been left closed and the power is off,' Molly said. 'Oh, God, the pong!'

They were housewives now and were bound to be appalled by such things, which didn't bother Tara in the least. They were fussing, all three of them, and annoying her.

'Thanks, everyone,' she said. 'You can go now, I'll be fine.'

But Claire was unpacking what she called 'a little picnic' which looked like a full state banquet, and a bottle of champagne was already popping its cork.

'You're very good to me,' Tara muttered, but they could hear the resentment lurking in her words.

Claire thought about saying 'What are friends for!' again, but decided against it.

'So,' said Liz, at her most brisk, 'are you staying down south from now on, Tara? Is the northern adventure over?'

'It wasn't a northern adventure,' said Tara. 'Don't be so patronising.'

'What was it then?' asked Liz, not at all put out by Tara's irritation.

'I was trying,' said Tara, 'to start a new life.'

'And you failed?' Liz asked. At least she made it into a question.

'You'd so like me to say yes, I failed, failed miserably, wouldn't you?' Tara said. 'Maybe I did *fail*, but it wasn't an exam. It was, it was a necessary process –' Liz laughed but Tara wasn't put off – 'and I was really happy, ready to move to a different place and start another job. I was getting it together and I had a car crash. And I haven't recovered yet, or decided anything, so shut up about failure, Liz.'

They ate and drank, and talked about Barney a bit, what an odd man he'd been. Tara didn't say much. Her dad had warned her about her 'uncle' Barney, telling her, when she was eight or nine, that he had 'wandering hands' where little girls were concerned and that if he tried anything she was to report back to him and he'd deal with it. But Tara didn't report anything back. She liked Barney, who was kind to her, and only ever wanted her to sit on his knee and put her arms round his neck. Her dad never did that. He didn't approve of arms round necks, or close cuddles. Her mum, her foster mum, wanted to give them to Tara but Tara didn't want them from her. So Barney gave her the contact she wanted and she was perfectly happy to sit on his knee every now and again. His hands never wandered any further.

At six o'clock, the picnic stuff was packed up, Claire efficiently putting remnants of quiche and salad, which was all that was left, into a tupperware container for Tara to have later. She'd already put milk in the ancient fridge and bread in the bread bin and some fruit in a bowl she first sterilised with boiling water, 'just in case'. (Germs were taken seriously by Claire, as the others knew.) 'Call us,' the three of them said. 'Call us at any time if you need help.' And they each kissed her, Claire on her forehead, as though she were a child with a fever, Molly on the cheek and Liz on the mouth, in a determined fashion, a sarcastic expression in her knowing eyes. Tara had a sudden vision of Nancy Armstrong recoiling in horror.

A month. She gave herself a month to recover fully from her injuries and then decide: the old life, the old haunts, the old friends, something, if she was lucky, near to her old job? Would all that ever be possible? Or the new life, the strange life she'd begun as someone else? She hadn't quite pulled it off but she'd got near to the transformation she wanted. The house in Cockermouth was rented for a year and though she had no job there she could still find one.

But she would have to visit her dad, her foster father, first. A visit she should have made long ago.

X

Alex Fraser was in his garden, watering his sweet peas, when Tara came. He saw her coming down the side passage which he'd left open, but gave no sign that he had. Let her stand there, leaning on her crutch, trying to look pathetic and arouse his sympathy. She'd been good at that. As a child, she'd broken her left arm, going too high on a swing and slipping off; as a young teenager she'd broken two fingers in a fight with another girl; while still in prison, he'd heard she'd broken a leg, not the one so recently broken in the car crash, falling down some stairs. (Falling? He wasn't so sure, but that was the official report, passed on to him for some reason.) Accident prone, then, that was Tara. But she was resilient, he gave her that. Endured pain stoically, healed well, bounced back. He couldn't help but admire her toughness. He'd sensed it from the moment she came to them, a scrap of a child but that glare blazing out from her eyes.

Why she'd come to see him he didn't know, but he was suspicious. What did she want? Not money, she'd said. Not accommodation – she had Barney's place for now. So what did she want? His wife might have known, she was good at sensing things, but he didn't and he was on his guard. Tara, he reminded himself, was manipulative. Mary had been sure that all the child needed was stability and affection, which would, she promised, 'turn her round'. But it hadn't turned her round. The strain and stress of trying to turn Tara round over years and years had, he was sure, been the trigger causing Mary's illness. Nobody could persuade him otherwise. He blamed Tara, and that was that.

He blamed her most of all for withholding herself from Mary's love. Mary was overflowing with love for all children, unable to accept the truth (that she couldn't have her own). Tara, even at three, had realised this instinctively and for the next fifteen years she exploited it. To Alex, it looked like a kind of revenge, but revenge for what? The child came to them in an almost catatonic state, scrawny, bedraggled but fierce. There were reasons for her appearance but no detail was gone into. They were only supposed to be fostering the girl until other arrangements were made. Two separate sets of adoptive parents started the long-drawn-out process of adoption, and twice it collapsed, to Mary's relief. She wanted them to try and adopt Tara themselves but he thought remaining as her foster parents was enough. Why? He didn't know. Maybe an innate sense of caution. By then, Tara was five, and physically unrecognisable from the girl who had come to them. Under Mary's care, she'd put on weight, her skin was clear, her lovely auburn hair shining, and she was dressed in pretty clothes, made by Mary's own fair hand.

So what was wrong with her? Because something was, and this 'something' became more troubling with every year. High-spirited? Possibly, but that wasn't all. Rebellious? Certainly. Perfectly normal. He and Mary didn't need to be told that. It showed some spirit, they said to each other, as a comfort. Once this 'spirit' found its direction, all would be well. Tara was clever and would go far. But it was the depth of her deceit that troubled them more than the smoking and drinking in her early teenage years. She lied all the time. Small lies, pointless lies, as a sort of amusement. Found out, she wasn't at all bothered. Confronted with evidence that she'd lied, she'd laugh and shrug and was entirely lacking in shame or embarrassment. It drove Mary to tears.

'Oh, don't be so silly,' Tara would say, quite cross with Mary. 'It was only a lie. I didn't kill anyone.'

'But *why* do you lie?' Mary would wail.

And Tara would say, 'Why does there have to be a why?'

Then there was her temper. Frightening. Tara could lose it completely. She threw things, anything to hand, breakable or not, and screamed abuse, her body shaking and quivering with rage. He would come home to find Mary white faced and tearful, the living room wrecked. They sought professional help, but it didn't help at all. Tara played these professionals with consummate skill, giving them what they wanted. She never showed remorse. Mary never got an apology, or a promise not to behave so violently again. He tried his own methods of dealing with Tara, since Mary couldn't cope. Physical activity, that was his way. Exhaust the girl, get rid of all that excess energy by encouraging her to swim and run and jump and throw. To some extent, it worked. Mary was protected. But then Tara began just disappearing. For hours. Where did she go, what did she do? She wouldn't say. They worried that she was getting into bad company but then she saved that little boy from drowning and suddenly she was in excellent company, friends with three nice, well-brought-up girls. They relaxed. It was a mistake. It was a shock, learning of what Tara was supposed to have done. His first thought was thank God Mary was spared this. His second was that his wife would have said, 'Go to her.' At that stage, he hadn't seen

Tara for something like four, maybe five, years, and he'd been relieved not to have done so. Her few visits, after she'd married this Tom, after Mary died, had been disturbing. She seemed to be blaming him for things of which he had no recollection. He listened, as Mary would have wanted him to, but he couldn't think how to respond to her accusations. He never really loved her, she said. He was 'scared of his own feelings'. What on earth did that mean? He thought, she said, that teaching her to swim and taking her running was all a father needed to do. He was distant, he'd rejected her love . . . On and on she ranted. It was deeply embarrassing. And why now, when she was married to this Tom? Nothing made sense. Abruptly as she'd arrived, she left, and he was relieved. He'd sat there, silent, observing her, wondering if she was in the middle of some breakdown. Well, maybe all the stability and affection she'd been given couldn't overpower how she was made. There was something about that thought which Mary wouldn't have liked, but he couldn't help it passing through his mind.

But when he was contacted by the police, he kept to the facts. Tara's upbringing was gone over and over, and then there came questions about her relationship with Tom. They were very interested in the early history of this, but he couldn't help them much. When Tara first met him, Mary had just died, and he was so lost and furious he took no interest in this new boyfriend. Yes, he had received an invitation to Tara's wedding, a register-office affair (which would have upset Mary) but no, he hadn't gone to it, nor had he replied. He expected it to be understood that he was too grief-stricken, this event coming so soon after his wife's death. The police seemed surprised that he hadn't actually met Tom. Not at all? No, not at all. Tara never brought him home. She never brought any of her boyfriends home. In the early days, when she'd started having boyfriends, and Mary was still well, it had been suggested she could invite them for tea. Tara had laughed at the idea. She said her boyfriends were her business, not theirs. But the police persisted: hadn't he thought he ought, as Tara's father, to insist on meeting Tom? He said he hadn't thought so. She was not underage. He no longer had any legal responsibility for her. He didn't tell the police that he had, in fact, once seen Tom. Once. In their local pub. He didn't go there often, only on a hot summer's day, when he'd been gardening for hours and the thought of a pint drew him. He wasn't a sociable chap, so he always sat apart from everyone else, nursing his pint in a dim corner of the long bar. A man came in who caught his attention because of the way he stood at the bar. The barman was busy, and this man banged a pound coin on the surface of the brass rim. His whole stance was arrogant. He had no patience, calling out, 'Service, please!' when his banging with the coin produced no response. He might, Alex thought, be foreign, though this impression was only based on the fellow's deep tan, if it was a tan, and his clothes. Something about his clothes . . . He looked somehow dishevelled, as though they had been thrown on in a hurry, and yet Alex could see they were not cheap clothes. His leather jacket looked like real leather and his shoes, though unpolished, looked like good shoes. Alex particularly noticed this because, for him, shoes had always indicated a certain status, something now lost with the arrival of the trainers he despised. Good shoes, it must mean something, worn as they were by a man he otherwise didn't like the look of. And then Tara appeared, looking so young and lovely, all brightly dressed in red, and she slipped her arm through this man's arm, and he drew her to him and kissed her, holding her tightly, too tightly. Alex left by the side door, beer abandoned, feeling slightly sick.

Yes, at that point he should have made himself known. He had no doubt that the man he'd seen was Tom, Tara's husband, a man clearly old enough, by the look of him, to be her father. There was something not right, and it wasn't only a matter of age. Tara, in that brief glimpse he'd had, seemed dominated somehow. But it was impossible. Tara did the dominating, always, of everyone. He thought about this years later, when Tara did what she did. He went to hear the court case out of a sense of duty, not to Tara but to Mary. She would have gone if she'd been alive, he had no doubt of that. Whatever Tara had done, Mary would have stood by her. So he went, every one of the days it took, though he resented his conscience making him do so. In the dock, Tara looked as she had always looked: defiant. Her head held high, her voice clear and firm in tone. She'd changed her hair, but then she'd been in the habit of messing about with it since she was thirteen. What colour had it not been? She was a blonde now, but the roots were already showing a dark red. Someone had brushed it smooth, or else, in that respect, Tara had changed. She would never brush her hair. It drove Mary to distraction, the mess of it, tangled and rumpled when it should, in her opinion, have been tidy. She was, he noted when she stood up, still slim, very thin in fact. No matter how much Tara ate, and she ate a lot, she stayed thin.

All this he noted, while listening to the barristers arguing their case. The prosecution had an easy time of it, what with the evidence so blatantly obvious and then, of course, Tara's plea of guilty, which more or less wrecked the defence's case, though they had a go at mitigation, and that was when he heard Mary's name and his own. Tara's time in their care was gone into in detail. He'd expected this, but what he hadn't expected was hearing that Tara had 'trouble' with her foster mother but 'looked up to and respected her foster father, to whom she was greatly attached'. He found he had said 'What?' aloud in his amazement. 'Greatly attached?' It simply was not true. This could only have come from Tara herself, but why had she made it up?

That was why he went to see her in prison, something he certainly had not intended to do, however much Mary's urging would have rung in his ears. There were limits, and he felt that by being present during the trial he had reached them. But now he had a specific reason to visit Tara and he had to go. He marched into the prison determined to be forthright, to say what he had to say, then leave as quickly as possible. He'd been going to sit down opposite her and come straight out with, 'What's this nonsense about being "deeply attached" to me?' But it didn't work out like that. She smiled at him, and said, 'Hello, Dad,' in such a soft, little-girl voice, and looked at him adoringly. Part of him knew this was acting, Tara putting on an act, which she'd done all her life, but another part of him couldn't help being touched. Maybe he'd been wrong, maybe he hadn't recognised that she was 'deeply attached' to him, in which case he had surely let her down. He coughed and spluttered, and asked her how she was getting on when what he wanted to ask was something quite different. He was glad when his time was up and he could leave. He never visited her again in all the years she moved between prisons and when he knew her sentence had been served and she was free he dreaded any contact she might try to make. But nothing, for practically a whole year, to his relief. What he was frightened of he couldn't work out, and there was no Mary to help him.

And now here she was, in his garden, standing watching him tie up his sweet peas.

'How did it go?' Claire asked. Her voice, on the phone, was breathy, not like her usual confident, clear tone. She'd said to Tara, when told of the approaching visit to her foster father, 'You'll let me know how it goes, won't you?' Tara agreed for the sake of peace, but hadn't let Claire know. Know what, anyway? She suspected Claire imagined she was going to confront the man with allegations of child sexual abuse or something scandalous, which was nonsense. If there had been any abuse, she herself had knowingly done the abusing, but, if she had, she hadn't seen anything wrong in it. She'd flung herself at him as a child and though he'd accepted her embraces he hadn't responded. Instead, after a moment, he'd carefully detach himself, without speaking. But she had seen the expression on his wife Mary's face though she hadn't worked out, then, what it told her.

'It went fine,' she said to Claire, 'we sorted a lot of stuff out.'

'Like what?' said Claire.

'Oh, stuff about Tom,' Tara lied.

Claire couldn't quite bring herself to ask what stuff. Anything to do with Tom was delicate.

'Well then,' she said, 'what now?'

'What indeed,' Tara said gravely, and hung up.

She was a little more expansive to Molly when she rang, mainly because Molly was more hesitant than Claire and said, 'Are you all right?' rather than asking how the meeting had gone.

'I'm fine,' Tara said. 'We talked about Tom and how he'd behaved and how my upbringing may have given him the wrong idea.'

'Oh,' said Molly, not following that up, 'well, I'm glad seeing him helped.'

But Liz wasn't going to leave such a statement unexamined. 'What do you mean?' she asked. 'What has your upbringing got to do with giving Tom the wrong idea? What wrong idea?'

'Well,' Tara said, 'once he knew I was fostered he deduced I had some kind of bad background, and that this made me vulnerable and needy.'

'Vulnerable, you?' said Liz. 'And we're all needy at eighteen. Come on, Tara, this is pure therapy-speak. It was a mutual physical attraction, that was all, simple.'

'No,' said Tara, 'it wasn't simple. I wasn't even really attracted to him at first, not physically. And he was so much older. He gave me a lift, remember? I told you all about it.'

her a diamond cluster ring, which she made him take back. Didn't he realise she wasn't a diamond-ring sort of girl? This amused him highly. She tried to ask him about what exactly he did, what his job was, but he just said that he was 'in the City' and it was too complicated to explain. Basically, he said, he shifted money about. She said her foster father would be interested in that since he was an accountant. Tom just smiled.

It hadn't seemed odd, at the time, that he didn't talk about his work in detail. Clever though she was, she knew she would have struggled to understand what he actually did. She didn't have the terminology to get to grips with high finance, just as he would have floundered if she'd tried to explain the excitement of chemistry. They both rather liked the fact that neither properly understood what the other did, but that they respected how involved they each were in their respective passions. It gave another element of mystery to their relationship.

But she never took Tom home. Alex was in deep, really deep, mourning for his wife, and when she mentioned, on the phone, the idea of introducing Tom to him he'd said he wasn't up to it at the moment. How *could* he have said that? That was what she'd gone to ask him about. How could he have refused to meet the man she was going to marry? It proved he didn't really care for her, that he rejected her, that he hadn't looked out for her. What might have happened if he'd met Tom?

Cross-examined him about his work? But no. Nothing. And though she sent him an invitation, he didn't come to the wedding. It was a small affair. Tom's parents were dead (he said) and he had no siblings (he said). The only people present at the register office were Claire, Molly, Liz, and a friend of Tom's called Clive, who was 'in the City' too. Claire had quite fancied him (he was the same type as Dan, whom she married soon after, tall and blond). Tara never saw Clive again.

The last thing her father said to her, standing among his sweet peas, was, 'Always blaming other people, always harking back to the past and claiming you were hard done by. You were lucky, my girl, you had all the care in the world and you didn't appreciate it.'

That was when she walked out of his garden.

Tara found herself thinking of Nancy Armstrong surprisingly often. She'd get sudden little images of the woman, close-ups of her creased, sullen face, so rarely lit up by any laughter or pleasure, and yet behind it was a lively enough mind, even if it had little to work on. Tara's fear was that she might have become a Nancy Armstrong. Hadn't she, after all, tried to become her, or someone like her? Someone who knew how to measure a cow? Who kept herself to herself, but who was strong, self-sufficient, in need of nobody's pity? But I am, Tara decided, I am in need all the time of, if not pity, empathy. I want people to understand how I feel, what I want, and nobody does. Why she'd ever for one moment thought Nancy Armstrong might do so was laughable. Nancy didn't want to *know* people. She was a practical woman. Her whole way of life was not to be involved with anything as messy as emotional needs.

Her stuff was still up there, in Cumbria, kept safe by some organisation whose name she couldn't remember but she had the inventory somewhere, the list of what had been taken from the car wreck and what she'd already moved to the rented house in Waterloo Road. Nothing of value, really. She could just tell them to bin the lot. It would be good to leave Barney's place, as she soon must, unencumbered with possessions. To have nothing would be a good thing – but there, she was doing it again, persuading herself that *to have nothing and no one was a good thing*. She knew perfectly well that this was not true. Hadn't she tried this, going off up to a town she'd never heard of, living in a place with no ties or memories or meaning for her? And it hadn't worked. She'd felt no happier, no more settled, nowhere nearer to finding her 'true self'. In fact, she didn't think she had a 'true self'. She made herself up all the time, as she always had done. It was exhausting.

'You told me I could call any time,' Tara said, 'so I'm calling.'

The voice at the other end of the phone was silent for a moment. Then: 'It's more than a year,' the voice said, 'and I'm afraid we are having to make cuts which means we have to be strict about rules.'

'I was told "any time",' Tara said. 'I need help. I don't know where else to turn. I'm suicidal.'

(She wasn't but she knew she had to sound desperate, and she was expert at that.)

The appointment was at nine in the morning. She made sure she looked as pathetic as possible, which wasn't too difficult when she already had dark circles under her eyes and hadn't washed her hair for ten days, so that it looked greasy and lank. Her clothes were on the edge of being bag-lady, a look which had taken some care to achieve. She hoped it would be the same Woman she'd seen before, in Workington, but it was a stranger, another Woman, which was a bad start. This one looked older, and harassed. She sighed a lot as she shuffled papers.

'You were doing so well,' she sighed. 'One of our success stories, we thought.'

'The car crash wasn't my fault,' Tara said.

'No, of course not, but it wasn't ours either.'

'What's that supposed to mean?' Tara asked, in a tone of voice sharper than she'd intended. The Woman was looking at her strangely, as though trying to decide something. She stared back, trying not to look defiant. Defiance was on the verge of aggressive – and being aggressive, she'd learned, towards anyone in authority was not a clever move.

'What exactly is it that you want from us?' the Woman asked.

'Help,' said Tara, 'like before. I want to move south. Well, I already have done, but I mean for good. And I need help, somewhere to live, a job, another new name and everything that goes with it.'

The Woman shook her head and smiled. Her smile, in Tara's opinion, was smug. 'We can't do that again,' she said, 'it's policy, in cases like yours. If you want to change your name again, you'll have to do the necessary yourself. I'm sorry, but there it is. It took a lot of work, you know, setting you up a year ago.'

Tara went on sitting there. The Woman looked at her watch, looked at the clock on the wall, and began to get up from her chair.

'I might kill again,' Tara said.

The Woman sat down again. 'Now really,' she said, 'there's no need to be dramatic.'

'I'm not being dramatic,' Tara said. 'I feel as if I could.'

'I'll refer you to someone,' the Woman said, but she didn't seem alarmed.

Tara had hoped she would be. Someone threatening to kill someone, anyone, should surely cause a fair degree of alarm. Maybe she should weep. She tried to, but for once no tears came on demand.

'Wait here,' the Woman said. 'I'll make a few phone calls and I'll be back with a name and number.'

Leaving the building twenty minutes later Tara tore the piece of paper with the name and number of a therapist into tiny pieces and stuffed them in her pocket. Then she rang Claire.

'I need help, Claire,' she said, making her voice shaky. 'I don't know what to do. No one will help me to get a new life again. That's all I want, just to start again properly this time.'

There was a silence, which was not promising.

'Claire?' she said again. 'Can I come to you, just for advice? I have to leave Barney's place tomorrow. There are tenants coming in. I won't stay.'

She shouldn't have added that bit, but it proved effective.

'Of course, sweetie,' Claire said. 'Ring me from the station and I'll pick you up. How long will you be, do you think?'

'About an hour and a half,' Tara said.

It was enough time for Claire to make a plan. The first part of this plan was to get Molly and Liz over as quickly as possible. She could not handle Tara on her own. She didn't like to admit this, but it was true. There was Dan to consider. He'd be livid if Tara was in the house again when he came home and though she wasn't exactly afraid of his anger she didn't want to have to deal with it. But neither Molly nor Liz responded to her SOS – that's what she told them it was – in the way that she'd hoped. Molly pleaded engagements with two of the charitable organisations she worked for, which she couldn't cancel at short notice, and Liz wasn't feeling very well.

'What kind of not very well?' Claire asked.

'Every sort,' Liz said. 'I'd be no use. I'd just be sitting there feeling awful.'

Claire wouldn't accept this as an excuse. Liz, she said, could surely manage to come for half an hour. 'I need you,' said Claire. 'I need you, and Molly.'

In the end they both came, though Molly was constantly looking at her watch from the moment she arrived, and Liz immediately collapsed on to the sofa and closed her eyes.

'Right,' said Claire, 'what can we do for Tara?'

'*For* Tara?' Liz said. 'We've done enough for her. It's more a question of what to do *about* her.'

'All right,' said Claire, 'what, then?'

'Just be generally supportive,' said Molly.

'And how do we do that?' said Liz.

'Well, just by trying to be understanding,' Molly replied.

'But,' said Liz, 'that's the point. Do we understand her? Do we believe her version of events, all that stuff she told us at the reunion? Do we believe that smart, clever, cunning Tara never sussed Tom out long before she said she did? And the murder. A bit extreme, no, a bit beyond understanding?'

'It happened,' Claire murmured.

'Oh, it happened,' said Liz, 'but my point is, we can't understand it, so "trying to be understanding" is a waste of time. We either accept Tara as she is, and help in practical ways, seeing her occasionally but not getting involved again, or we decide enough is enough, and make no effort to keep in touch.'

'But we're her oldest friends,' Claire said, 'we can't desert her.'

'We can,' Liz said.

'But we won't,' said Molly, 'not completely.'

They were sitting in silence when Tara arrived, still wearing the deliberately dreary clothes she'd worn for the interview.

Liz sighed.

'What's this?' she said. 'Little Orphan Annie day?'

'Yes,' said Tara, 'but it had no effect. They won't help me, except to send me to one of their tame therapists.' She slumped on to the floor, back to the sofa, where Liz was still lying.

'And what did you ask them for?' Molly said.

'Basic needs,' Tara said.

'But, Tara,' Claire said, 'you've got enough money for basic needs, you told us you had.'

'Not for living in London, without a job.'

'London?' Claire said. 'You're going back to London, after . . .'

'Yes, after,' Tara said. 'It was a mistake to leave. I'm going back to the old me.'

'With some refinements, I hope,' Liz said.

'Yes,' Tara said. 'I was wild and impetuous, I didn't think things through, but I do now. I'm totally reformed.'

Nobody said anything. Eventually, Molly, rather nervously, said she really, really would have to go. She got up and gathered her things, dropping her scarf as she picked up her bag, and then her bag as she tried to wrap her scarf round her neck with one hand. 'Oh, help!' she said.

'Molly,' Tara said, 'can I come and stay with you whenever I need to?'

'Of course, sweetheart,' Molly said, and there was a quick embrace before she rushed out, flustered. Slowly, Liz levered herself up.

'I'd better try to get home before I completely collapse,' she said.

'Can I come and visit soon?' Tara said.

'Soon? How soon?' Liz said.

'That's so like you, Liz, really welcoming.'

'I *am* welcoming, when I'm ready to be welcoming,' Liz said, not at all put out.

'So I need to give you notice?'

'Most certainly,' said Liz. 'Lots of notice, then I'll think about it.'

Left with Claire, Tara sighed heavily. She watched Claire gathering up the coffee things they'd used.

'Mrs Neat and Tidy,' Tara said.

Claire said nothing, just completed filling the tray and disappeared with it to the kitchen. Tara waited. Back she came, standing in the doorway looking at her. 'Tara,' she said, then stopped.

'Yes?' said Tara. 'You were going to say?'

Claire shook her head.

'Thought better of it?' said Tara. 'Very wise. That's what I'm going to do in the future, think before I speak. Claire, can I stay the night here, tonight? I don't feel like going to Barney's place. I'll pack up there tomorrow and go I know not where.' She laughed at that last bit and said, 'Oh, God, hark at me.'

Slowly, Claire came and sat down beside her. 'Tara,' she said, 'Dan will be home in an hour or so, and I'm afraid he – that is, there might be a problem. I mean, of course you can stay, but he's not going to welcome you, let's put it that way, and—'

'Let's not,' said Tara. 'Let's face it. Dan hates me, always has done. He thinks I'm a bad influence. Well, maybe I have been, though you're much too secure for me to have had much effect. If you want me to go, because Dan won't like me staying, fine, I'll go. Nothing more important than abiding by a husband's wishes. Is there? I always abided by Tom's, until I didn't. I didn't even realise I *was* abiding by his wishes. It took me ages. I thought I just wanted to do what he wanted to do, I thought we were in perfect agreement. Making Tom happy, pleased with me, was all that mattered. And then, so slowly, I started to notice that I was doing what Tom wanted to avoid disappointing him. Little things at first. Choice of restaurants, that kind of trivial thing. And then bigger disagreements, like where we'd go on holiday. He liked big, flash hotels in Spain and France and I didn't. He liked sitting by pools, drinking, having sessions in the spa, and I wanted to explore and really see a country.'

'Well,' said Claire, hesitantly, 'that sort of argument is normal, isn't it, between married couples? I mean, Dan and I—'

'Oh,' said Tara, 'Dan and you . . . there's no comparison. You don't get what I'm on about, Claire. You didn't know Tom. You didn't know how any challenge to his will enraged him. As long as I was docile and adoring and admiring, he was fine. But I couldn't keep it up.' She smiled, enjoying Claire's confusion, put on her thin jacket, and gave Claire a peck on the cheek. 'I'm off,' she said.

'This is awful,' Claire said. 'I didn't mean . . . I don't want you to think . . . Oh, I should never have said what I did . . .'

'I know the feeling,' Tara said, and left.

*

Barney's place was soon packed up. Next morning, Tara loaded her bags into the second-hand car she'd bought at the local garage, and set off slowly to London. She was pleased that though the traffic was heavy, her confidence seemed undiminished by what had happened. This car had automatic gears, so she didn't have to use her still-painful left leg, now out of plaster but stiff. She was going back. It was the only thing to do.

'Have you heard from her?' Claire asked Molly.

'Yes,' said Molly, 'I'm shocked. The idea of it. What was she thinking of?'

'Well, it makes a kind of sense,' Liz said, 'facing up to things, that sort of attitude. And it's where she was happy, well, happy for a long time.'

'But, Liz,' Claire said, 'she can't go back to that happiness. She wrecked it.'

'No,' said Liz, '*he* wrecked it, as I understand it.'

'She'll never have got a flat there, or even a room,' Molly said. 'That area is phenomenally expensive now. She wouldn't even be able to park – she hasn't got a permit.'

'Oh, stop it, Molly,' said Liz, 'this is Tara we're talking about. She'll find ways and means, you'll see.'

They hadn't met for a while. Liz's not-feeling-well had proved to be a virus from which she'd only just properly recovered, and Molly's youngest had come home suffering from chickenpox and needing her tender loving care. They were all uneasy, none of them having heard from Tara since they'd seen her at Claire's a month ago. The mobile phone number they had for her was no longer in use, so they had to wait for her to contact them, as she surely would. They were all expecting to be surprised. But then, when Tara did text them, they were disappointed *not* to be surprised. The information given in their texts was brief and to the point: 'Studio flat found in old house. Job serving in a pharmacy starts tomorrow.' Not much to analyse there.

'I can't see Tara as a shop assistant,' Liz said.

'We couldn't see her working in a factory,' Molly said. 'Anyway, she's got a job, she's got somewhere to live. Let's stop fretting about her. She'll contact us again when she needs us.'

'Exactly,' said Liz.

She was here, in the same house they'd lived in years ago. It had changed internally, of course. Each floor was now split up into these studio flats, merely one-room apartments, with a tiny kitchen in an alcove and an even smaller shower room behind a plywood wall in a corner. The conversion had been cleverly done, though, giving the impression of space. There was no furniture, of course, which helped this impression along, and so did the new laminate floor, and all the white paint. No curtains or blinds or shutters on the windows. No need, when the top floor was so high up. The room was twenty-two paces, front to back, with a view of lots of greenery out of the rear window. She would furnish it sparsely, none of the clutter Tom had accumulated.

She knew who she'd been, here. It helped her, being here, to understand what had happened, how far she'd come since those days. Too far. But she couldn't go back and do things differently so all she could do was go forward, take another route to the life she should have had. Standing there, in that empty room, she tried to empty herself of all the rage and hate she'd felt when Tom's 'business' was exposed. She should have done this over the last decade – she'd been given enough opportunity – but she had resisted hollowing herself out. Time, now, to do it, to be Tara again (no more pretending to be Sarah Scott), to take the good parts of herself and use them to subdue the bad parts. If it could be done.

She went to the window and looked out. Tom used to do that a lot, but she never knew what he was looking at, or for, so intensely. In the early days she would come up behind him and put her arms round his waist and lay her head on his back. He was solid and strong and she loved this. She'd given him an easy death. Nothing bloody or violent. She'd been friendly that night, suggested they eat together again. Some pills, the right pills, pills he was ignorant enough to believe were merely painkillers so kindly provided by her for his headache. Then alcohol, wine and spirits, over a good dinner. Then sleep. Then waiting several hours. Then making the phone call for the ambulance. Then the autopsy. Then herself confessing. But Tom was safely dead. Her humiliation, the humiliation of having been completely fooled by him – she, the smart, clever Tara – at an end. She'd felt no regret. Some fear, yes, but no regret. She still didn't feel any, no remorse at all, except for wishing she'd seen through him sooner.

This, she knew, was what puzzled people most. It puzzled her, too. Again and again she trawled through those years of being with Tom, looking for signs she might have missed, trying to work out if she'd overlooked the significance of certain words, actions, even expressions on his face. But no, nothing. Her only sense of unease had been about the money rolling in. The newspapers were full of 'people in the City' being paid vast amounts, but even so. She commented on this, and he said, 'Are you complaining? I work hard.' She wondered if it was this 'hard work' that was making him more and more irritable. And he seemed suddenly nervous, the very opposite of how he'd always been, developing strange little tics around his mouth which he clearly wasn't aware of. The silent treatment got worse, too – it was as though he couldn't bear any noise.

She decided he must be ill. He'd lost weight, and looked increasingly drawn. But any suggestion that he should maybe consult a doctor was met with fury, and so was her advice to take a break. He laughed at this idea. It wasn't a happy laugh. He wouldn't talk to her about what was worrying him, claiming he was perfectly OK and she should stop fussing. For months, she put to the back of her mind the growing suspicion that some sort of drug use might be involved. It would explain his agitation and then the spells of seeming vague, unsure where he was. She knew that he used cannabis, and she'd long ago had to accept that it never seemed to do him any harm, and he wasn't going to give it up. He'd tried to get her to smoke it with him but she'd refused, saying drugs were a total no-no for her, though she didn't tell him why, didn't confess why she was afraid of them. Maybe she should have done, but all her life it had felt too intimate a thing to tell anyone about her mother. When it came out during her trial it had caused her such intense pain that she could hardly bear it. Anyway, she'd never told Tom. Only now could she see how significant this was, what it should have told her about her relationship with him.

But if he was using something stronger than cannabis, she found no trace of it. She looked for clues, but there were no marks of syringes on his skin, no suspicious bruises. She had to dismiss drugs being the cause of his strange moods. She hoped they would pass before their marriage entirely disintegrated. Then one day, she found him crouched in a chair, weeping. It was such a relief to comfort him, to urge him to tell her, at last, what was wrong. 'I'm in a mess,' he said. He told her he'd got involved with a group of men. They thought he'd cheated them, and maybe he had, just a little. He'd been too clever, got into 'certain deals' without realising the consequences. After he'd told her this, he wouldn't say any more. Her questions went unanswered. She could sense the fear in him without knowing what caused it, but it seemed impossible to credit that all this terror was just about money and some negotiation that had gone wrong. It took courage to demand to be told the truth. She asked him, point blank, if these 'certain deals', which had apparently landed him in such trouble, were drug deals. He didn't reply. So she knew.

She should have left him immediately. She should have sought help, and a place to stay, from Liz or Molly (not from Claire, definitely not from Claire). But she didn't. She stayed, waiting for something to happen which would force her hand. Maybe Tom would run away. Maybe the police would arrive. Meanwhile, she hardly saw her husband. When they were both in the house, they ate separately, they slept separately. Few words passed between them.

Her silence was now as deep as Tom's, but it was of a different nature. She thought constantly of what drug dealers were responsible for and her revulsion grew. She felt all the time as though she was boiling up inside, that the pressure of her hatred would make her explode. She would not leave Tom: that, she decided, would be cowardly. It would make her guilty too. So she had a choice: either she went to the police (though she had no evidence to give them) or she dealt with Tom herself. She knew she was not thinking straight but she deliberately ignored the whisper of a sane voice within her that told her that killing Tom was mad, mad, and wouldn't make the slightest difference to the supply of drugs throughout the world. But still she wanted to do it. Why was that so hard for others to understand? And she gave him an easy death.

She began to unpack the few things she'd brought with her. She was not now ruined, or cowed, though she acknowledged that she shouldn't have taken the law into her own hands. But it had seemed to her that her own hands were perfectly capable. The judge, sentencing her, had made a big thing of how cold-blooded she'd been, and she had. It hadn't been a crime of passion. On the contrary, it had been carefully calculated. Killing was straightforward so long as it was understood what the consequence would be. She'd understood that, and she hadn't cared.

She'd thought of killing herself afterwards but felt no inclination to. Prison was not attractive – she'd had no illusions about what would await her – but she'd thought she could endure it. And then years later, she would start again.

She'd done it, too, only not the right way. She'd wasted time, trying to eradicate herself and turn into another woman when what she should have done, what she was now going to do, was be herself but a better self. All the experts she'd been seen by had worked so hard to call her past to account, and she'd gone along with this. But it was a mistake. Constantly revisiting, re-examining the past didn't help at all. It didn't bring her to the state of remorse they wanted. The past mustn't be allowed to flood into the present and the future. She was determined to put a stop to all the sudden, inexplicable images which constantly threatened to overcome her. Some were banal to the point of stupefaction, but some were frightening, from a far past she couldn't identify. She would have to develop a trick to deal with them.

She would invite Claire, Molly and Liz to her flat – soon, but not too soon. Not all together, not the first time. She fully intended to keep in touch with them, and show them that she valued their concern. And she would make new friends. She wouldn't cut herself off from new contacts simply because she was afraid of what the cost would be. She felt a faded version of her old self, but then, on the verge of real middle age, it was to be expected. She still, she reckoned, had time to prove herself as someone more worth caring about than a woman who had killed her husband and didn't regret it.